As STORM CLOUDS Gather

As STORM CLOUDS Gather

CHARLOTTE COLES

For my sweet husband, Charlie Coles.
You encourage and inspire me. You are by far
the most positive person I've ever known.
~I love you with a whole heart.~

CONTENTS

ACKNOWLEDGMENTS

I honestly must thank my husband first, for always being there for me along life's journey and believing in my dream to write. Through the thick and thin of it all, we are bonded together like the pages of this book. I love your positivity, compassion, and loyal nature. You are much like Levi in this book, a lasting presence through the ages—watchful and protective. You're still my best friend after all these years.

Thank you to my daughter Bethany, who proofread the rough draft of this story and held nothing back in her corrections and feedback. That's my girl; you always can rise above the adversities and find your footing, much like Awna. It was so much fun to have you be a part of this work.

Thank you to my son Cody, who inspires a balance to the world. Your giving nature encourages me, as well as others. Even in the chaos of life, you find not just a silver lining but the golden thread, giving me the thought that you are much like Alon in this book.

Thank you to my brother Mike, who helped me write my first poem about a red train; it seems that poem seeped into my heart and never let go. I used your name in my book as Chef Michael, thinking of your Sunday morning breakfasts.

Thank you to my sweet mama. You have always been there for me. I am so very blessed to have you in my life. Your kind demeanor and love have always made me feel peaceful. I pondered that you and Faith Banks are much alike.

A big thank you to all of our children and their families, who have supported my dream to write. Your encouragement has meant so much to me over the years.

Finally, to Selah, my beloved 8-pound Yorkie who lived as my precious fur baby for over sixteen years and thus inspired my fur friend in this book. You, my sweet girl, will now live on in the pages of this book forever.

In memory of Ira Martin Jr.

Daddy, thank you for encouraging me to write. I used to get a little agitated with you for draw-ing cowboy illustrations on the pages of my sto-ries, but you know what? I sure do miss them.

The Bible Scriptures in this book are true and have withstood the test of time; God's Word will always remain so. They are yes and amen.

Thank you, Dixie Phillips, for believing in my writing abilities and coming alongside me to write our children's books. I'm forever grateful for all I've learned from you. You are a true treasure, sweet friend.

To my special friends: I think of the Tylers, who have always been supportive of me over the years. Thank you for your love and kindness during life's twists and turns; I am forever grateful for your hospitality and kindness.

A special thank you to Rachel Porter and the staff at Christian Editing & Design Publishing Studio. You've done such wonderful work with *As Storm Clouds Gather*. A special shout-out to my personal team from CED: Bethany Clark—project manager, Megan Fuller—line editor and coach, and Shannon Herring—book cover designer and formatter. Thank you, team, for your amazing talents and faithfulness as we worked together on this book. May God's blessings chase you down.

I will admit that there may be some of my own self-lived miracle accounts from the Lord above in pages of this book, accounts that I've witnessed during my Christian walk. Thank you, Lord, for your faithfulness.

Furthermore and foremost, I pray this book will bring God the glory, showing readers that you too are the apple of God's eye and can obtain the wonder-working warrior power through Jesus, just like the character of Awna.

To all who read this book, may our prayers bind together over the enemy, bringing peace to this world, and may the saving grace of God call to the hearts of man.

Although my characters may remind me of traits similar to those I named above, this is a work of fiction. Names, characters, places, and incidents either are products of my imagination or are used fictitiously.

You will find that satan and lucifer are not capitalized in this book, nor will those names be capitalized in any of my writings.

Put on the whole armour of God, that ye may
be able to stand against the wiles of the devil.

For we wrestle not against flesh and blood,
but against principalities, against powers,
against the rulers of the darkness of this world,
against spiritual wickedness in high places.

Wherefore take unto you the whole armour
of God, that ye may be able to withstand in
the evil day, and having done all, to stand.

Stand therefore, having your loins girt
about with truth, and having on the
breastplate of righteousness;

And your feet shod with the preparation
of the gospel of peace;

Above all, taking the shield of faith,
wherewith ye shall be able to quench
all the fiery darts of the wicked.

And take the helmet of salvation, and the sword
of the Spirit, which is the word of God.

— Ephesians 6:11–17

ARMOUR OF GOD

Helmet of Salvation
Breastplate of Righteousness
Belt of Truth
Shield of Faith
Sword of the Spirit
Shoes of Peace

CHAPTER 1

MODERN DAY

I watch, studying him from a distance, knowing not to get too close; I am afraid of being revealed. I have already sensed that he entered the area, so I am ready. I know what must be done to survive. I have found survival to be a funny thing. When you are drowning, you fight for air; when you are backed into a corner, you find whatever may be used as a weapon to fight, anything to overcome the enemy! Sometimes, just outwitting your enemy is all that is needed. However, in this case, I know I will be safe for the time being, for his whole demeanor has changed as I continue to watch him from a distance. He is carousing among the fair ones, who are unaware of their possible secret demise of being inbred by an offspring of pure evil.

He has come to kill me, and he would have if he found me earlier, before I felt his presence. But, as the odds would have it, things changed. Cruelly, some might say, but I can only feel a twinge of grief for his inevitable suffering. It is his facial expression that has given him away. He is a tall breed, standing upright at close to seven feet tall. He probably told the fair ones that he was some famous basketball player to cover for his height, for they always want to blend in. Down through the ages, their height has changed. In the days of David, the Bible speaks of Goliath standing over nine feet tall.

I too must blend in as best as I can with the humans. My words and thoughts are formal, flowing through my mind from ages of spoken languages, yet when I converse with my human brothers and sisters, my speech is but a reflection of how they speak and make conversation. I am a chameleon, just like the tall, handsome one enticing the fair ones. The difference is that I change things for the good, and he changes things for man in the worst-known ways, for he was born with evil intent.

Genesis 6 describes this intruder's ancestors:

And it came to pass, when men began to multiply on the face of the earth, and daughters were born unto them, that the sons of God saw the daughters of men that they were fair; and they took them wives of all which they chose. And the LORD said, My spirit shall not always strive with man, for that he also is flesh: yet his days shall be an hundred and twenty years. There were giants in the earth in those days; and also, after that, when the sons of God came in unto the daughters of men, and they bore children to them, and the same became mighty men which were of old, men of renown. (Genesis 6:1–4)

Long ago, a small band of angels made their choice to follow lucifer into a revolt against God Himself, and lucifer (satan) deceived some of the angels in Heaven with his lies. They were cast down to earth, where sin and evilness made their way into human DNA, changing God's unique design for humanity. If there was good in these angels before the fall, there is no goodness left; their evilness has intensified with time. Their offspring, like this tall breed, have come to corrupt humanity with even more evilness.

In biblical times, these Nephilim, as they have been referred to, migrated to Canaan, which is in modern-day Israel. The Israelites overtook them, but only by God's hand, and only then did the Israelites possess the Promised Land.

Over time, these evil fallen angels, or, as I call them, "fallen ones," were thought to be wiped out, but a few survived, hiding in high caves with their offspring. This hideous evil clan, known as Moloch's Clan, eventually moved through the Middle Eastern countries and then crossed the seas, inhabiting many other countries. Their goal was to procreate with humans, just as this vile creature seated near me is trying to do. The more evil they infest into the world, the more that good people suffer.

This is my story and how I have come to be; I am an offspring of the fallen ones. Do I feel that it is fair?

NO! I just inherited the DNA within me, just as you have inherited your DNA from your family.

This was never God's intention when He made man, but He gave humanity free will to make their own choices. In fact, humans were supposed to live forever; they were never meant to die like they do now.

As I ponder all of this, I'm astounded by the lost opportunity of the humans.

God wanted to commune with His creation, just as He had visited Adam in the Garden during the cool of the day. He wanted to know how His creation felt with each step. Even if they dashed their foot against a stone, He wanted to know about it. Such love our God has for us.

Adam and Eve changed the course of humanity through their disobedience and sinful nature. They believed the lies of satan, for he had tricked them. Their sin started the fall of man; their spiritual eyes were blinded by the enemy, and they started seeing with a fleshly vision. Thus, this disobedience separated them from God. Instead of living forever with God, the sin embedded itself within man like a virus. Now from their sin, this virus has spread to all of humankind, and all of humanity will surely die.

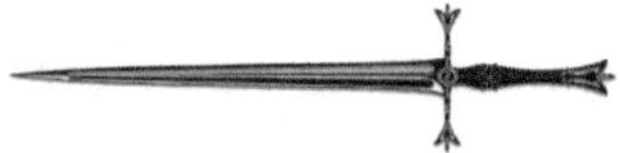

Being a female and offspring of the fallen ones makes me a rarity, for very few were ever born. From the stories I heard as a small child, the early female offspring from the clan were often defenseless and killed because of the forceful nature of these enmities and due to our having small frames.

I have a type of DNA that ages far slower than my human brothers and sisters. I did not fall under the human curse of death of one hundred and twenty years but have retained much of my half-original Heavenly design; however, I am not corrupt, and my human side is redeemed.

As I stated earlier, very few of the original angels from the fall remain, for they are in chains until the Great Judgment. Even so, there are just enough of their offspring, imps, and horrid demons left to cause chaos on this earth. Those who remain are my foes, and we fight until death. I have been set apart to do God's work, protecting humans against this evil. I will cast this one in my presence from this earth; he too will be held in spiritual chains until the Great Judgment.

This intruder is part of Moloch's Clan. I usually know when they are close to my territory. They cannot say the same for me, however. It is God's protection over me that covers and hides me from their intentions. Sometimes I know hours, days, or even months before they come into my territory. When they finally sense that I am near them, the fight is on, accompanied by raging storms.

I glance over at the offspring; he is having a good time, not a care in the world. The time for battle has not yet come, but as I take notice of the clouds starting to form in the sky, I know it will not be long.

Sometimes I feel unworthy of my lot in life, yet I can feel God directing and leading me as I defend myself and others for the cause of good. Today, as I observe this intruder as he entices the fair ones, I understand my need to survive. I am a protector against the evil caused by inbreeding and conflicting human DNA.

I too am a warrior of old. My name is Awna. At present, I am in modern-day Bermuda at a small café named Simon's, located near Cambridge Beaches. Simon's overlooks the clear blue-green waters of Bermuda. The warm, gentle breeze glazes over my skin; it calms the churning anticipation inside me, the anticipation of the fight and the unknown. Will this be my last day to survive these battles, or will I live another day?

As the clouds darken, looking ominous as always before the fight, I sigh. The tourists, unaware, chat and mingle with one another as the waitstaff busy themselves attending to the customers. Things seem normal with the boats moored in the bay; all is peaceful except for our rogue visitor and the churning clouds above. As he talks to the women at his table, I know he has more in mind than casual conversation; after all, his goal is to create more beings like himself.

His face is more handsome than most, almost angelic, as if he could do no wrong. His tall frame and alluring good looks work as a deterrent to finding me, as he has become sidetracked. He has let down his guard because of his lust.

His eyes are dark and piercing with a soft sparkle or glint that gives way to a smile. His teeth are straight and white like the fallen snow. His hair is pitch-black with a slight wave and hangs inches past his neck, near his shoulder. He often uses his hands to rid his hair from his face. His skin appears darker against the gauzy white shirt he wears.

His muscles bulge beneath his clothing, which allures his prey into his web of lies and destruction. For all appearance's sake, he is "tall, dark, and handsome." His voice has a French accent, further alluring the females to his attractiveness. I could hear vague bits and pieces of his conversation. The fair ones laugh at his possibly inappropriate jokes. A charmer for sure on the outside, but a vile obstruction of sinful nature on the inside, evident as he chats with his audience.

I order my morning cup of coffee, along with fruit. I read *The Royal Gazette*, Bermuda's local paper, and catch up on the neighboring news. The breeze touches my face again, and I close my eyes longingly. *Lord, please take this battle from me, I pray. I just entered this territory not long ago; my heart yearns for this peaceful place, my sanctuary. I only pray to stay here for a while longer and rest. Lord, I do so need a rest; you know how I struggle with these battles.*

There is spiritual silence, but I know in my heart: *Yes, Lord, that is why I was spared. . . .*

I let out another sigh, already knowing the answer.

You must take care of this one. . . .

I finish the fruit and sip at my coffee. I glance above the paper, and that is when I see his face changing. One minute he is laughing, showing his broad smile, and the next, his face becomes distorted as what looks like pain envelops him. He shifts in his chair as his stature stiffens. I have a rush of panic, which surges through my chest and then to the pit of my stomach.

I can only think that he sensed that I am near. All the years of my disguises, training, discipline, and readiness in these circumstances must have failed me. Surely he would not have recognized the disguise of a frail-looking old man with thick glasses who sat reading the newspaper while sipping coffee. My disguises are very keen and unique for such events.

I am ready to bolt. I know he is quick and can easily lay hands on me. I must steady my breathing. *Lord, help me,* I pray.

In the very instant that I was going to make a run for it so as not to have innocent people involved in this fight, I feel glued to my chair. I cannot move; it is as if I am paralyzed. In my spirit, I know that God holds me still so that I might only witness what happens next. For months, as this intruder has edged closer to me, I have fasted and prayed. I am ready for the battle, prayed up, led by God's hand, but now God holds me still.

This tall offspring leaps to his feet, tipping the table and chair to the ground. In my moment of stillness, I hear a growl escape him. As for his ready prey, the fair ones gasp in surprise. The onlookers watch in amazement as his demonic appearance and actions betray their thoughts of his beauty.

I watch from the corner of the newspaper as the humans crowd together, and the two he was at the table with cling to one another. One man stands to confront the intruder for his outburst only to be pushed aside like a feather. Not only is he large in stature, but he is very strong. As he starts to sprint toward the beach area, I quickly finish my coffee, leave money on the table, and silently fall into a sprint at a distance behind him. Thankfully, it is early morning, and a lot of the tourists are not out yet; plus, the pending storm will keep most indoors, at least for now.

He moves toward the cliffs and wooded areas that surround parts of the surf. He runs miles, until neither he nor I have much breath left at all. He rounds the corner near Horseshoe Bay and climbs onto a cliff. I take shelter along the caves near the sandy beach where I can see him from a distance.

The cliffs overlook resorts but offer only a small distance between them and this demonic activity. My concern for the humans grows. He stares out at the water for minutes, as if listening, until it comes. That low growl that I heard back at the café rises to a roar and then gives way to a scream. It fills my ears, and its sound is long and deep. To bystanders, it only blends with the thunder rolling in closer and closer. The sound I hear speaks of grief and pain, of losing one of his own. From the looks of his face and demeanor, I guess it is a family member. I watch him for hours until his body lies prostrate on the ground. I am hidden now within the mouth of the cave.

As the ocean waves gently caress the shore, I feel the spray the waves leave behind.

At the Lord's urging, I steady myself and rise to my feet.

I know he will soon leave this region, for he has been struck a mighty blow. Losing a loved one is one thing, but losing a member of your family after centuries together is quite another. Unique bonds form when there are so few of your own kind left, and it is wrenching to lose one. I should know; I have no one left except for Selah and occasionally Levi.

The task before me is still great, although my enemy is at a complete disadvantage. I can take him out easily, and yet it brings me no joy. If I were to let him go, he would only return, bringing others with him, which would make the battle even more intense. Plus, I have already been instructed. I ponder the past hours and start to pray again; in the stillness of my prayer, I receive the same answer.

I climb up the side of the cliff. The storm is upon us now. The rain pelts my face, and lightning flashes as I walk toward the edge where he lies. I stand over him, and he looks at me, still not recognizing me, for my disguises are so clever and enhanced by the glory of God. He lifts his tall frame from the ground with a look of disgust on his face. His hatred is for humanity, and I know he still does not recognize me. He lifts his hand to strike me dead, but as I lift my hands to Heaven, the glow that surrounds me is unmistakable now.

At first, he shows utter surprise at the predicament that he is in—vulnerable—like a deer caught in headlights.

Then he tries to rouse strength that has evaporated from him, but due to his grief, he is incapable. The power of Heaven drapes itself around me, and God's divine hand of protection is unmistakable.

He knows he has no chance now and that his foolishness has taken him to this place. I begin to pray. My prayer covers the past, present, and future, and this enemy has no place here in the present.

The glow and glory of God begin to shine around me, high up on the cliff. It is evening now as the setting sun tries to creep through the dark clouds. The glow appears to be part of the spectacular scene displayed on the island. The storm clouds quicken yet again, covering the sun that tries to override the clouds to no avail as the thunder rolls closer and closer to the shore.

The fight between us begins.

I ask him his name, but he ignores my question.

"You must tell me your name; I command you this in the name of Jesus Christ of Nazareth!"

He looks past me into the distance, pausing before he speaks. "My name is Roman."

His eyes turn red, ablaze with disdain at the mention of Jesus, but he knows the command must be followed. He knows he must finally bow to Heaven. He tries to touch me to feel the glory that his ancestors once felt, but the ancient barrier is covering me, protecting me against the enemy.

In my youth, when casting these imps into Hell, I made mistakes. Sometimes I did not fast enough, and the prayer cover was not thick enough, and they accidentally touched me and felt the glory. When this happened, they lashed out with more power. Or worse, I had to witness the fury of their sinful nature, playing before me like a movie. It was horrid, the things they had done. Unmentionable sins that I have tried to forget but, at times, haunt me still.

Even without their touching me, I still can capture glimpses of how they lived their so-called existence; this only helps me continue the fight.

The storm presses upon us in full force. The lightning flashes with the severe sound of thunder pounding into the shore, with high winds, and more rain following. The glory of God is now all around me, and my enemy is able to see the real me. My long dark hair which reaches my lower back glistens in the light of God as it drapes to frame my face. The storm blows my hair to and fro, but my small frame stands mightily in the presence of God.

The full armour of God can be seen upon me now. The armour is made of bronze and gold, and the breastplate of righteousness covers my torso and protects my heart. A sparkling emerald jewel shines on my breastplate. A bronze helmet of salvation protects my head from injury but also the thoughts that can penetrate my mind. My feet are adorned with boots of bronze, shod for the preparation of the gospel of peace. A belt of gold is girded around me with truth and purity. I raise my bronze shield of faith that can withstand the fiery darts of the enemy. As I raise my golden sword, the Word of God echoes from its blade. As I begin to pray in the Spirit, the language of Heaven sounds for the perseverance and supplication of all saints. My Heavenly tongue reaches Heaven's throne, and the fight is on.

He rises to his feet, and his dark eyes penetrate his stare. The hatred on his face speaks of a life spent with the evilness inside him.

He lunges toward me; I hit him with my shield as what looks like a lightning bolt erupts, sending him sideways.

He gathers himself and growls as he runs toward me. My sword is ready; as I slash through the gauzy shirt, his blood quickly rises to the surface. This only seems to anger him further. I retreat to a nearby rock to evaluate his next move, wanting to end this fiasco.

He staggers, disoriented, as if he were a blind man searching but not seeing, seeking but not finding.

I run toward the side of him. Leaping from another rock, I raise my sword, and as it comes down upon him, it pierces his heart. I remove my sword from his body and crouch low beside his fallen vessel. One hand steadies my shield as I hold it to the ground between us. My other hand is on my sword, the blade raised behind me. I start to pray, and the Word of God continues to echo from my sword into the storm.

Although his hatred is deep, the power of the presence of God is stronger, and the hate soon fills with remorse and disturbing images flowing through his memory. The acts of immoral and despicable conduct flow through his memory as accusations build against him. The glory surrounds his fate as he lies dying, ready to meet God. Although I have pierced his heart, it will take time for his audience with God, for the piercing of his heart has paralyzed him. He fights, trying to move his extremities and fight for his existence, but his heart beats slower and slower.

Doom and sorrow fill him now as a whirlwind begins to envelop him. The wind spins around his body, yet warmth runs through my own body as the depths of Hell's fire rage close to me. He senses his termination and demise are near. He will soon join the others who have gone before him into a maze of torture for their wicked deeds.

I wait; the power is upon me while the Lord deals great judgment on this offspring of a fallen one.

Sometimes the audience with Heaven takes longer; sometimes the judgment is swift; I never know. Some battles are shorter, while others are brutally longer. I continue in prayer, asking for God's hand of protection over me as the process continues. Suddenly the wind increases, and with it, I feel an electricity tingling through my body and know the end is nearing.

Roman's eyes meet mine. I can see sorrow, regret, and remorse for his wicked lifestyle: the murders of innocent fair ones, even innocent children, due to his hatred of humankind.

The wind changes. Instead of going around us, it surges forward, and with a flash of light, cloven tongues of fire surround us and, with precise, exact accuracy, zap their victim.

I fall to the ground, exhausted. My armour is still upon me physically and spiritually. Human eyes may have seen what happened, if anyone is near, but the storm has kept them away. I take long, deep breaths, for my vision is foggy, and my body is weak. I look around as the fog clears and the darkness finds its way around me. Indeed, for this one, the fight was short, but the judgment took longer.

Roman is gone within a flash, in a blink of an eye. I kneel, praying for the redemption and salvation of lost souls. I also pray for their needs; they will never know the spiritual battle fought for them and how many prayers cover them, keeping them safe from the enemy every single day, every single moment. All I know concerning Roman is that there is one less evil in this world.

I sit there on the cliff, holding my armoured knees, staring out at the Bermuda waters while waiting for all of my armour to disappear. My bodily armour and sword are always the last to go and remain for a short time after any battle.

The gentle flow of waves now caresses the cliffs with its spray. The distant sounds of people talking and laughing can be heard echoing over the waves. The storm is over, and the humans are coming out again.

Finally, I feel a tug in my spirit, and I know it's time. I stand and lower my sword to the ground, and my armour and sword disappear simultaneously. The ocean breeze feels soothing against my too-warm skin, an effect of being so close to the scorches of Hell. I finally have the energy to stand on my shaky legs. Looking around, I find the wig close by; it is short, gray, and cropped like a man's. I sigh and shake off the chills that threaten me.

After such events, I am always a little weak and chilled for hours. At least now I can rest, but only for a while.

Knowing that Roman has suffered his end, his clan will travel to the place of that loss to search out the cause of his demise. It will take preparation and time on their part to retrace his steps here. Nonetheless, they will soon know it was this location, and they will know it had to be me, the one they have sought for past centuries. If not for God's protection, as well as the Keepers, I would have been gone a long, long time ago. Or would I?

The Keepers are the holy ones set upon the earth to protect the humans and the good order of things. Over the years, I've recognized some of the Keepers and know that they were hand-picked by Levi just for me. Some originally traveled with the Israelites to the Promised Land, years before the birth of Christ. In those days, the Keepers guarded God's temple against idolaters and evildoers. They also guarded the High Priest. They were at one time alive, just like other humans, but they were exceptional humans with a dedication to God and His holy ordinance. Upon their death, some became guardian angels, some became Keepers, and to tell you the truth, I'm not sure if I can tell which is which. They are designated to protect me as I protect the humans against the clan of fallen ones and their offspring. They have watched over me from the time I was young. My story is as ancient as they are. They are ranked higher than humans, just like other Heavenly angels, but are appointed to the earth to protect the secret things of God. I must trust that God will direct them in leading me, and I can tell you He nor they have ever let me down.

I sweep my hair up into a quick messy bun atop my head, adjust my masculine disguise to look a bit more feminine, tie my shirt in a knot to one side, and roll my baggy pants above my ankles. I tuck the wig and thick glasses into my pocket and set out for a seven-mile hike back to the cottage.

The night air is crisp for island weather, and I pass tourists wearing hoodies as the ocean breeze sweeps through the palms. The breeze serves to clear my head as I walk along the road and shore, tracing my way back to comfort, solitude, and my normal. I hike up the hill to my home, situated near the island's hook. I see the lamps that dimly light the living room, and I left the outside porch light on, feeling that my return might be late. The cottage is more secluded from the tourists than other cottages, and that is okay by me. I appreciate my privacy. The closest cottage to mine is on the other side of the hook.

Cambridge Beaches, Bermuda, is within the locality of Sandys Parish. There are nine different parishes in Bermuda, and the interesting part is that they used to be called tribes. This part of the island rents houses to newly married couples, and the couple nearest my home just arrived a few days ago. Cambridge Beaches is notorious for weddings and honeymooners and is known for its beauty. To me, it is a place I call home and have for a long, long time.

There is a loneliness that constantly plagues me. There is still much work to do in this area; still, it seems I have a hole in my heart that will never be filled. As I turn the key to my front door, the loneliness follows me inside.

CHAPTER 2

GLIMPSES OF THE PAST

Selah greets me at the door, the one faithful fur friend I have in this world. No, Selah is not a military-trained OPT 85-pound German Shepherd, nor is she a 130-pound Rottweiler. Standing before me is my small but fearless 4-pound teacup Yorkie. She is brown with incredibly beautiful blonde highlights mixed into her coat. Her long hair touches the ground, which means she must have daily grooming attention. She has a cute little pink nose and big brown eyes that are good for begging. Selah is a great watchdog; she has warned me more than once of impending danger. It is as though she reads my every thought, probably because she is special like me.

"Hello, my sweet little girl." She barks and twirls, her eyes never leaving me.

I take her outside, where she immediately sniffs the grass. I have a garden area alongside my patio where I grow a few veggies and herbs. There's fencing around the property that separates the nearby cottages; I can see some rentals in the distance associated with the Cambridge Beaches Resort, and this is a perfect place for Selah and me to blend in. The house itself is far too large for just us two, but it is sufficient for our needs.

I have been here for six months this time, loving the days spent in bliss, rest, and retracing my memories. My memories are especially important to me, mostly because I am alone. I constantly retrace the years, remembering each moment as if it were yesterday.

I take Selah inside, give her a treat, and settle in for what is left of the night. I am still feeling weak, so eating anything is out of the question. I make hot tea, turn on Mozart, and stare out of the large, open French doors from the living room. The doors give way to welcome breezes, which make the long sheer white curtains sway back and forth. The storm has passed, but the remnants of sprinkling rain continue as the crashing waves can be heard in the distance.

Regaining my strength a bit, I sip my tea as I stroll around my home, taking in the familiar surroundings, while Selah sleeps peacefully on the couch.

The living room holds overstuffed, lush white furniture made for comfort. The hardwood floors glisten in the dimly lit room, giving way to a peaceful surrounding. The cathedral ceilings have a roomy appeal, which makes the grand piano in the corner appear as a small object. A large wall library adorned with a ladder is dedicated to an array of books I have read over the years.

The sunk-in living room has four stairs that make way up to a massive dining area and kitchen. I am the only one to sit in the dining area, but I change my seating daily to give the furniture the wear it needs.

To the left of the living room is a large office; it too has French doors with a balcony overlooking the waters. There is a downstairs bath that could have been mistaken for the main bath due to its size. Off from the kitchen is a large laundry room with timeless-style shaker cabinets, shelving, and a table for folding clothes, all resembling the kitchen cabinetry.

The attached two-car garage holds a 1955 Mercedes-Benz 190SL convertible and a new leather Vespa Bermuda scooter. Small vehicles are necessary on the island; after all, the country itself is around twenty-one miles long. The roads are not wide enough for large vehicles, which brings reasoning for Bermuda scooters. Each family in Bermuda may own only one car, and only if they are residents. Tourists are not allowed to drive a car in Bermuda either, making scooter rentals a must.

At the top of a massive wooden staircase is a large loft that curves back toward the front of the house, encompassing a huge master bedroom with another outdoor balcony overlooking the Atlantic Ocean.

From my bedroom, there is a large secret room attached to the master bath. A visitor would never notice it unless they knew where to look. Inside the secret room, there are racks of clothing, appearing much like a small boutique. The room holds wigs, hair extensions, glasses, contacts, makeup, shoes, purses, luggage, and many disguises and gadgets that are all part of the décor. To the right side is a dressing room. To the left side is a large hidden safe holding many passports, driver's licenses, ready cash, and important documents.

Beyond the master bedroom, there are still three more bedrooms with baths, all giving way to an oceanfront or side view of the water. All the bedrooms are furnished with the finest of furnishings, a poster bed in one, a monarch Vispring bed in the next, and a daybed in the middle room.

Recently, on this trip back to Bermuda, I turned the middle bedroom with the daybed into a place where I can paint. It's a room where I can create and a space to have peace. This room looks like an art studio with pieces ready to show at a grand opening. It also, like the master bedroom, has a balcony where I can open the French doors and paint from the balcony.

The master bedroom furniture is also monarch in a distressed antique white. The décor has a Bermudian beach theme with pops of turquoise colors on the pillows. The walls are adorned with pictures of seashells and beach scenes that I have painted. The Turkish throw rug beholds beautiful colors, while everything else remains white. The furniture in every room is massive and speaks of another time, all made of vintage material. The outside of the house is white with a hint of pale pink along the edges, made of slabs of limestone erected to withstand the harsh tropical weather. The roof of the house is like other roofs in Bermuda, designed to harvest water; each home stores water in tanks because of the lack of fresh water in the area.

The home is luxurious and extravagant, much more than any one person could ever need, but my homes are all such as this one. I have homes all around the world, each just as unique as this one. The houses speak of the geographic landscape in which they sit. I do not need or want anything—the Keepers make sure of that—but I never use or take more than I need; I am frugal.

The Keepers have land and properties all over the world. Some of the properties have houses, condominiums, furnished apartments, or flats. There are also underground housing units with all manner of items that one might need to survive a great catastrophe. The bunkers have airing fans blowing into fake windows, making the curtains move, much like the ones moving in my living room in Bermuda right now. A person could live the rest of their life in complete comfort in one of these bunkers if they did not mind being alone or having fake sunlight the majority of the time.

My living quarters in the underground bunkers are much like the cottage here in Bermuda, having a gym facility equipped with stationary bikes, treadmills, weights, resistance bands, swords, and weapons. Some even have a running track. Honestly, I cannot even imagine the Keepers ever using any of the workout equipment, but I do. I spend most of my time training spiritually and physically. I must. I always need to be ready for what is next.

The Keepers do frequent the underground living communities and tunnels, but whenever I meet a Keeper, we are only cordial. On my adventures, I often pass a Keeper, and we each nod, never speaking, but there are no other humans in the underground areas. They make sure that I have everything that I need wherever I am. Still, they never ask; they just know.

The Keepers come into my life now and then. I never know when to expect them, but I mostly feel their presence before I see them. They are not family, but they are the closest thing that I have to one; they feel familiar. A few Keepers are able to take on human form as they choose, for my sake and others, bringing to mind the Scripture in Hebrews 13:2: *"Be not forgetful to entertain strangers: for thereby some have entertained angels unawares."*

Moloch's clan is the enemy. They, along with their offspring, are influenced by lucifer (satan or the devil, as some call him). Unfortunately, I am an offspring of Moloch; he is one of the original high-ranking fallen ones and an evil enmity. I came to be after he violated my mother, as she was one of the fair ones taken hostage by them. I will never call Moloch my father, for God is my only Father, and I will always claim the Heavenly and earthly mother's part of my DNA, and no other.

Although I am a female with an exceedingly small frame, unlike the male offspring of the fallen ones, God has truly gifted me with special strength to fight evil. This is why I am constantly in training. Moloch's plan has always been to replenish the earth with his offspring, in hopes of overtaking the earth. That has not changed, but something in the Heavenly realm has changed, putting these creatures more on edge.

These entities only prove to be a constant burden of trials, tribulation, and all manner of sin for humans as they crossbreed. However, a human who pleads the blood of Jesus over their life and believes that Jesus is the Son of God is safe and sealed. The believers must always be watchful for satan and his crew, for they are always looking for whom they can destroy.

My mother was given to a fallen angel named Alon, a somewhat high-ranking peacekeeper in the clan. He was strong and smart. His name in Hebrew meant *Oak Tree*, and he was strong like the oak. He was not evil like the rest of the fallen ones but just trying to survive.

Alon asked Moloch if he could have my mother. Secretly, he wanted to protect her from the clan. He knew what they would do to my mother; he knew my mother's fate would soon meet with demise. Alon always kept a close, protective watch over her, and the two lived near one another at the edge of the clan territory.

Alon even looked more human than the other fallen ones, who could distort their looks seemingly to whatever suited them. When Moloch agreed to give my mother to Alon, there was a condition that any offspring would be

Moloch's. Alon agreed, never even considering intimacy with this fair one, for he felt soul-wrenching remorse for his unknowing part in the revolt against God.

Alon kept all of this to himself, of course. He protected my mother, Anissa, but she will forever be my *Eema*, the Hebrew name for mother. Alon watched over and took care of her, and the two became close, like that of a deep, true friendship. Alon told my mother about Heaven and all that he had seen and how he had been deceived into following the evil ones into rebellion against God.

He realized he had been deceived by Moloch only after it was too late. Moloch had asked him to be a witness, to bring peace over a minor disturbance between Moloch and another high-ranking official in Heaven. Alon always wanted to keep the peace, and he went to help willingly. By the time the revolt happened, he was in the wrong place with the wrong people at the wrong time.

After realizing Moloch's plot, Alon prayed, agonized, and even tried to escape the grips of satan and Moloch, but to no avail. It was too late; God had already cast them all down to the earth. The earth was not where Alon wanted to be; it was not his home. Still, even in his anguish, he wanted no ill fate to come to this fair one or any of the fair ones. Anissa was not afraid of Alon, but she was terrified of the clan. Anissa believed in God and His goodness; she believed that God would deliver her from this evilness.

Alon may not have been a human like her, but Anissa considered him a dear friend. Alon was so high-ranking that no one would dare cross him. As the days passed, Alon saw how the others glanced at Anissa with lustful eyes, never hiding their evil thoughts about her. Although he knew their thoughts, they could never map out his. It was a gift from God that his thoughts were protected from their minds. Alon pondered all of this in his heart and began thinking of a plan.

CHAPTER 3

MEMORIES

Iknow I should let Selah out; after all, I've already spent over an hour lost in my thoughts.

"Do you need to go out?"

Selah jumps up from napping and barks. We make our way outside; the rain has cleared, and the stars can be seen twinkling like diamonds in the sky. I can hear the laughter of the tourists and smile, knowing the charm that Bermuda portrays is breathtaking. One keeps this beauty within their heart like a treasure to protect, long after they leave. Selah quickly runs back inside for her treat. I make more tea and settle back onto the sofa, where Selah curls up in a ball beside me. I quickly drift back into the past, bringing memories of my earthly parents before me.

Many conflicts and fighting erupted between the clansmen as boundaries were broken daily. Alon knew in his heart that he must leave with Anissa. He talked to her about his concerns but also expressed a plan of escape. Anissa agreed and was eager to leave their place.

One day while the clan was distracted by the offspring and evil games that they often forced on the fair ones, Alon and Anissa slipped away. Their journey would require traveling hundreds of miles together. Alon did not require sleep, while Anissa needed sleep, food, water, and shelter. These needs could pose a deadly problem for the travelers.

The clan would surely send the offspring after them. The offspring had great strength and could travel quickly, but even they required some rest. Alon decided that he must carry Anissa while she slept to stay ahead of the offspring. It was not a problem for him, for he was large in stature and just as strong. Alon also had to be incredibly careful not to meet up with humans. They would see Anissa with him, and then there would be a fight to the death over her. The humans did not like these fallen ones or their offspring and frequently tried to kill them. They were large like giants, and that made it very hard for the humans to conquer them. Alon did not want to give Anissa up; she had become his only companion in this lonely, strange world.

When the two first left the clan, Anissa had thoughts of escaping even Alon, but his constant kindness and care for her were reassuring. She also knew that he was her only protection against Moloch. The humans would be no match for them. She made up her mind that God had given Alon thoughts to notice her and free her from bondage, so she would stay with Alon for life or until the Lord stirred her heart otherwise.

Together Alon and Anissa crossed rivers, valleys, and mountains until they finally found rest, but this rest came only after they had traveled hundreds of miles. Alon felt safe with the distance they had put between themselves and the enemy. He had also erased his tracks as they traveled and sent other tracks in different directions to outmaneuver the enemy. Weeks and months had passed before they finally stopped. They made their new home high up on a mountain where sharp-edged rocks would keep inhibitors away and where Alon could observe from miles away any enemy coming toward them.

He provided for Anissa and cared for her for two years on the mountain; their common goal of staying alive only served to deepen their friendship to that of family. Just when the two thought they could take a breath from worrying over the enemy, the unfathomable happened. Anissa started showing signs of being pregnant, and a year later, I was born. The gestation period for this fetus was much longer than that of human gestation, taking years for the human DNA to bind together with the genetic makeup of the fallen ones, but eventually, it did create a fetus.

Alon knew that Anissa had been violated by Moloch but thought he had saved her from further harm. He never once considered that she was with child when they first escaped. After all, Anissa had lived with the clan for months before Alon took notice of her. It was no wonder that Moloch had agreed to Alon taking her into his camp and only asked for the offspring; he had already known she was pregnant. Moloch could sense it; he always knew.

Alon had never been like the clan, for he was good and not lustful like them. He stayed pure and without fault, and constantly tried to communicate with God. The evil thoughts and deeds of the clan were so unlike his demeanor, and at this point, Alon determined in his heart that evil would never trick him again.

Alon knew a child only added risk. He knew that my Eema and I would always be in danger because of his promise to Moloch. Moloch would know; he always knew when an offspring was born. He would come for the child and stop at nothing to get it back. The child was valuable to Moloch, and there was little Alon could do to stop any misfortune, being so outnumbered. He knew, if found, they would be overpowered by the clan.

Alon pleaded with God to hear his prayers, but he heard no answer in return. Anissa prayed, begged, and pleaded with God for help. She prayed that the enemy would be scattered and confused while searching for her and Alon. They found that, although God would not answer Alon's prayers, He did answer Anissa's prayers. She had been redeemed because she was human. Alon, on the other hand, was an angel, and a fallen one at that, banished to the point that God did not hear his prayers anymore. The knowledge of this was dreadful and saddened Alon greatly, but he would always love God regardless and would forever continue his prayers.

One night, Anissa felt the Lord speak to her through a dream. She dreamt of a tribe of many, many people that she would soon join and would be protected by their numbers. She was saddened by what she must do—leave her dear friend—but she had to share with him what the Lord had shown her.

When Anissa finally mustered the courage to share her plans, Alon was devastated by the news. He cried upon the rocks; this word was too much for him to bear. He wanted to die, but death would not find him. He cried out to God repeatedly, but still, all was silent. He continued to pray harder, even if he heard nothing at all back. Day after day, week after week, he would never stop his prayers. He wanted God to know how sorry he was for trusting Moloch, and he begged God for forgiveness.

At first, great sorrow surrounded the two of them, for their future was so uncertain. It was not knowing from one day to the next if they would be found by the clan that caused the most anxiety. I was born during this time of fervent prayers. My birth brought a new joy that seemed to funnel through our makeshift family. It was when they held me and watched as I made funny faces that peacefulness and love found them.

One day while Alon was hunting for food for Anissa and me, he saw them—a large group of people traveling.

He observed their daily routine; he watched as manna rained down from Heaven for them. He remembered the manna, for it was Heaven's blessed food. More peace flooded him. These were the children of God that Anissa had seen in her dream. Alon watched for close to another year as this group continued around and around the mountain called Sinai.

Month after month, it was as if this group was moving in circles, looking for something. *What could they possibly be looking for?* he often thought. Alon knew that God had answered Anissa's prayer, for there was safety in numbers, and the hand of God's protection was on these people. He knew Moloch would not go near them, for the power of God had put a strong hedge and a boundary around them and this mountain. They were protected by a cloud by day, signifying God's covenant with them as they followed the cloud daily. At night, Alon watched the cloud as it turned to fire in the sky, giving them light in the dark wilderness. This was the safest place on earth for his earthly family, with God's protection surrounding these people.

Anissa waited for God's timing. While she waited, I grew, but very, very slowly. For years, I was tiny in my Eema's arms. I looked like a toddler, but I was ten years old. I could also speak and reason as an adult. My mother grew older, but Alon never aged. I continued to age so very slowly. My mind was quick and beyond anything that Alon or my mother had ever witnessed. I had a special sense of things; I also knew things before they happened. The knowledge inside me was growing faster than my tiny body. I ran alongside Alon as he hunted for our provisions. I could close my eyes and sense the life around me and tell him where the life force was. Neither of us wanted to kill an animal, but there were times when we could not find enough berries to live on. During some of those times, the manna from Heaven rained down on us too. It sustained us; God's hand of protection was upon us.

I could communicate with Alon in my mind, and yes, this drove my mother crazy, but that is how Alon and I communicated with one another. He taught me much about life, Heaven, and the afterlife. He shared details with me about the places he had seen and the many different dimensions of Heaven. He taught me secrets that I have never revealed to anyone.

Alon instructed me with the words of God and coached me to quote them against the enemy. He trained me to be a warrior and to fight with handmade weapons. I was instructed on how to prevail against evil in the enemies' weakest areas. I learned many tactics on how to war against Moloch's clan, for Alon knew that one day I would have to fight for myself and that my existence depended on it.

My mother taught me how to cook, clean the camp, and take care of myself. She taught me the secrets of the humans. She taught me about love, morals, values, and rules that I must live by. She also taught me the Word of God and how to use my knowledge to conquer my spiritual enemies and bring peace where it was needed.

The day came when it was time to join the multitude. My mother was incredibly old and had become very frail and weak. Alon watched as I helped her down from the mountain to meet the others. There were so many people that it was easy to blend into the midst of them. No matter how far I strode from Alon, I could still hear his voice. We talked, and he helped me to know what to say and do around these people.

Our feet were dusty from the sand. It was hotter in the valley than on the mountain, so Eema had to adapt. We paced ourselves, walking during the dust of the day; even so, this took a toll on my mother's health. We fell into step with the others in this tribe of people.

A few days passed, and before long, my mother was asked to have an audience with the elders. Their main leader's name was Moses. My mother told him that she had fallen behind the group because she was old. She shared that she was related to me and that we were family, knowing he would never think she was my mother with what looked like such a significant age difference. The elders never inquired about my parents but accepted us into their band of safety.

Moses and the elders readily fed us, cared for us, and sheltered us. I had such a hard time adjusting to all these people, never having been around anyone but my Eema and Alon. I watched their every action and their talks, absorbing everything around me.

Eema continued to pray for guidance; she knew her time on this earth was limited, and she had to make final preparations for me. It was a comfort for her to know that Alon and I still communicated constantly; it was also a comfort for him. They talked to each other through me, and it was of great comfort to us all. As Eema prayed for wisdom with more fervent prayers, God answered her once again. She was to take me to the Levite priest, who would know what to do.

The priest listened to my mother's story, and she held back nothing. She told the truth of all that had happened to her by the fallen ones and that I was an offspring raised in the ways of God. The Levites met and discussed amongst themselves all that the priest had learned from my mother. Then they allowed us to join their group; ironically, the name Levi means *to join*. These people were intrigued by me and kept me close, fascinated by my knowledge and special ability to pass the peace to others. They cared for me and taught me an enormous amount of knowledge concerning God, as did I with them.

Soon after this, my sweet Eema died peacefully in her sleep. I was devastated, to say the least. She and Alon were all I had in the world; my only comfort was that I still had Alon. Even though I could not see him, he was there with me, comforting and guiding me. He too was tormentingly upset by the death of my Eema. I felt it in his thoughts; we were both shattered, but God sustained us once again.

This is how I came to stay with the Levites' priest. One of the priests, named Levi, named after his tribe, was in constant communication with Moses as he spoke to God.

Levi was not the highest priest in the Tabernacle, but he was the one that most people talked to and confided in. I was closer to Levi than any of the others. I loved Levi like family. Although he was a lot younger than the other priest, he was respected by everyone around him. After Eema died, he was the one who continued to care for me. For many years he taught me all that he knew about God. He searched for the deeper things of God, not settling for surface information like many of the others did.

One morning, I awoke to a scurrying of the priest; something was amiss. I searched for someone to tell me what was going on. I finally followed two older priests who were also close to Levi. They had stopped at Levi's door, whispering. When they opened the door, I slipped in behind them. There lay Levi, sick with fever.

I recalled that I had not seen him for a few days but never thought much about it; he was always so busy. Once the priests saw me, they tried to shoo me away, but I stood my ground. When Levi saw me, he motioned for me to come to his side. I could tell that he was extremely sick, and I reached to put my hand on his forehead to ask God to heal him. Levi reached out quickly and held my hand away from his forehead.

I remember his words like it was yesterday. "No, child; it is not meant to be."

Tears escaped my eyes; I did not want him to die. Everyone died, but that did not mean that I had to like it or even accept it.

"Please, Levi. If I ask my Lord God to heal you, I believe that He will!"

"No," he whispered as he drifted back to sleep.

I stayed by his side for days, bringing him sips of water and broth. I cried by his side way into the night, not wanting this to happen.

"Levi, I need you. What will I do without you? I'm all alone," I cried.

Between my tears, I saw him open his eyes.

As he lay there, he nodded for me to come closer. I knew his time was near; he was trying to whisper something to me. I inched even closer to hear his last words.

"Awna, be watchful," he gasped in a weak voice. "Be watchful as storm clouds gather!"

When I looked into his eyes to ask him what he meant, he was already gone.

Our plans are not God's plans, nor His ways our ways, for His ways are higher than ours. Therefore, I knew I should not question what was happening, but my little heart was broken yet again. I did question. I did ask, and I did get angry.

I was devastated by the loss. My heart hurt like when Eema died. I missed my mother and Levi both so much that I honestly could not distinguish my grief between them. I had basically lost Alon, my mother, and now Levi. Alon reminded me that he was still there, but it was no comfort to me at the time, for my best friend had died.

I ran far away from camp; it was deep into the night when I had finally cried all the tears that my body would allow. "God, why are you taking everyone from me?" I shouted, but there was no answer for my grief. There was only stillness while the stars twinkled in the sky and the moon shone bright.

This was only the first of many, many people that I would watch die the fleshly death. No matter how many of my human brothers and sisters go, I am saddened each time because I know they were supposed to live forever.

CHAPTER 4

THE ANOINTING OF A WARRIOR

Moses had passed by now, and Joshua oversaw the Israelites. God had instructed Joshua that he would be the one to possess the Promised Land. I was now thirty years old but looked like a young teenager, still on the small side.

One night as the Israelites came closer to their promised land, also called Jericho or the City of Giants, we heard that the city was closed. How could that be? It was such a powerful city. No one was coming in or going out of the city. The Levite priest instructed me to go listen to the conversation between our leaders.

"Awna, stay in the shadows. You must not be seen," instructed Segal, another priest.

I crept past the guards that stood watch around the tent of the leaders. They were distracted, talking to one another. I went around to the backside of the tent, waited, and listened to the plan that was being devised.

The fighting Israelite men were to march around the city of Jericho every day, once a day, for six days. The priests were to carry trumpet horns, as well as carry the Ark of the Covenant. The priests carrying the trumpets were to go before the priest carrying the Ark of Covenant, and they would blow the horns while they marched around the city.

I returned to the Levite camp and told them what I'd heard; then we discussed our own plan.

The Levite priest decided that on the night before the seventh day, I was to come along and accompany him, for the priests knew I was a trained warrior. I'd been trained not only by Alon but also by Levi and a small handful of trusted warriors in the camp. They were impressed by my skills and fearlessness; they also knew what my mission in life would be, for the Lord had told them. Maybe they also knew it was the anger that drove me, but no one ever mentioned it. Instead, they would use it to our advantage against the enemy.

The plan was the same as the other days, except that today we were just to march seven times around the city. At the start of the seventh time around, the priests were to blow their horns, and the people of God were to shout. They did just that, and as the horns blew and the people shouted, the walls of Jericho started tumbling down. While all of this was happening, I slipped away from the group to wait for the evil ones to come out of the city.

This is where I saw Moloch's clan for the first time. They were part of the original fallen ones with their offspring. They were tall like giants. I'd heard about them my whole life, and now they ran from the ruined city. I chased them unnoticed because of their fear of the millions of Israelites who had just taken their city. I chased them into Debir, better known as Lodebar.

Other warriors I had noticed followed me; we all were dressed for battle. A massive storm started forming as the city of Jericho began to fall. The clouds darkened, and the wind blew hard, with rain, thunder, and lightning covering the whole area.

Through the wind and rain, I could see the creatures closer now. They were large beings that looked somewhat human. Their faces were different, though. Their eyes blazed yellow, their torsos were long, and their arms and legs were bulky and looked out of proportion. Their faces were pointy, and their skin looked gray and wrinkled. They hissed at each other like angry felines. They all stood above nine feet tall. Alon was tall like them, yet he neither looked nor acted like this angry mob. These creatures were all demonic.

They spoke a different language, but somehow, I understood it and was able to anticipate their next moves. When the battle to overtake these creatures began, although it was my first battle, it was much like my battle with Roman. I had fasted and prayed before the battle, and when we took the city, no matter how much I tried to stop it, my grief drove me to fight and fight hard against these fallen ones for what they had done to my Eema. The loss I'd suffered was almost unbearable, and I truly didn't care whether I lived or died.

The battle started. It was intense, and as I fought, I heard Levi's last words spoken to me: "Be watchful as storm clouds gather."

I looked up into the dark sky and knew it had been a warning for me concerning this evil, for the storm that covered the land now seemed different from the storm before the fight started. We fought the enemy, and as I lay there slightly shaken, a whirlwind came out of nowhere and enveloped the enmity as he lay on the ground. The wind was furious against me as I struggled to my feet. The fallen one closest to me struggled to stand in the whirlwind, so I pierced his heart with my sword. A bolt of lightning struck the fallen one and took him away.

I approached more of the fallen ones and their offspring with my sword and did the same thing. As the creatures lay on the ground with the whirlwind swirling around, the lightning bolt struck each one and took them as if they were never there. Each bolt of lightning took one from this earth, and God used my sword to help accomplish His purpose. I heard the Word of God echoing out of my sword.

In the end, we had conquered the enemy and cleared Jericho of this great evil. Jericho was just a city in the land of Canaan, but it would now be home to millions of Israelites who could live in the land promised to them. Today this land is known as present-day Israel.

What we did not know was that, before the battle of Jericho, Moloch and a handful of the original clan, along with some offspring, had fled to a different region. They had sensed the battle and the loss that would occur on that very day and escaped across the waters.

After the battle, my young but injured body limped back to camp, unseen in the darkness of the night. The Levite priests prayed over me in the Tabernacle. It was then that the Keepers came to me for the first time. They looked much like the Levite priests but were somehow different. I was put into my first deep dormant sleep, which lasted until after the crucifixion of Jesus Christ.

The battle of Jericho and my first dormant sleep played a significant role in my existence. My awakening from that sleep was when my armour first appeared. It was as if God clothed me with His glory, awakening me to who I was created to be. His love shines on my breastplate armour with a Bareket stone, better known as an emerald, which represents the tribe of Levites. The Hebrew word for Bareket means *lightning flash*. It was at this point that I became an anointed warrior.

I never heard Alon's voice again after the battle at Debir. It was there that I knew I had lost him forever. This is how I know the anguish of the clan when one of their own is lost. I realize now that it was Alon in the shadows with other warriors who had followed me into the battle. It was there that I believe he protected me with his own life when I was cornered by two offspring.

At the time, I was so emotionally torn that I felt that my heart was being ripped from my body, which is probably why the Keepers put me into the dormant sleep. I had lost Eema, Levi, and now Alon. I had fought a terrible battle, and the pain was unbearable for me.

Oh, Eema! It has been so long since you passed, but my love remains so strong for you; no matter the years, my heart still aches. I paused as the emotion wrapped around me.

And Alon, thank you for loving me and teaching me! I miss you so much, I whispered.

Now I force myself out of my thoughts and memories from the past. I sit on the sofa, looking out into the black night, far different from the Israelite camp and my first battlefield.

The sounds of Mozart comfort me as I store the memories back into the safe recesses of my mind. I must always retrace my steps; it is vital. Otherwise, I feel that I will lose myself entirely. It also gives me peace to think about my Eema and Alon often; they must always be tied to my memories. It seems to make me stronger.

My memories are quickly interrupted as Selah moves off my lap to stand and stare at me.

"Yes, Selah, once again, I'm lost in my thoughts." Hours have passed as I reminisce.

Selah reminds me it is time for bed. I turn off the lights along with the memories; a few hours of sleep would be nice, for that is all that I require. We head to bed, and Selah curls up next to me. The warmth of her little body sends me fast asleep.

The dreams are so real to me; it is as if I never really sleep but just go into another place for a few short hours. As I drift into sleep, he is there. I am used to seeing him in my dreams. He is the only one of the Keepers who communicates with me. When it is time, the other Keepers will come for me, but it's never him. I never know when they may come. It could be one hundred years or less, sometimes more than one hundred.

These Levite priests have passed the knowledge down through the ages to care for me so that the quest will continue. Their quest: keep me alive. Yes, keep me alive even thousands of years to fight this evil enmity and to keep the purposes of God.

The Keepers sometimes arrive where I might be working, if I have taken a job just to pass the time. Or they might arrive while God has me on a mission or a special errand that needs to be done in an area. The Keepers may pose as coworkers, or they may even be grocery clerks put in place just to keep an eye on the territory. They always know where I am. I can never hide from them, nor would I want to. I mostly know them, but there have been times

I've had just a feeling but am not entirely sure it's one of them. Regardless, I never feel threatened.

I trust them with this legacy that must be carried out, protecting my human brothers and sisters from the ancient enemy, the enemy of the souls of man. The Keepers sustain me, which is how they have kept me alive for so long. Once a mission is complete, they pray over me, and I pass into a long dormant sleep, only to revive one hundred years or so later. Either way, they control some of my situations, or, as I have often thought, maybe all of them.

At times when the clan comes too close, the Keepers will put me into a dormant sleep so that the clan loses track of me. It throws the clan off, even to the point of thinking I am gone, never to return. Moloch can sense when I am back in action, warring against his imps or offspring, although that takes him a while. Then he is back on my trail, sending out his evil ones to do his bidding. I have become one of the clan's most hated ancient enemies.

I am restless in my sleep, and as the fogginess clears, he is clad in the clothing of the Keepers, but his smile shows the difference. Most of the Keepers are "matter-of-fact," with no expression. Levi and I use our minds to communicate.

"How are you?"

"I'm fine, but I feel lonely," I speak.

His expression says he understands, and he nods.

He then asks about Selah, and suddenly she appears in my dream.

I smile. "Yes," I say. "She's fine, as you can see."

Levi gave Selah to me as a companion at least seven awakenings ago. Selah lives like I do, also with dormant sleep.

He tells me I can stay in Bermuda for a while longer. The Keepers will watch the perimeter and give me fair warning when it is time to leave. I am thankful. I need to just live, breathe, and rest in between these battles.

As I think these things, he nods. He steps forward toward me, then stops and raises his hand, as I do mine. Our hands never touch, but the energy that flows between us is powerful.

I say, "Goodbye, Levi," but he is already gone.

PAST AND PRESENT LACED TOGETHER

When I awake, I feel happy. I look at the clock: 5:00 a.m. Early mornings bring me joy. Bermuda is my resting place. It's the only place where Levi has met me in a fleshly form since we lived in the Israelite camp. At the time, I did not know it was him. I feel so connected to him, and all I know is that I trust him with my whole being.

The day is sunny; the breeze is gentle. Of all the places I have been in the world, Bermuda feels like home. Maybe it's the mystery connected to this place; maybe the place is also connected to me.

I think I will go out today as myself—the small, tiny girl with long dark hair, piercing dark eyes, and olive skin tanned by the sun. It feels good to be myself and not in disguise. I stretch and wonder what the day will bring. I am so happy and peaceful knowing that I can remain here for a time. Usually, when the Keepers tell me I can stay in one place, even if it is for a brief time, there is much to be excited about. It is freedom at its best.

Selah is as excited as I am to start the day. We go downstairs and open the doors to let the fresh air flow through the house. I start the coffee and then take Selah out for business. I grab the *Morning Gazette* from the front step and then mosey toward the veranda to read. A distant neighbor waves; I wave in return. It would appear to others who may take notice that my cottage is a rental since it looks like so many different people come and go. There's the older Asian-looking man who is deaf and must sign to communicate. Thus, I do not have to communicate at all unless someone knows sign language. There's the elderly lady who finally came for her dream vacation but is in too much of a hurry to chat. So many people come and go from Bermuda that they never stay long enough to realize that it is just me staying at this cottage in many different forms of disguises.

I drink my coffee while Selah smells around, leaving no stone unturned. I gaze out into the beautiful turquoise waters; a peacefulness floods my soul. Basking in the moment, I can't seem to help myself. I am once again lost in my thoughts and memories of Levi.

It was the late 1800s, and the only way to Bermuda was by ship or boat.

It was the same cottage on the hill, overlooking the waters in Cambridge; it has just been updated, renovated, and expanded upon over many years. The same gentle waves caressed the pink and white shores, but everything looked so different. I was waiting for him, dressed in a long pale pink Victorian gown; white lace covered the outer shell. My hair was piled on top of my head and adorned with a matching bonnet, and I clutched a parasol under my arm. I traveled by horse and buggy to meet him.

After my arrival, I waited a few minutes and then dismounted the carriage and tethered my horse to the hitching post. I saw him standing near the stairs of the balcony. I started to walk toward him, and his smile deepened; clearly he was happy to see me. Our eyes met. I stood there for a moment, taking in this memory that at any moment I knew could end. I believed that we were meant to be together forever and that nothing could ever separate us, not life or death. It was the only time in my existence that I have given in to human emotions for a friendship or really for anyone except for my Eema and Alon.

He was an officer in the British army, so handsome in his uniform adorned with medals. I met him at the balcony. We turned and made our way down the newly erected stairs of Fort Scaur. The fort was built to protect the Royal

Naval Dockyard from enemy invasion. The position of the fort was a thought-out process in protecting the island—a watchtower, so to speak.

He had the day off duty and wanted to spend it with me. We picnicked along the cliffs, just chatting and catching up on the news within the island and beyond. Later, we splashed our feet in the water as children, laughing, not caring. From the beginning, he knew I was a bit different, and I think he sensed that I have secrets I hold dear. Still, he did not care; he enjoyed my company anyway. He listened to my vague answers and never acknowledged the times when I was gone from the area without a word. His companionship was always comforting.

It had been one year since our friendship began, and truly that is all it ever was, but it was as deep of a friendship as I ever thought possible with a human. As the evening sun started to go down, he took my hand as we walked along the shoreline. We then took a carriage to the Royal Naval Dockyard beach, where his whole demeanor changed once we arrived.

The thought crossed my mind in all our visits that he had never taken my hand until today. I wondered why this day was different. Regardless, I enjoyed the closeness to another person.

I was right. Life would never be the same. Our day took a turn that would haunt me for a lifetime. They came, hunting for me like animals for the kill. It was a vicious fight. I nearly lost the battle, for in this battle, some of the main clansmen came for me. It was the first time in my long life that I was vulnerable to the enemy. My soldier and I both fought hard, but in the end, they killed his fleshly body, and he died protecting me. My spirit still grieves over his fleshly death. I know in my heart that this is why I fight the enemy so hard, for all the loss and tragedy that their evil brings.

After Moloch's clansman and his demons killed my friend's fleshly body, things went back to the way they were before. The unbearable loneliness and the nightmarish dreams all came back until the night when my dreams started to change. This time, he appeared alive in my dream. He spoke to me and wanted to know how I was doing. He was and still is very real to me.

During the times we walked on the beach, picnicked in the newly planted botanical gardens, or developed a friendship during that year, I did not know that he had been sent to me in human form. I found this out later when he started to visit my dreams.

He had been sent to build trust and a friendship with me and to protect me and Bermuda's small country. In his earthly form, I had no idea that he had been the one watching over me since I was a young girl traveling with the Israelites. It was Levi of the Levites; he had now become a Lead Keeper. His mission after his death in the Israelite camp became to protect me throughout the generations. He had become my guardian angel sent from Heaven. He was not part of the angels who had fallen, like Moloch's clan. After his death, Levi became one of the holy angels, which was fitting since his life spent here on earth was dedicated to the priesthood.

As my memory flows back in time, I realize now that the Keepers knew that the fight at the Royal Naval Dockyard beach would be different, with the enemy's strong entity reaching across Bermuda. They were ready for battle even though I had not sensed the immediate danger as I normally do. Even the Keepers had no idea that Levi himself had taken on an earthly form to help protect me; only God knew.

As the storm erupted, it brought the demonic force in, and we were both almost taken in the fight. Levi, however, fought without condition or choice, and the punishment was great. My friend and short-lived companion was lost. I grieved at the thought that I would never see him again.

The Keepers came for me after that battle. My spiritual weakness and wounds were great, but the emotional agony was even greater. The Keepers left me in a dormant state far longer than usual. When I awoke, things were different for me for quite a while. I was very lonely, and there was a silence in my prayers. I could not rise to do my intended work, not until Levi started visiting my dreams. One night he brought Selah into my dream. When I woke up the next morning, Selah was there, a real fur baby. Levi was not.

CHAPTER 6

FRIENDS

My thoughts have wandered yet again, but I am barked back into reality by Selah, who needs my attention.

After my daily prayers and meditations in the Word of God, and a vicious workout, we finally get started on our day. Selah and I take the scooter, me on the seat and Selah in her basket. She loves to ride. It is good to have her for companionship and just someone to talk to. If I did not talk to her, I believe I would have no voice at all, for it is sometimes days, months, and—yes, I hate to admit—even years before I use my voice even to say hello to another human. Amazingly, Selah alerts me when something is not right; she is my little watch angel.

The scenery is breathtaking along South Road; the clear waters sparkle as the palm trees sway in unison. All of it is refreshing to me, and the warm breeze that brushes my face feels majestic, like the scenery. We ride to Gibbs Hill Lighthouse, high atop a hill in Southampton Parish. The view is breathtaking here, one that was also enjoyed by Queen Elizabeth II when she visited Bermuda in 1953. The lighthouse is one of the oldest cast-iron lighthouses in the world.

There is an old telephone booth from the past that sits at the side of the building, but I have no use for it. I have no one to call. While cell phones are so commonplace now, the phone booth serves only as a great photo opportunity.

The restaurant and gift shop are inviting, so we stop in. I've read in *The Royal Gazette* that there are new owners at the lighthouse, and I am not sure of the pet policy, so I tie Selah outside, much to her dismay. She barks and draws attention.

A young man looking to be in his mid-twenties comes around the corner of the restaurant; when he reaches Selah, he kneels to give her a pet.

"You can take her in; there haven't been many tourists today."

"Are you sure?" I ask.

"Yes, my grandmother won't mind; she loves dogs. Hi, my name is Will Banks."

He reaches out his hand. I do not like to touch others because I can see into their lives and the sin that dwells within. I reach out my hand anyway and then quickly think of who I am today. Oh yes. I am myself.

"Hello, my name is Awna."

As I shake his hand, I feel only peace, and I smile, knowing instantly that he is a believer in Christ. Peace warms my being, and the human connection feels refreshing.

As Will looks at Awna, he thinks, *She's a beautiful girl. Her smile is warm, showing straight white teeth. Her dark hair shines as it glistens in the sun. Her skin is flawless with an olive complexion. She is a tiny girl, yet her beauty somehow outsizes her. Those big, deep dark brown eyes display a glint of sparkle, with full, thick lashes that adorn oblong-shaped eyes.* He continues staring until he realizes that those dark eyes are staring back at him. He looks away quickly, the heat of embarrassment touching his cheeks.

Awna is taken aback by his staring at her, but they both quickly recover when a woman comes out the door of the restaurant. She walks over, and Will introduces his grandmother, Ms. Banks. She is a friendly sort with a jolly laugh and a heavy British accent, much like Will's. Her hair is grayish, almost white, and shoulder length, swept back away from her face. Her face shows signs of aging. Her eyes are steel-blue but gentle. She loves Selah and wants to hold her. Selah, of course, eats up the attention. *What a ham,* I think.

Ms. Banks looks at her grandson and sees the embarrassed look on his face. She does not know what she just walked into, as far as conversations go, but she does know that Will has embarrassed himself somehow. Ms. Banks only smiles and takes the small dog inside to spoil her a little more.

I buy a ticket in the gift shop to go up into the lighthouse. I sign the guest book, as many others who visit do. I see signatures from US states and all over the world: Virginia, West Virginia, Ohio, Georgia, Alaska, and then from many countries in Europe and Asia. These were all recently represented in the guest book.

"I'll look after the pup, give her some water, and keep her company while you go up for a look," Ms. Banks offers.

I hesitate but know that Selah would throw a fit if all was not well. It is odd, I ponder, how Selah acts so comfortable with our newfound friends. *Funny, but I feel the same way. It is the love of God between us*, I think.

It has been many years since I have taken the 185 spiral steps up to the top of the lighthouse; it gets my heart rate pumping as I quickly ascend. It feels so good to have peace, even if it is for a brief season. At the top of the stairs, I relish the view as the island and the shoreline meet. It is a welcoming sight. The blue-green waters give up the secrets that lie below, and schools of fish swim in harmony to the beat of the ocean melodies.

I breathe in deeply as the breeze envelops my body. The sun and its warmth are comforting. I am suddenly brought back to reality as Will stands behind me.

"It's amazing, isn't it?" he speaks.

"Um, yes, it is," I say.

"I noticed in the guest book that you signed your home as Bermuda."

Who would have known he would look? Why would he look? I wonder.

"I don't think I've ever seen you before."

"Well, I travel a lot," I say.

"My family's cottage is near Cambridge Beaches in Sandys Parish, so I come home when I can, which lately hasn't been a lot."

"Oh, wow. So you live kind of close to here? Maybe, what, like fifteen minutes?"

"No, no," I say, acting like I am serious.

Will frowns.

"It's more like seventeen minutes."

We both laugh. Will looks around at the view, trying to be nonchalant.

"So, you're a Bermudian?" he inquires.

"Kind of. I guess you could say that I think my family came in with Admiral George Somers."

We laugh again. *What am I doing, trying to act like a comedian?*

He must have thought this was funny yet very unrealistic, the way he was shaking his head and still chuckling.

In my heart, I know my history is somewhat true, since I had been sent here shortly after Admiral Somers founded the colony of Bermuda. In those days, some military and civilians were building a township. The Keepers instructed me to rest here in a much smaller, less formal cottage, one that blended in with the cultural surroundings.

"So, what type of work do you do?" Will asks.

"Umm, you might not believe me if I told you."

"Give me a try," he says.

"Well, okay, I am somewhat of a corrections officer. I travel around looking for the bad guys, bringing them in for justice."

He laughs, contemplates for a moment, and then looks me up and down, as if knowing my small frame is not fooling anyone. Then he says, "No, really, what do you do?"

I give the truth, and you choose not to believe me, I think.

"Okay, I am into missions. I travel all around the world. I'm a teacher to those who need to learn, and I just help where I'm needed." That explanation seems to go over a little smoother.

"Wow, where have you been?"

"Well, Asia, Europe, the Middle East, the United States, and Russia. Just wherever I'm called. There are needs everywhere, you know."

"Do you speak any foreign languages?"

"Yeah. Some."

I'm thinking to myself: *Not some, but all.* There is not a language that I do not know. I even know the Heavenly language Alon taught me.

"How long are you staying?"

"Well, I'm not sure. I could get word today or tomorrow and must head out, but hopefully I can stay a few weeks or maybe a month or so. I'm taking a vacation right now."

"Hey, if you're going to be here for a while, come and see me at Bermuda College. That's where I work most days; I also do some construction work on the side. There are a few openings at the college. We need some long-term subs; what do you teach?"

"Oh, I'm endorsed in a lot of different areas, like foreign languages and criminal justice. Believe it or not, my favorite subject is history," I say. I quickly change the subject. "So, what do you teach there?"

"I teach hospitality management. I mean, we do plan to live in Bermuda for at least the next five years on our workers' permits," Will says.

I smile, knowing the value of what he teaches at the college.

"Great field," I say. "This is definitely a great place to teach the younger generation about tourism and the trades."

I look out again at the ocean, and he leaves me to my thoughts. We both stare at some recreational boaters enjoying the waters.

The silence is broken by Selah's barking.

"I better see what's going on with her. She has separation anxiety at times. I can't leave her for very long."

We travel back down the narrow spiral stairs.

As I start the descent, I feel it. The reason for Selah's barking is a warning. Will and I see a couple climbing the stairs, and as we maneuver around them, I feel Will, who is near, take my elbow protectively. I almost shrug away but realize he feels it too—that uncomfortable feeling you get when evil is near. My senses heighten, and I look the two visitors in the eye as we approach each other to pass. I pray silently: *Lord, protect me from the evils of this world.*

The couple stare back at me. I look away after making eye contact and concentrate on the stairs. These two are just evildoers who are unsaved, and they are not my fight.

My fight is much bigger than these two. I have found it better to ignore those who are ignorant.

As we pass each other, the male bumps into me. Like a bully teasing me, he gives me the death stare.

I look at him politely and say, "Oh, excuse me. I'm so sorry. I didn't mean to bump into you."

His glare is angry as he responds, "Just watch where you're going!"

His tone is sharp. My sweet and kind demeanor can be felt by all, and as I look into his eyes, I silently speak peace into his spirit without a spoken word or touch. At first, his dark eyes deepen into a frown of defiance. His whole look is a bit unnerving with the demonic artwork and piercings his body displays. His unruly hair is long and unkempt, as is his facial hair.

However, his negative attitude is quickly extinguished when he feels the peace that I pass to him. His look says it all. First, there is bewilderment, and then an unexpected smile creeps over his harsh features. The girl tugs his arm.

"Come on!" she says. "Baby, what's wrong?" She then looks over at me with hatred in her eyes. I keep moving down the stairs as Will stays close.

As we round the corner, I see Selah sitting in a chair with Ms. Banks. Selah is snarling and giving me that look, the look I have come to love. Her look says, "I told you so. You should have listened to me when I barked the first time."

I pet her head, and she calms as quickly as the guy on the stairs.

"I'm sorry for that," Will says. "You never know who's going to come in."

"You are right about that," I say.

"What happened back there?" Will asks.

"What do you mean?"

"That guy? Do you know him? What was his problem?"

"Oh no, I don't know him, never met him before in my life. Maybe he just woke up on the wrong side of the bed."

"Or maybe . . . he didn't have his usual cup of joe this morning; I don't know!"

We both laugh and walk toward the dining area. I quickly thank them for the walk down memory lane. As Ms. Banks comes in for a hug, I notice the beautiful cross necklace she wears. That is why I feel so comfortable with them; they are truly believers. I thank them for allowing Selah to visit with Ms. Banks. We say our goodbyes, and out the door I go, promising to come back soon.

CHAPTER 7

EVIL IS NEAR

As Selah and I head down the winding road down from the lighthouse, I am not comforted. The quick curves and turns are much like life: they come for you when you least expect it. The man on the stairs is part of the sin that has crept into the world. He is tall, but not an offspring. He is only a descendant of the fall of man. Yet he has no clue as to why he is so drawn to evil. He has chosen a life of sin, and he will be doomed if he does not call out for forgiveness and get right with his Maker.

Although my fight has, from time to time, included some of these types of humans, it is not by choice. Usually, I can control the situation by silently speaking peace to the small amount of good that resides within them. They have no sense of why, but they will submit to the peace that is offered. I have come to realize that many humans have no idea why they instantly hate the good and react negatively. On the other hand, just like with Will and his grandmother, the believers feel something too. It is a discernment of the spirit. I also must add that not all tall humans are part of this evil, for I have met a lot of good humans, godly humans, who just inherit the genes of height with no evil intent within their souls.

Selah and I drive to the botanical gardens in Paget to walk for a while. I put her into my backpack and zip open an air hole.

"Selah, stay quiet," I say.

She understands and settles down in the airy mesh fabric. I walk along the maze of flowers and shrubs. I breathe in the aroma of the exotic blooms; I allow the smells to renew me. I gaze upon the magnificent, brilliant colors that so entice the eyes.

The color and elegance of the Bermuda passionflower with its purple petals and the hibiscus with its bright purples, yellows, and reds catch my eye. These flowers also bring back the memories of former days. The bright pinks and the hues of yellows speak calmness to my spirit.

I decide to sit for a while in a nearby Banyan tree that has an ingrown seat or something like a scooped-out bed. I take Selah out, and she rests on my belly. It feels good to be myself. The disguises of my life are so frequent that I almost lose myself sometimes. I must use some disguises for days, weeks, or even months at a time when I am on the trail of the enemy, and these take a toll on me.

We rest for a while and then walk through the gardens. I put Selah back in my backpack. I hear a low growl escape her, but I shush her as we pass a guided tour. The Bermudian tour guide smiles and welcomes me to join them if I'd like. I thank her but decline. Bermudians are such friendly people. Everywhere you go, the locals are helpful and hospitable; even the children are raised to be so, for it is their livelihood.

The Bermudian environment has always drawn me back as a place of comfort. The borders of this country, however, must be kept safe from the enemy, just as all borders around the globe need divine protection. Any territory is vulnerable to the enemy at any given time, which is why the crime rate is rising around the world.

I walk the thirty-five acres and feel revived. It is late March and still in the off-season of tourism; the crowds are not what they will be from spring through summer. The temperature is in the high sixties, and there's not a cloud in the sky.

Oh, God, what a beautiful haven. I do so enjoy this special place.

I pray and tell God every thought that I can think of and every feeling that I feel. I know He enjoys communion with me because I feel His response in every fiber of my being. The breeze catches my hair, and I am reminded once again that I am me, and I am free to be me, for now.

I turn and hear another low growl from Selah. As I stop and collect myself, I feel it too. I look around seeing no one, but I know they are there.

"Let's go, Selah," I say. I walk cautiously but normally back to the scooter. I put on my helmet, tuck my hair within, and put Selah in the basket. I then strap her into the harness for safety but do not shut the basket.

I feel their presence before I even turn; I know it is the couple from the lighthouse. His troubled demeanor speaks volumes to me even though we don't say a word.

I feel a tap on my shoulder, and I pray a silent prayer: *Lord, blind their eyes so they do not see us, as you did with the prophet Elisha against his enemies.*

I turn, but who they expect to see is not there. Their eyes see someone else entirely.

I know this immediately; the look on their faces tells the story.

The woman hits the man on his shoulder.

"Where'd they go, Ethan? She's obviously not an old Japanese woman with a white Pomeranian dog. You can't do anything right!"

"Rosie, I'm sorry. I followed her right here. You saw it, right?"

Rosie starts peering around. Since they see me as a Japanese woman, I begin to speak to them in broken English and add an Ojigi greeting (a Japanese bow). My smile holds as the two look baffled. They quickly look toward Selah and then back to me and begin to move to the left near the restrooms to search for me there.

"Have good day," I say, and I get on the scooter and stroll away.

I hear the tall male say, "Look around. She can't be far."

I am shaking inside; I cannot believe what just happened. I am sure now that it was these two I sensed following me in the gardens. What do they want, and how long have they been following me?

The danger I was in was enough to blind their eyes as to what they were really seeing. That rarely happens unless the humans are very evil, if imminent danger is near, or if I need to slip away quickly. In those situations, I ask the Lord God to blind their eyes to what they really see. He did this in biblical days with Elisha.

In 2 Kings 6:18, an army of men tried to capture Elisha. He asked the Lord to blind his enemies' eyes, not fully, but just so they could not see him or their surroundings properly. God is no respecter of persons. What He did for one, He can do for another to benefit His kingdom.

Selah and I head for home but take the long way, stopping a few times to be sure that we are not being followed. Back home, I am so restless that Selah and I decide to take the car out for a drive; I just need to escape. We ride around Bermuda, stop at lookout points, and take in the beauty around us. We then take the ferry to Hamilton, park the car, and walk around.

We stay until early evening. It is just what we need. We walk by the beautiful shores, dip our toes into the waters, and enjoy looking at the small schools of fish nibbling at my feet. I laugh and feel my mood lighten as I watch Selah swim farther out, her little paws paddling hard. She looks like a wet rat and quickly swims to meet me. The sky is now changing, signaling late evening, so I gather our towels and wrap us up. We take the ferry back home, where we settle in for the night.

As evening starts to take its place in the sky, I turn on the classical music. Bach always soothes me. I drink my tea and read, and I do feel peace. No breeze is blowing the curtains tonight, only the rumble of the music and the house sounds.

It is early into the wee hours of the morning when I finally drift into sleep, but he is not there.

I wake up with a start, knowing that he did not come to visit my dreams. He is always there! Something is wrong. I feel it deep within my spirit.

I am unnerved by the current events: the lighthouse, the gardens, the tall male who is not one of them. Who and what does he want?

I stay in for most of the morning, focusing on meditation and prayer. I spend two hours in prayer, seeking direction. I feel peace about my current location and situation, though I have a twinge that something is amiss. I have learned that I would feel more uneasy if I were in any immediate danger. Still, something is up. I do know that much.

I complete an intense jog around Sandys Parish to prepare myself for the next venture. When I arrive back home, Selah is still sleeping in her bed, so I make my way down to our secluded beach. Three-fourths of the way down to the sand, I take a right toward the small stepping stones that create a path. Bermuda cave ferns cover the mouth of a cave, and a large, thick industrial door is hidden amongst the ferns.

There is an antique iron padlock on the door, which I unlock, and then I turn on the light switches on the right-hand side of the building. Rows of lights become illuminated seconds apart from each other, unveiling a massive room built within the cliff of the cave. One advantage to having the cottage high up on the cliff is that there is lots of space left below the rock.

The underground room is large. It serves as a bunker in case of hurricanes and tropical storms but also houses a new fifty-nine-foot Tirranna cigar boat, made for speed. Attached near the opening of the cave is a separate garage door that houses a solar-powered boat ramp that can extend out into the water. When I am ready to bring the boat in from the water, I use a remote that opens the garage door. The extender ramp automatically retrieves the boat and stores it back in its proper place. To the side of the boat is a Jet Ski, which is great for water sports, taking a ride, or getting from one side of the island to the other. It too has a ramp that works the same as the boat ramp.

A room at the back of the boat garage stores nonperishable food and water. The Keepers always stock the area before I arrive at any destination. If I use anything, I also replace it. To the right of the room is a workout area full of different rowing machines, treadmills, bike machines, weight benches, and a personalized Tonal Smart Gym that adapts weights for the user.

A small solarium room with a lap pool and hot tub next to it are positioned near the back of the room. The lighting is different in the pool area; the heated water is blue. I can choose night or day features for the ceiling and windows. Stars adorn the night sky, with a moon displayed in all cycles. During the day, the sun shines brightly, and birds chirp as they sing their songs. Although the plants and flowers are not real, they appear to be, and each has its own authentic smell.

A five-foot tunnel is at the back right of this well-thought-out room. It connects to a door and then to a very small apartment, furnished just as nicely as my cottage on the hill. The apartment has the same fake windows so that I can change the scenery to appear as if the viewer is outside. I can make my view be the beach, the mountains, the desert, or any place at all. It all looks so real that it gives me feelings of security and peacefulness.

I work out for a few hours and then shower at the apartment, change clothes, and make my way out of the shed, remembering that I need to let Selah out.

I relock the cave door, and as I am leaving this underground playroom, I amuse myself as I realize I always refer to this area as my shed. The Keepers are all about my training and my comfort, but truth be known, I am comfortable anywhere in God's creation.

Once back at the cottage, Selah and I sit outside on the veranda, where I begin searching on the computer. I check out the weather for the rest of the evening: mid-sixties. Perfect. I check out the current and local news, and there is nothing alarming.

I decide to go to Simon's to be around people and enjoy an early dinner. Even if I just have coffee, the idea sounds good to me. When a person is constantly alone, they must force themself to go out and be around people; otherwise, they become reclusive, sad, and depressed. Ask me how I know. . . .

Before I leave, I take Selah out to do her business. She gives me a funny look as she snorts.

"No, sweet girl. You cannot go this time." I fill her water bowl and leave a little dry food for her.

"Selah, watch the place. I'll be back." She whines but does not make a big fuss as she moseys to her bed.

Simon's is only slightly busy. With the winter months behind us, I see mostly locals and a fair number of guests and workers on permits, but still, nothing like the warmer weather crowds.

The wedding season will start soon, and the sixty-five thousand locals and workers will grow to six hundred thousand with all the tourists. It is a very dense flood of people for such a small area, but no one ever seems to complain. It brings money to this small piece of paradise.

I order, and the waiter makes small talk. "How long are you staying? What beautiful weather we are having . . ." and such. I smile and comment, not wanting to converse.

I have seen this waiter here several times and heard others mention that he is a culinary arts college student here on a worker's permit. He is hoping to get a feel for the cuisine and learn as much as possible while he is here.

The executive chef comes out and makes his way around the small crowd, asking if the food is to our liking. *Of course it is*, I think. Not only is it wonderful food, but the scenery is breathtaking. Chef Michael makes his way over to me, and I glance up and smile.

"The food is amazing, Chef!"

"Thank you. I hope you enjoy it," he says and moves on to the next table.

"I always do." I smile and return to my meal.

Chef Michael is a small-town boy from a farm in the States, near the eastern coast. You can learn so much by just listening to people around you.

It is a calm afternoon with greenish-blue hues that give a surreal appearance. From where I am seated, I can see the shallow shoreline and the fish swimming close enough for recognition. I see a hogfish with cream and red coloring. The purple band along its elongated nose is a quick giveaway. These fish are rooting for worms in the shallow waters.

Looking out at the moored sailboats, runabouts, and small fishing boats gently waving back and forth in the water, I think it's as if the sea cradles each boat, rocking them to a lullaby.

I am lost in the views when a young man sits at a table around the corner from me. At first, I pay him no mind, until I hear his voice. It is Will.

Yes, I think. *Now I can really see what he is all about.* Watch and listen: that has always been my motto.

He orders water, a fish sandwich, and a side salad. *Healthy enough*, I think.

I hear him unfold a newspaper, probably *The Royal Gazette*, to read as he waits for his meal. I peek around the corner as two young girls look his way and smile. As they leave, he nods with a friendly smile and goes back to reading. The waiter returns, they speak pleasantries, and the waiter leaves.

Will gets a call on his cell phone and answers.

"No, I've had no luck yet," he says. "I'm going to look around Cambridge. That's where she said she is staying, in her family home."

A flash of alarm goes through me. *Is he talking about me?* I listen intently now, on high alert.

"No. There is no sign of her. I've asked around the area, but no one seems to know her. Hey, if she's still on the island, I'll find her."

CLICK! And that is it. He continues reading, so I pay for my meal and exit unnoticed.

Now what? I know I felt a kindred spirit when I met Will and his grandmother. I leave the restaurant, now feeling betrayed by my own judgment and silly for the thought of new friends. Just goes to show that you cannot trust anyone.

The walk back to the cottage seems long. As I pray for guidance, I know my only loyal friend is God above. My mission and my mere existence are all for Him. Even if Levi never visits my dreams again, I will just have to accept that.

At home, I read the Word of God aloud, I pray, and I ask for peace with these new circumstances and a clear mind for whatever comes next. Hours pass as I sit here. A calm comes over me, and I know the presence of God is overshadowing me. I have never felt such peace as I feel in this moment. Truly, this is a sign that all is well again.

I am confused. I am calm with my peace from God, but I also cannot shake the restlessness inside me. How can I feel both of these feelings at the same time? I have so many feelings lately.

I move to the veranda to look at the beauty of the waters and think. After a few minutes, I feel compelled to take the boat out.

Okay, Lord, what's going on? I know this is you. Can you give me any hints about this?

There is silence, but in the silence, I know I need to obey.

"Come on, Selah. We are going on a boat ride!"

I don't have to ask her twice. She loves to ride, whether in the basket of the scooter, in the car, on the Jet Ski, or by boat. It matters not how she rides, just as long as she gets to be a part of the action.

Selah's such a good little traveler, I often think.

We enter the shed. As the lights come on, I click the remote, and the opening for the boat slip begins to open. I pick up Selah, and we get into the boat. I look for her life jacket, put it on her, and then put my own on. Although we are both strong swimmers, there is no need to take risks or chances.

As the boat touches the water, I turn the engine over and move away from the opening of the boat slip. The roar of the motor purrs in the breeze. I look out farther, and the white caps are jumping from the water. The breeze has also picked up. I move farther into the water away from our beach area, always cautiously looking for jutted rocks.

We ride the waters of Bermuda close to the eastern shoreline, in the St. George's region. We are still out in the waters far enough to enjoy the moment but able to keep an eye on the shoreline. I feel energized as I gun the throttle. Selah ducks under the passenger seat, digging in her heels. I slow and circle the boat back around the point, heading along the west side near H20 Watersports. As we pass by H20 Watersports, I take in the view. I see the anxious faces of renters of skiffs, Jet Skis, sailboats, snorkeling equipment, and basically anything that floats.

I slow my craft as an overwhelming sense of danger creeps into my spirit. I know there's no danger for Selah or myself, but I feel something ominous for a human brother or sister.

"Oh, Lord, lead and guide me," I pray aloud.

I keep a watchful eye as we travel near Mangrove Bay National Park. I look into the clear waters below the boat and can see the bottom of the ocean. I drive on slowly and look around. I see no one but feel uneasy. As we pass the bay, I spot them, and my heart skips a beat. There is a legion of Portuguese Man o' War. These creatures travel in groups of a thousand or so. They look a lot like jellyfish but are siphonophores; they work together as they travel, searching as one for food. Some of these creatures have tentacles reaching over one hundred feet long.

Why are they this close to shore? This is unusual, just like my not seeing Levi lately. Are these strange occurrences somehow related?

We are nearing Sugar Cane Point Beach, a family-oriented beach. I see a boat in the distance, and then I spot them, and my heart sinks. A group of snorkelers swims from their boat right into the path of a multitude of Man o' War. I pick up speed. As my heart rate increases, I feel the Holy Spirit all around me. Now I know my reason for the unsettled feelings, and I am on a mission.

I blow the horn of my boat to alert my human brothers and sisters and to hopefully scare away this legion of stinging floaters. I look into the waters below as we speed toward the area, but the creatures are still all over the place.

Selah starts barking and runs toward something on the boat. I slow and turn to find her inches from stinging tentacles. The Man o' War has hitched a ride on my boat.

I immediately stop the boat. "Come here, Selah." She backs away from the beast, obeying but still barking. I look around the boat to see what I can use to get the thing off of the boat. I spot the fishing net in the back of the storage compartment. I put Selah on the driver's seat to keep her safe and quickly leap onto the passenger seat and then to the back seat. This beast has extra-long tentacles that are moving all around the floor of the boat. Even if it lies dead in the boat, its tentacles will still be able to sting its prey.

Selah continues to bark. I hear a scream in the distance and know that someone has already been stung by the creatures. I quickly wrangle this one into the net and throw it overboard. Returning to the driver's seat, I move the boat toward the snorkelers.

There are blood-curdling screams, along with shouts for help. It seems that all the swimmers have been stung. Four people are in the water, and Man o' War are all around them. I throw a life ring out to them. One young man is calling to the others to grab hold, but the stings are so excruciating that they don't hear him. They are all flailing in the water.

I blow the horn to get their attention and then throw out another life ring. Three of the four grab hold, and I tug them to the steps of the boat, helping them aboard. All three are badly stung. I move to the glove compartment to retrieve the first aid kit. I then find the bottle of vinegar I keep in the boat for cleaning. I start pouring the vinegar on the wounds.

I hear one of the young ladies on the boat shouting and pointing, "He's going under!"

The fourth snorkeler is already under the water, flailing.

Lord, protect me from the stings, I pray. I then dive in.

I swim under the water through the tentacles and find the man floating downward. Even in the water, his body looks swollen and blistered from the multiple stings. He seems to be in the middle of the group of creatures and still has one attached to his leg. I gently pull it off, and it swims away.

Lord, please protect him from further stings and save him, I pray.

I grab him under his arms and swim back to the boat. Even in such pain, the other three help me pull him into the boat.

Very calmly, I feel for a pulse, but there is none. I begin compressions, praying silently the whole time. I turn toward the young man standing over me.

"Call 911," I say.

"Our phones are on our boat!" he yells.

I look back around, and the two girls are kneeling, crying, and one is holding the young man's hand.

"Please don't leave me, Dillon!" she sobs as tears roll down her wet face.

I continue compressions. I know that his time is short; this young man will either live or die. It is all up to the Lord above. Everything in me wants him to live.

The other young man, even in his own pain, tells me he will take over. I search his eyes and know he needs to try. Even if the young man dies, his friend will know he's done all he can.

"Oh, Trent, please help him. Please!" the young lady holding Dillon's hand begs.

Trent starts compressions on his friend while I put my hand on Dillon's forehead and bow my head to pray.

"Nettie, I'm trying! Come on, buddy; don't leave us!" Trent shouts.

I feel a power being released into Dillon's body and know my prayers have been answered.

I immediately put vinegar on his wounds and instruct Nettie and the other girl to apply the vinegar to their wounds. I grab a bucket and dip it into the ocean water and then tell them to use the water to unleash the venom.

"Don't rub the area," I implore, jumping into the driver's seat and heading toward the other boat.

"Where are your phones?" I yell over the roar of the boat engine.

Trent looks up from administering CPR. "They're in the zippered bag in the back of the boat!"

I move the boat close to theirs and jump aboard their vessel. I retrieve their bag and throw it onto my boat.

Nettie grabs the bag to find her phone and calls 911. The operator stays on the line with us and continues giving instructions.

"The rescue boat will be here in two minutes!" Nettie relays. "Jennie, let me help you."

Neither girl is concerned with themselves; they continue to put water on the wounds of Dillon.

Water finally spurts from Dillon's mouth. We roll him over to his side, helping him get the water out of his lungs. The others are overjoyed that their friend has life again. They act like all will be well, but I feel unsettled. I look toward the shore to see if help is on its way yet, but it is not. I take a deep breath and close my eyes.

Lord, lead me, I whisper.

Dillon is weak and cannot seem to breathe correctly. He keeps grabbing at his throat. I again run to the first aid kit and grab an EpiPen. I administer the shot into his thigh, and his breathing immediately settles into a good routine.

We hear the sirens before we see the rescue boat. As they near our boat, the EMT workers can't believe the terrible situation of these young adults.

The EMT workers come aboard our vessel and start examining everyone.

One of them looks my way. "Ma'am, were you stung?"

"No," I say.

"How did you not get stung?" Nettie asks.

"They were all around us. You jumped in, and they were all around you too," Jennie adds.

"I guess the Lord watches over those who help others in a crisis," I say.

Jennie and Nettie nod simultaneously. "Amen to that!" Nettie responds.

Later that night, I try to sleep, but the events of the evening play over and over in my head. The young snorkelers had been so brutally injured. Pacing around the house, I think about how Dillon would have died if I had not obeyed the still, small tug in my heart to steer my boat in their direction. Maybe they all would have died, having been stung so many times and not being able to get back to their boat. I am thankful that the Lord God used me to help them. The care they showed one another and the hugs they all offered me later still play in my thoughts. Dillon could not hug me, though; he grabbed my hand from the stretcher, thanking me for helping save him.

At the rescue, the EMTs told the snorkelers how lucky they had been. The spring is when they see the Man o' War in this region, but never had they seen them this close to the shore. The EMTs also gave me confidence that, although the injuries were bad, the quick thinking and action on my part had saved the snorkelers. Dillon would remain in the hospital for further treatment, but they felt sure he'd make a full recovery.

I listened but knew in my heart that it had nothing to do with my quick actions and everything to do with God's healing power and mercy. "Thank you so much, Lord, for putting me in the right place at the right time," I pray aloud.

By now, Selah is fast asleep, not a care in the world. I try to lie down, but still I toss and turn, anxiously awaiting sleep. I want to see him, but as hard as I try, I cannot find sleep, nor can I find Levi.

Days pass. I stay inside, willing sleep to come. I need to see him. Even if only in a dream, it would mean everything to me to see him.

The days quickly give way to weeks. Still, nothing.

I know I have to get ahold of myself. Honestly, I have not eaten or slept enough to even dream, yet there is still no sign of Levi. Something is amiss, for sure. How could I have felt so much peace just days ago and now be overcome by the helplessness I am feeling? I have to do something about this instead of wallowing in uncertainty.

Could this be what they call *depression*?

Selah, on the other hand, plays, eats, and sleeps as if she has no worries in the world. She tries to console me, but I feel so lost in thought, as if a brain fog has taken over me. What could have happened to Levi or even the Keepers, my only family? I know I have to pull myself out of this, but it is easier said than done.

Stress has overtaken me. For weeks now, I have fasted and prayed, and still, no answers.

I feel a pit in my stomach and know something is very wrong, so I intensify my workouts. I swim laps in the pool until I have no breath left. I work every machine in the shed for hours until my muscles ache.

It is now a Wednesday, close to midnight, and I have no peace. Selah is snuggled in her bed and only lifts her head as I go out the French doors to the balcony. I am so unsettled. How can I feel this way in this beautiful paradise full of adventure and unimaginable beauty? How can I be this troubled, not only in my spirit but, it would seem, in everything?

I decide to go down to our beach. I light the tiki torches and kick off my shoes to feel the sand between my toes. The coolness and grainy texture stir me. I decide a midnight swim could be refreshing. I swim out into the water, and as it glistens over my body, the full moon acts as a light, guiding my way.

I swim toward the ocean and then turn back toward Cambridge Beach. I tread water and gaze at the cottages. I hear laughter at the beach; it must be a group of tourists or workers who just got off their shifts. Sometimes I wish I could be normal, but that is not who I was created to be. Plus, there is no point in wishing; that would get me nowhere.

I watch the beach interactions intently, hoping to feel happy, but my loneliness only grows. I swim back to my side of the beach. By now, I am tired because I have overdone it. My muscles ache, and my breathing is labored.

I look at the steps and just cannot attempt the climb. I go to the shed, retrieve a blanket, and use the air compressor to inflate a small boat. I climb in and paddle into the water. I lie there in the boat, staring up at the stars. The gentle water sways back and forth. I pray and plead with God to send Levi back to me, but there is silence. I float out near the cliffs and throw a rope around one of the jutted rocks. I lie back and finally fall asleep.

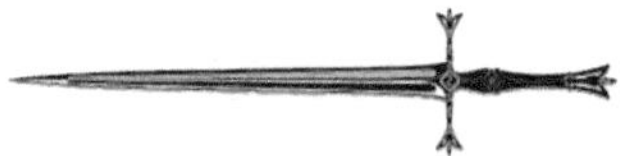

The next morning, I awaken to the sound of the workers driving into work, most likely at Simon's. I listen to the scooters' tires on the pavement as they crush a few pebbles and sand. Sound carries on the water; I guesstimate that it must be around 5:30 or 6:00 a.m. I am cold and shivering. The water has gotten cooler overnight. I maneuver my way back to shore and shiver up my steps to a much warmer environment. After feeding and letting Selah out, I shower. Then I fix myself something to eat.

There is one can of soup left on the shelf; I have not been to the store in a while. Soup and crackers will be my breakfast. I have to force myself to eat, but finally, I finish the meal. I feel dazed but not tired.

I decide to go out. If the Lord has given me peace, then the imminent danger must be over.

Maybe I should use a disguise? I think. No, whatever is happening, I will face it as myself, and face it head-on.

I dress in a beige cotton pullover dress with a bit of lace around the V-neck and three-quarter-length sleeves. I put on matching spandex shorts, just in case I ride the scooter. I pull my hair into a swooping ponytail and then into a messy bun and adorn it with golden hair clips. The humidity has jumped, so I smooth in hair serum to calm down any frizziness.

"No, Selah, you're staying here." Selah whines but then settles down in her bed near the gas log fireplace that I never use. I shuffle into a pair of brown leather thong sandals.

I take some money from the safe and put it into a cross-body purse. I then strap the purse over my arm and neck and retrieve my messenger bag, which is filled with water, snacks, and my iPad.

Standing in the garage, I cannot make up my mind which to drive: the car or the scooter. I choose the scooter and drive to the ferry. Once on the ferry crossing to Hamilton, I sit and watch the people. They are oblivious to who I am. I divert my attention to two teenage girls giggling and telling each other their deepest secrets and how they feel about this or that.

I think: *I am saving you from an evil that you would never think is possible. You have no earthly idea, and I am glad you do not. Enjoy yourselves, laugh, and have a full life.*

I think all of this as my own heart aches.

Hamilton hosts an abundance of eateries and shops with enough to keep a girl's mind off all the stresses of the past weeks.

I go to a quaint coffee shop called Java Joe's. I order a mocha and then move to a table near the corner window. I grab my tablet from my bag and begin to surf the web. I research the crime in the area; there's nothing too much out of the ordinary. A Bermuda scooter has been stolen; a reward is offered if found.

There is an ad from a church seeking shelter for a homeless single mom and her child currently living in the caves. I memorize the address so I can help her through monetary funds.

Why haven't I thought of doing something like this before?

I watch as couples sit together, laughing and enjoying each other's company. Everyone has somebody except me.

I long for companionship, but I know my life does not support that kind of pleasantry. My life is dedicated to a cause, and that is just the way it is. Still, I watch and listen curiously to how couples speak to one another. I relive the conversations in my mind, pretending it is me with a friend laughing and giggling, just as the young girls were on the ferry.

I look around, truly observing the people around me. I honestly do not think I have ever really looked at them as real people; I have always looked at them as helpless victims. As I observe, I see college students completing homework assignments, mothers with their little ones, a fussy baby that must be teething, a lonely girl sitting by herself, just staring into her coffee cup as if the weight of the world is on her shoulders, and two older retired ladies talking about the past and catching up on their families.

As I watch the young girl sitting by herself, I begin to feel what she feels: loneliness, rejection, uncertainty, and thoughts of suicide. I lift an urgent prayer for her. *Lord, I do not know her, but I see her. I feel her pain. Would you ease this hurt that is within her? Please give her peace, hope, and joy again.*

One by one I look around the room and feel what each of these people feel. I begin to pray for these human brothers and sisters. Here again, I have never really thought about being that connected to them. It is now as if my eyes are open for the first time. We are all on this journey, and yes, the journey is hard, but joy and happiness are here for the taking. Each person could find joy in God if they would only listen to their spirit within.

I shut my eyes, and I can hear their spirits calling out. *Oh, God, let their spirits awaken. Let them feel you, and give them your peace.*

When I open my eyes, peace surrounds this place, and even the workers start smiling and acting like it is the Christmas season.

A wave of joy continues to flow. One man answers his phone and announces that he has just become a grandfather; he buys everyone in the place a free coffee. The sad girl I prayed for minutes earlier, her face now shines like an angel, and her smile is brilliant. Joy truly shows on her face. The baby stops fussing and begins to coo, looking at its mother with such love that the mother's face changes from aggravation and helplessness to a sigh of relief and motherly love. People began to change their moods.

What a happy place to be, I realize. *Lord, thank you! You answered my prayers so very fast.* I've never realized that God could pass the peace to a whole area through me without my being right next to a specific person.

I pay for my mocha and thank the man for my free refill, which I take in a to-go cup. As I pass people on the street, I smile, and they start smiling back.

Wow, what a beautiful day. I start to feel what these people feel for the first time in my existence. The fasting and prayer have done wonders. Not only can I let go of the old way of thinking, but God is showing me a new thing.

I stop in at a boutique called Atelerie. It has an airy, pink feel that smells of clean ocean air. The store sells everything from plates and gifts to jewelry and clothing. I buy a white cotton top and a blue jean skirt with silver jewelry to match. In the back of the store, I find a small array of pet supplies and clothing. I buy Selah a small chew bone and a blue jean jacket to match my skirt. What will Selah think? I don't know if she will like my purchases; I've never bought her clothing before, but why not?

I shop around many other boutiques and then eat a late lunch at The Pickled Onion on Front Street.

By the time I leave Hamilton, it is evening. The day has passed quickly, and I'm finally feeling a bit tired. As I take the ferry back to Cambridge, I truly enjoy the scenery around me. The evening sky with the sunset looming and even the waves from the ferry catch my attention. It is like my eyes are being opened to new sights.

I am not so focused on the fight but on life itself. The waves hit the ferry, and the spray splashes on my face. The water feels cool against my skin, and evening gives way to night. I close my eyes and breathe in the salty air, which fills me with peace.

I exit the ferry and stop by the grocery store on the way home. The quaint store has everything I need. I buy salad fixings, steamed veggies, a loaf of artisan bread, and fresh fruits for dessert. All are fresh, homemade, and organic. I buy a little more than I need because I do not like going to the grocery store. My garden usually tides me over, but I've already eaten everything in my garden. I load the groceries into the scooter's cargo storage, fill Selah's basket, put what is left into my messenger bag, and hang bags on my handlebars.

Just as I am getting on the scooter, someone grabs my arm. It is him, the man from the lighthouse, the same man with the girl at the botanical gardens. At present, he is alone.

I am startled, but I stand firm. I stand with courage and assurance that I will be fine.

Then I feel it happen: peace fills me, and I pass it on to him. His eyes fill with tears, and he begins to weep.

I do not know what might happen next, so I say, "Let's move to the umbrellaed tables over here to get out of everyone's way."

He looks around, and we both notice that a few people at the store have begun to stare. It would appear to those passing by us that this is a lover's quarrel, so people move on. I do not feel threatened by the man this time; things seem different somehow.

"What have you done to me?" he asks.

"What do you mean?"

"Ever since I passed you on the stairs at the lighthouse, something has happened to me." Tears stream down his face, and I really notice him, unlike our first encounter.

I note that his face is not hardened anymore. His eyes are not as dark and piercing; they are now soft and humble. He no longer looks like he wants to hurt me.

"Let's sit and talk for a moment. What's your name?" I ask.

"My name is Ethan."

"Hi, my name is Awna."

He wipes his face with the back of his hand.

"So, Ethan, tell me what has changed."

He takes a breath and begins his story. "My girlfriend, Rosie, and I came to Bermuda with a plan. We were going to steal enough money from some of the rich houses on the water and then find us a child. We were willing to kill if we had to."

"What do you mean, find a child?" I ask.

"Rosie can't have children. We've been together for five years and have seen many doctors, but we don't have money for all that in vitro stuff. We can't adopt, because we both have records. You know, we've been 'in the pen.' So, we decided to take from the rich people here in paradise." He points to the mansions on the banks and cliffs.

Ethan then sighs and looks down, his wild, greasy hair hanging in his eyes.

"We figured we could steal enough stuff and sell it. Then we'd nab a kid between two to four years old, you know, so they wouldn't remember anything. There's some of those homeless children that we even thought about grabbing."

His hands start to shake as he continues.

"We had the houses cased out and even saw one kid we could take. Then I passed you, and something happened. Everything changed. I told Rosie I couldn't do it. She got mad and took all the money we had left, and I guess flew out of here. She called me a coward."

I look at Ethan, tall and bulky with a muscular build. Now he just looks frightened, crying like a child.

"Things may not change right away, Ethan, but I can assure you that if you give your heart and life to Jesus, you will find the peace that you so desperately crave."

There is silence, but I continue. "God will bring you to your destiny if you trust Him."

"I want to trust! And I want to change, but I'm not a good person, Awna."

"Ethan, God makes all things new, if we just believe."

"How? Believe what?"

"Believe that God sent His Son, Jesus, to die for your sins and that He took your place, Ethan, so that you may live. The evil in this world is great, and I'm telling you that it won't be easy, but it will be a better life. Have you ever heard about Jesus or been to church?"

"I used to go to some church as a child; my foster parents made me. I haven't even thought about it for years."

I lead him in the Sinner's Prayer, and tears of forgiveness flow over the years of the forgotten man. We sit and talk a while longer. I answer his questions, and when I think he is on the right path, I give him some money from my purse for food and for a place to stay.

"Awna, I can't pay you back."

"It's a gift, Ethan. Just make sure you stay on the right path. No more stealing or thoughts of taking a child!"

I get up to leave but do not feel released. *Okay. Lord, what now?*

I take a deep breath. "Ethan, if you decide to stay in Bermuda for an extended vacation, I'd be happy to help you grow spiritually."

This broken man quickly accepts. As I drive away, he agrees to meet me for lunch a few days from now at the botanical gardens.

I shake my head as I board the ferry. *Why this? Why this now, God?*

I am not so sure about this new turn of events. I never like to commune with people, but I know I have to trust God in my every movement. I am not even sure that Ethan truly meant his acceptance of Jesus, but who am I to say? It is, after all, between him and his Maker.

As I reach the curve to the cottage, I hear Selah barking. She stands at the living room window, wagging her nub, so excited to see me. I never stay gone from her this long. Has she always been this excited to see me?

Even Selah is changing. Something has definitely started to change for both of us since Levi's absence. My heart aches at the thought of him; he is my protector and my only friend. Why is God suddenly directing me on such a different path?

As the breeze overtakes the cottage on the hill, I stand in wonder at the day I've had. On the balcony of my bedroom, I gaze at the night sky, taking in the beauty and the stars that shine like sparkles in the sky, as if dancing to the tune of Heaven's songs. I close my eyes and let the breeze sweep through me. This same breeze creeps through the house and makes its way into every room. It overtakes every nook and cranny of my being. I feel rejuvenated and alive, like when the Keepers wake me from a deep dormant sleep.

I open my eyes to find a light surrounding me; my Heavenly Father shines His light and love all around me. I stand basking in His favor and know for sure something has changed.

CHAPTER 8

TRUST

The next morning, as the sun glistens across the blue waters, a calmness like I have never felt before fills me. I feel such peace and decide to venture out to Simon's for breakfast.

Simon's is not that busy this morning. I read *The Royal Gazette* while sipping coffee when a familiar voice speaks over my shoulder.

"There you are; I've been looking for you!"

I look up to see that it is Will!

"Oh, hello, Will," I say coolly.

"May I sit?"

"Suit yourself."

I wonder why fear has not overtaken me, or why I don't have an uneasy feeling. He sees my confused look and quickly moves on to an explanation.

"Umm, well, after you left the lighthouse a few weeks back, the guy that bumped into you on the stairs came to the lighthouse asking questions about you. He had gotten your name from the guest book in the lobby. My grandmother and I thought we'd better try to find you to make sure you were all right. I have been all over the island looking for you, and I came here a couple of times but couldn't find you. This was my last try before I called the authorities; we thought he may have done you harm."

I believe him. In fact, I know in my heart that he is telling the truth.

"Thanks, Will. It turns out he did find me."

I could see the shocked look on Will's face.

"Oh, it was nothing. He just needed help finding something; it's all taken care of."

The look on Will's face tells me he is not sure about my answer, but he decides to let it go. I quickly offer to buy him a coffee, and all seems forgotten.

I search his eyes and his mannerisms, and I conclude that he is still a nice and trustworthy person.

I lift a prayer for confirmation and feel peace.

I give in to centuries of loneliness and begin to laugh and talk about everyday life. Will has a bit of dry humor that catches me by surprise as he waits for a laugh or response to his silly, funny ideas and stories. I smile when needed and even add an occasional laugh.

"So, do you live close to Simon's?"

"Umm, yeah, just up the hill a little way."

My answer is interrupted as Chef Michael passes by.

"Good morning; is everything all right here?"

"Oh yes!"

I smile, and Will nods approval as the young chef asks our names.

"Yes, I've seen you both here. Are you here on work permits also?"

"My grandmother and I run the lighthouse for the next five years at least, but yes, we do have work permits."

"Yeah, I know what you mean. I came back last July: peak season for tourism. They needed an extra hand, and next thing I knew, the executive chef left, they hired me on the spot, and here I am for the next four years too."

"How about you?"

Both heads turn to me as Chef Michael poses the question.

"Oh, umm, I'm here for an extended vacation. I'm actually a Bermudian with a long family lineage from here. But I'm into missions, so I'm gone quite a bit."

"Yeah, why not choose the most beautiful place on earth for a home place," Will says.

"I agree; you've got my vote on that," says the chef. "Well, I'll see y'all around. Enjoy your morning."

"Thanks," we say in unison.

As Chef Michael leaves, we are left to stare at each other, as if to say, "What's next?" An awkward silence fills the space until Will speaks up.

"Well, it's Saturday and it's a beautiful day. Would you like to go for a hike or go to the beach?"

I am totally caught off guard.

"Oh, I really should get back. Selah needs to be let out, and this is my . . ." I was going to say, "It's my day to clean or wash my hair" or something similar that I've heard humans say.

My hesitation is enough that he holds his hands up and says, "It's okay. Maybe another time. I understand stranger danger."

"What?" I say. "Oh, no, I didn't mean that."

"Well, Awna, you don't know me from Adam's house cat. I could be a hitman, a robber, or some criminal for all you know."

I burst out laughing. "I know you are none of those things; you would never have gotten a visa if you were."

"Oh yeah? I could be hiding out as a fugitive or pretending to be someone I'm not. Who knows. It's the kind of place for it, you know? You meet someone, tell them you're a doctor or rich gamer, and then you're gone in a week, and no one ever knows the truth."

"Sounds like you've had practice at this!" I say, shaking my head.

"Oh, no, no. I just watch TV."

We both laugh, and I mean I laugh for real.

I feel more trusting of him as we talk. I am so lonely without Levi; I just need to talk to someone.

"Okay. Let's go hang out for a little while, but I do have to bring Selah along. She'd just be devastated if she missed the opportunity to spend time with a crook."

I have NEVER, I repeat, NEVER, let anyone this close, not since Levi, let alone allowed them to know where I live. What am I thinking? Now my stomach turns to knots, nervous for what?

Regardless, I must trust in the confirmation of my prayer and the peace that I feel.

Selah is shocked when she sees Will but licks his face in utter jubilation. Will picks her up and rubs behind her ears, her favorite spot. When he puts her down, she turns circles in complete puppy folly. Once on the floor, she turns her head sideways, looking at me as if to say, "Have you lost your mind? Well, I'm so glad that you did."

Will is mesmerized by the so-called family cottage. It is more spacious than any one person needs, and it is impressive, high on the cliffs, overlooking the greenish-blue waters. He peers at the tall, vaulted ceilings and fine décor in the family room.

He observes the clean, airy cottage, and the shiny hardwood floors mirror his smile. The history of Bermuda adorns the walls; the pictures of the past are amazing. Books, entire collections of Shakespeare, and an array of music symphonies (Bach, Beethoven, Strauss, all the greats) fill the large wall library.

"Wow!" Will says, raising an eyebrow.

"Umm, what can I say? My family loved collecting books and music."

"Okay, when you said cottage, I thought 'small and cute,' but you didn't say anything about a huge, impressive mansion overlooking the adorned beauty of this fair

Island. Umm, so much for the so-called cottage, my lady." He bows as if I am royalty.

"Oh stop, silly. My family has been part of Bermuda for a very long time. It was not so costly when they built this place, and as time passed, the family renovated and expanded."

"Okay, I'd like to rent this when you're away on missions. I'm just saying."

Will wanders around, and my thoughts instantly go to my secret room upstairs. The door locks automatically once closed, and unless you know what you are looking for and how to push it to unlock it, you will never know it is there. I feel safe with him looking around. I know he wanted to.

"Go ahead and look around. I can sense your nosiness." I laugh. "Would you like some tea?" I shout in my best British accent.

"Sure!" he says as he moseys around. "You really need to work on that accent."

I do like this banter of fun from this human brother. I make the tea as he tours the lower level. Then, as if he cannot contain himself, he points up.

"May I?"

Before he takes the first step up the stairs, I shake my head in approval.

"I'll come with you while the water heats," I say with a smile.

Will seems to love the upstairs as much as he likes the downstairs. He strolls toward and out of every balcony to get a glimpse of the ocean, where he pauses, taking in the beauty.

When we get to my studio, he just stops and stares at the paintings.

"You painted these?"

"Yes."

"Wow, Awna. They're magnificent!"

He continues looking around the room. He touches a few canvases on the wall and then stops to notice some of my creations still on the easels. My work consists of clouds, sunsets, the beach with sand, seagulls, banyan trees, flowers from the botanical gardens, fish, and places around the island. All my art in every part of the world represents where I am at the moment. He stands gazing at my collection as if taking it all in.

"Awna, these should be in an art gallery. Do you sell them?"

"Oh, no. I paint just for fun."

"You're very talented; the colors look so real," he comments, touching another painting.

"Thank you," I say awkwardly.

After his tour, we make our way back downstairs. I pour his tea, and he motions to the piano. "You play?"

"Yes," I say shyly.

"Let's hear it, then."

I blush, hesitate, and then finally stroll over to the piano, putting my tea on a coaster. I sit down, closing my eyes to think of what to play, and then decide on "Für Elise" by Beethoven. He sits on the sofa and watches intently as I perform the piece. At the end, he claps.

"Bravo, bravo! Wow, that was awesome!"

I start talking quickly to divert the attention away from myself, totally unprepared for this praise of my talents.

"You know, it's sad that 'Für Elise' was never published during Beethoven's lifetime. It just goes to show that what we do right now may take on a powerful meaning later on." Will looks down thoughtfully, contemplating what was spoken.

"So true, and to think he was deaf yet composed such amazing musical pieces. God sure pours out His blessings in such unique ways," he says.

"Amen to that."

I smile and retrieve my tea from its coaster as we make our way to the patio. Upon my opening the French doors for Selah, who stands ready to bolt, the breeze makes the curtains dance in a rhythmic, excited expression. It is as if the whole house is alive, and I honestly feel more alive too.

We sit on the lawn chairs and gaze at the water while Selah smells and explores outside. The waves rhythmically slosh upon the cliffs as the sound surrounds us, as if part of a symphony. There are very few big waves that make it to the shore on this side of the island; it usually has to do with boats.

If you like waves, sometimes large ones, you would have to go to Horseshoe Bay, Sonesta, or Hungry Bay to experience them. That is where all the water sporting events take place. It is just the way the island is shaped as to which side will have more waves.

We sit for a bit and make small talk. I reveal the thoughts I've just had about the waves.

Taking it all in as he looks around, Will notices the stairs. "Oh my goodness. You do not! Come on! No way! Of course, you do." He speaks his thoughts aloud.

"What?" I say, frowning.

"You've got your own private beach!"

I shake my head and roll my eyes. "You want to see that too, I guess."

"Absolutely!" he exclaims. "Remember, I'm nosy," he smiles.

We stroll down the tiny steps that give way to the beach adorned with heavy-duty outdoor chairs, a table, an umbrella, and a fire pit. Of course, there is also "the shed" that most people would not even notice.

Will, of course, does notice and is impressed by swimming floats, towels, sunscreen, floating devices, and a kayak. He is thrilled by the fact that there is a cave inside the cliff, and by the fact that I call it my shed.

In reality, he has no idea about the extent of my shed because I don't turn all the lights on. The lights that I do switch on give the impression that there are just a few things in the front of the shed. And once Will sees the kayak, he immediately asks to take it out.

"Of course," I say. "Enjoy!"

I grab a magazine from the shed and pretend to read. Selah and I glance up, watching this peculiar young man. He laughs at himself as he playfully almost tips over. The gentle waves rebel against him as he paddles farther out of the cove. He tries to balance his way through. I laugh at him as a small wave hits him, and he wipes his face but continues to paddle.

"You have done this before, right?" I yell.

"Umm, well, no, I haven't, but I've always wanted to!"

"You have to balance yourself."

"What?" he questions.

"You have to balance yourself," I say, standing this time. Okay!" he yells back.

I have always been nice and cordial to people. After all, that is why I am here: to help protect them. But I have never had a friendship, nor have I wanted a human one, except for Levi. I am perfectly fine with the spiritual friendship that Levi and I share, plus the occasional visits from my Keeper.

Until the 1800s, when Levi came into my life, I did not know the joy that having a friend could bring; he was all that I needed to get through the loneliness of life. The battle is still all I have ever really known. To protect these weak, frail, yet intriguing humans has been my life. Yet they have no idea of the evil that surrounds them or the fact that they need protection at all.

Spending time in prayer, fasting, working out, and training sums up my life. But one of the marvelous things to see is when God moves, working amid the humans. Now that is an experience that I would not want to give up.

Lord, would it be possible for me to have a friend? For that matter, is it possible that I could know how to be a friend?

Peace engulfs me as the thought penetrates my very soul. *I will try, Lord. Thank you!* I say to myself.

Will seems to be getting the hang of the kayak; he has now been at it for about an hour and looks like a pro. Although Will looks lanky, he does have muscles; I did not even notice any of this before. His wet hair is pushed back away from his face as he paddles from one thing to see to the next. He is like a curious kid with a new toy.

Will's cell phone rings and a picture of Ms. Banks pops up.

"Hey, Will. Your grandmother is calling."

"Answer it!" he yells back.

"How?" I ask.

"You don't know?" He turns his head with utter disbelief.

Who would I ever call? I am great with computers and technology, but I have never needed a phone to call anyone.

"Ugh, all right." I pick up the phone and fumble around with it until it answers. "Hello?"

"Will, that doesn't sound like you?"

"Oh, no, Ms. Banks, it's Awna."

"Oh, Awna, he found you. I'm so glad; we were very worried about you."

"Yes, ma'am; Will told me, but I'm okay. Thank you for checking on me. Will is kayaking right now; I am watching him from the beach."

"He's what?" There is a pause, and then she says, "Oh, all righty. Well, you two have fun."

There is another pause as if she is not sure what else to say. Nor am I.

"Umm, okay, we will," I reply cheerfully.

"Tell him he doesn't have to call me back since he found you."

We end the call, and I feel warm inside that someone cares about my well-being. *Wow, here is another feeling.* These feelings are something I am not in tune with.

I look up after hanging up and see the kayak upside down, but Will is nowhere in sight.

"Will!" I yell.

I scan the shoreline around the kayak, but I see nothing. Fear threatens to rise within me, but my instincts kick in. Along these cliffs are rocks hidden underwater. I know where they are, and they are near the overturned kayak. I run into the water and dive under, searching the underwater cliffs.

There he is, floating helplessly under the kayak. A rope I sometimes use to tie the craft had wrapped around his ankle and somehow attached itself to his foot. He must have tried to tie off to the rocks with his foot. I remove the rope and lead his unconscious body to shore. Still, no emotion or fear engulfs me as I get him to shore.

I do not use CPR. I just simply lay my hand over his heart and call out a prayer.

"Lord God of Heaven and earth, Lord over life and death, please help my new friend, Will. Please restore him and heal him, in Jesus's name."

In that instant, water gurgles from his mouth, and I roll him over, patting him on his back so the water can escape. His breathing is labored as I help him sit up. He is embarrassed, and the moment seems extremely awkward. Will looks like a surfer with light blonde hair, light blue eyes, and a lanky build of around six feet tall.

I am sure his ego must be bruised, I think.

"Umm, thanks, Awna."

He shakes his head, releasing the water from his ears, gagging, and spitting.

"Take slow, deep breaths," I say, helping him to a chair. He keeps coughing. I run to the unlocked shed and grab a bottle of water and another towel. Once he seems stable, I swim back into the water and grab the kayak by the rope.

Normally, I would have jumped in an overturned vessel, once righted, but in this instance, I do not want him to feel any worse. I carry the kayak to the shed and put it on the rack, and when I come back out, I see him sitting in the chair with his head in his hands.

Will looks up when he sees me coming back. "You know, I tied off with the rope on the rock. I put the rope on my ankle to enjoy the fish swimming by, but somehow I guess my balance was off and I flipped over. Maybe the rope got hung up on my ankle? I really don't remember what happened."

I walk closer to him. "Oh, Will, your head is bleeding, so my guess is that you hit your head on a rock. You probably passed out. You could have drowned, Will. Just sit tight. I'll be right back."

I head back to the shed to grab a first aid kit to clean the wound.

I say a silent prayer so that I do not scare him. I pray as I touch the wound, which is rather deep; he probably needs a few stitches. As I lift the prayer in my mind, the Lord flows healing through my body, and I feel the release that flows through my fingers while touching the wound.

The blood flow stops, and the wound closes, just as if it never happened.

"Okay, Will, you're all cleaned up." I put a piece of gauze over the wound, just for show, even leaving a trace of blood on the gauze. Blood is all over the towel, and drops of blood are on the sand. "I wouldn't bother it for a few days if I were you. You know, let it heal."

I throw away the bandages, and we sit and talk for a bit longer.

"Well, I'm really embarrassed," Will says.

"Oh, don't be silly; this could've happened to anyone."

"Yeah, but it usually doesn't happen to me."

"Well, that's because it usually happens to me!" I laugh, knowing I am not telling the truth.

That reassures him as we both laugh. Selah comes down a few steps from where she was sleeping, looking suspicious.

"It's okay, sweet puppy. Come here."

She jumps to my lap as we sit and watch the waves touch the shore. We talk for about fifteen more minutes; then Will says he had better get going. We walk up the stairs and into the house, where Bach plays softly.

Will frowns. "I don't remember you turning on the music."

I smile. "Well, you did hit your head."

He looks confused.

"Yeah, calm down. It's on a timer," I retort, smiling.

"I can't believe the girl who doesn't have a house phone or a cell phone has a computer, a gigantic house, security cameras all around, the best sound equipment, flat-screen TVs, and the best of everything."

"TVs which I hardly ever watch," I interject.

"You don't have a cell phone, but you travel the world. Isn't that enough reason to have one?"

"My goodness, Will. Does it bother you that much that I don't have a phone?"

"Well, as I take all this into consideration, you should at least have a landline."

I think about how observant he is and smile.

He smiles right back. "How am I going to get in touch with you or call you?"

Then we both laugh. "I've just never felt the need for one," I shoot back. "I don't have anyone to call."

Whoops. Why did I say that?

He pauses with concern. "Awna, you mean there isn't anyone that you need to keep in touch with?"

This is exactly why I never get close to my human brothers and sisters; they are way too curious, or maybe just too nosy. I am a quick thinker; I have had a lot of time for such things, but at this moment, conversing with a real live person on a personal level, I feel caught and cornered.

"Will, the phone plan I'd have to get would be so expensive. I may live in this big old house, but I'm very frugal. Plus, I move all around the world, and the distant friends that I may encounter are in foreign villages with no cell service. Plus, I have internet here, so what more do I need?"

Will looks around. "I think you can afford it, and even a satellite phone if needed." He continues and smirks, "I mean, maybe you don't want to stay in touch with me?"

"Let me check your head again. You might have had a greater injury than at first glance," I retort, playfully moving toward him.

Will frowns as I giggle like a schoolgirl.

"Okay, okay. I promise to look into it," I say, just to appease him.

"You never answered my question, Awna."

"What do you mean?" I answer as sweetly as I can muster.

"Do you have family or close friends?" he repeats. "You really don't have anyone to call?"

"I . . . umm." The sudden sadness fills my spirit, and the truth is all that is left. "No, Will. I really have no one except Selah."

I cannot believe that I have just confirmed this for him, but for some reason I trust him.

"My mother passed away years ago. She was an only child, and I am an only child. I have never actually met my father, but I know who he is. Besides, I have my Heavenly Father, and that is enough for me."

Will ponders this as he walks to the door. "My grandmother said you were alone. She always knows these things, but she also said you were not alone, whatever that means, and that she felt a kindred spirit with you."

I smile, and it is genuine. "I know. I feel it too with both of you."

With that, he leaves, and I am once again alone. Not really alone, though. I have God and Selah, but. . . . Sadness creeps back in as I think, *And I used to have Levi.*

The next morning, the breeze is brisk. The curtains in the living room blow out from the panes. I look at the clock, and it is nearly 6:00 a.m. I look at the outdoor temperature gauge—fifty-eight degrees. Yes, there is a bit of a chill in the air. Our Bermuda broadcast from ZBM 9 News says it will be brisk the next few mornings but then get warmer each day.

I pause, standing very still, as a chill overtakes me. Something is different. I have never been able to feel much difference in my body temperature, just enough to notice when it is slightly cooler or warmer. This usually occurs only after a fight, but then it feels like shock-shaking. Sometimes, when I get out of the water, I can feel there is a small difference.

Those feelings have never compared to this.

I think back to the other night when I was swimming and became chilled and shaken. I have never thought one thing about that.

I frown as Selah barks and runs around me. "You feel it too, Selah?" She barks in agreement.

I close the doors, light the pilot light, and turn on the gas logs in the fireplace, as this is the only source of heat in the cottage. I then make coffee, one of my comforts in this life. While the living room begins to warm, I grab a blanket and sit outside, thinking about the latest events.

Oh, Lord God, I need direction. Please help me know what to do, how to do it, and how to adapt to these new events and friends. I pray for Levi; I pray for his safety. Where is he, Lord? What has happened?

Oh, Lord. Let the words of my mouth and the meditation of my heart be pleasing unto you, I whisper.

As I pray and meditate, the prayers rise from my spirit, from the deepest part of me. These are the prayers I have learned over many, many centuries.

I pray in the Heavenly language taught by Alon, and when I finish, hours have passed. The sun has crept high in the sky. It must be noon; the house is now warmer than the outdoors, so I turn on the air conditioning. My goodness, this has become awkward trying to figure out my comfort zone.

Selah and I quickly get ready for the day. I plan to meet Ethan at the Gardens between 1:30 p.m. and 2:00 p.m. I open my secret room and walk around, looking at the disguises, wigs, clothes, makeup, and jewelry all awaiting the next page in this drama. I step through the hanging clothes to where the fireproof safe stands and unlock it with the combination. I take $5,000 from the money box and record it in the ledger. I then put the money in an envelope and print his name on it.

For Ethan.

I tuck a note inside.

Ethan,

May God bless your path and bring you into His fold with great understanding.

~Awna~

This should be enough to get him back home and then a little extra to get an apartment. Hopefully, he will get a job and a fresh start in a small town somewhere. The rest is up to him.

While in the safe, I write out another check for $20,000. This one is for the single homeless mother and her child I read about the other morning while having coffee.

I have memorized the address of the church from the ad:

The Evangelical Church

1 Mission Road

Mt Pleasant, Bermuda

I have been to the church before. It has a beautiful tan exterior with a hint of pink undertones and white trim all around. On my first visit to the church, I sat in the back pew so that I could be in and out and go unnoticed. The beautiful couple who pastored the church seemed trustworthy; I knew the money would go to the woman.

I close my eyes and pray, "Yes, Lord, let it be so."

I also retrieve from the safe a deed to Bermuda Bay Club Condos, another benefit from the Keepers. I write and attach a letter to the church to explain what the money and condominium should be used for, and then I enclose the key. This should do nicely; the young lady and her child will have a home and a fresh start.

Before leaving, I continue to research. I have noticed something new about properties in Bermuda during this visit and kept the information in my files. These properties were not here on my last visit to Bermuda. This particular deed, the paperwork states, is non-tangible property, meaning it is much like a timeshare, stocked with furniture and necessities. On the other hand, nothing personal is included: no cars, stocks, bonds, and such.

Several of the property descriptions include pictures. One shows a large building with small vacant one- or two-bedroom apartments. These are in a nice neighborhood with manicured landscaping.

Then I see it, and chills cover my body. There is a picture of an amazing playground. I search for information about the area. There is a daycare within walking distance, and a new resort looking to hire a few new employees. I know without any doubt what I am supposed to do with this property.

I write another letter to the church and include my directives for that property. I want the church to gather as many homeless families as possible from around Bermuda. "Find the mothers or fathers living in caves begging for money in their rich homeland. Put them into these properties." I know it will be nowhere near enough space for all of them, but at least it is a start.

One thing I have learned through these many years is that God loves His children and has a plan for them, just like He has a plan for me. In the letter, I also ask that workplace readiness counseling be provided for these homeless people to help train them for interviews and jobs.

Today I choose the scooter to meet Ethan. I put Selah in the basket and shut the lid slightly to protect her from the sun and heat.

"Here's our water bottles, Selah," I say as I nestle them in the basket.

I stop by Champs Variety Store. They have recently added a deli, and it is right on my way out of Cambridge Road. I grab some ready-made sandwiches and chips for lunch with Ethan. Selah makes room for the items. She snuggles to the side of the basket and, as usual, never makes a sound as we travel.

The breeze blows through the botanical gardens, making the trees turn this way and that, as if they are part of a marching band. The flowers keep time, swaying to the identical beat.

I look toward the Camden House as it stands on the premises in all its glory. It gives way to a spectacular view, with its old colonial look speaking of an era long, long ago. The delicately painted shutters are like bows on a gift, ready to be unwrapped. A person knows they are near royalty as they gaze upon its beauty.

I watch the hummingbirds sip the nectar from the colorful flowers while the island canary flutters by me singing such delightful tunes, telling the story of her day to all who care to listen. I watch families and couples stroll around hand-in-hand, arm-in-arm.

I sit on a bench and wait under a massive tree with roots spilling far beyond the normal venue. In fact, it looks like there are many trees clustered in an area. In reality, it is just one, the Banyan tree, much like the one I lay in the last time I was here. I think about what I will suggest to Ethan. He needs a plan of action when he makes his way back to the States.

An hour passes, and I eat my sandwich, sharing a bit with Selah. I feed the birds the bread from Ethan's sandwich as I wait and begin to doubt that he will even show.

I wait and wait, to no avail. Hours later, at 4:30 p.m., I leave. I have a bad feeling about this. *Lord, I pray that Ethan's salvation prayer was real and not prayed out of desperation, only to fall on shifting sand.*

On our way back home, I stop by the post office to mail the deed and money to the church. Then I hesitantly make my way to the cellular store. If for no other reason, I could use the smartphone as a minicomputer. Staying alert to the crime in the surrounding areas always gives me an advantage over the enemy. As Moloch's clan hunts for me, they always leave a trail of crime behind them. It would be handy to have the phone for news, information, quick weather reports, or just to play games.

Who am I kidding? It would be great to stay connected with my new friends.

I choose a no-contract plan. Sure, I have to pay more, especially with the international plan, but I never know where my next move will be. The employee puts the global SIM card into the phone. This way, no matter where I travel, I will be able to communicate with Will and Ms. Banks. If I am going to dream, I will dream big. Plus, I like knowing people care about me. *What is it with them, anyway?* I had no idea people could care so much.

After getting hooked up with my new phone and, yes, practicing a bit with its gadgets, I decide to drive to the lighthouse. Actually, I feel compelled to go. It is indeed a new phone, after all; I have to get their phone numbers.

The extra breeze today feels good on my face. As I travel up the winding hill, Gibbs Hill Lighthouse comes into view. I round the corner and park beside the phone booth, my favorite little spot. It is close to 6:00 p.m. now, and I am just in time for an evening meal. I creep in and grab a table without being noticed. I do not see Will or his grandmother. The server takes my order and gives Selah a little bowl of water. I put her out of sight in the booth to not cause any disruption. Only two other customers are in the place, so I do not think anything will be said.

I eat and wait around, still not seeing my new friends. I consider asking the server about Will but decide to just head home. As I am walking out, I hear his voice. He is standing in the office behind the restaurant. I smile and almost reach the opened door when I hear Will say to Ms. Banks, "That's impossible!"

They hear me and turn. Just as I step into the doorway, their faces go white, as if they have seen a ghost.

I am not very in tune with people, so I do not know what I have walked into, but they both stammer over their words.

"Awna!" Ms. Banks smiles politely. "We were just talking about you. What did you hear, dear?"

I stand there with a blank look on my face, not knowing how to respond. Will closes the gap between us and shuts the door.

"Awna, can we talk for a moment?"

My stomach does a flip-flop, another feeling I have never experienced. "Umm, sure." I know enough to stay silent and let them do the talking.

Will starts the conversation.

"I guess . . . let's just start with the accident. I know I hit my head and that there was some blood because it was on my shirt and the towel. When I came to, blood was even on my hands. I'd felt it and knew that it was a deep wound, but when Grams took the bandage off, there was nothing except a trace of blood on the bandage. No blood was matted to my hair, either. There was not even a sign of a wound, and, for that matter, it never even hurt after I left the beach."

They both look at me for a response. There is none.

I want to run, but the Lord holds me still. I look at them both. They stand, awaiting an answer.

"I don't know what to tell you, Will, but to say, 'Praise God for His healing power!'"

When Ms. Banks speaks, her words are soft and soothing. "We are not trying to make you feel uncomfortable, dear. We're just a little confused and curious as to the facts as we see them."

She pulls out a large, old, tattered book and opens it to a specific page. The date she points to is 1846, and there are old, old photographs.

I now really want to run and flee from the truth.

I know what they have found, but the Lord holds me paralyzed and does not allow me to move. I try to keep no expression on my face but then opt to go with a confused look. After all, what they have found cannot be possible, not in their world.

Ms. Banks comes closer, showing me the tattered book and its pages, as well as the guest book I recently signed. The photos she shares are from 1846.

"You see, Awna, we've found a most striking resemblance between you and these photos."

Ms. Banks pushes the photo close to me. In the photo, I am trying to avoid the flash of light from the photographer's bulb; nonetheless, my image is caught in the side of the photo.

My memories flooded back to that place in time. It was the year 1846, and the Gibbs Hill Lighthouse was being constructed by the Royal Engineers. The island was so excited to have this new lighthouse, and it was a sight to see, with its sturdy cast-iron statue. It was one of the first lighthouses in the world to be made of such material, and it had been a magnificent undertaking. People all around the island came to watch the progress. At 354 feet above sea level, the lighthouse has always been a beacon of light for ships and fishermen to safely sail the Atlantic seas at night. The cliffs and rocks that jut out of nowhere along the Bermuda shoreline make for such an adventure but can also be deadly to people aboard boats and ships. Gibbs Hill Lighthouse has been a safe beacon for many travelers, cargo ships, and other sea vessels.

I just stand there and let them talk. I will see what they come up with.

Ms. Banks begins: "The pictures of this beautiful young girl hold a striking resemblance to you, as well as these signatures in 1846 when the construction was complete. And look here again in 1846, as onlookers signed the old books."

I pretend to act interested and curious as Ms. Banks continues.

"Yes, I see what you mean," I respond.

"And here's another one in 1953, when Queen Elizabeth visited Bermuda as part of her round-the-world tour. I found all of these as I cleaned the attic last week. I was comparing the visits made by people from around the world as well as the locals who'd been part of memorable events in Bermuda. I just happened to look at our recent logs after viewing the photos and compared the logs with modern-day visits. I found that your signature is oddly the same as the past signatures, all just signed, 'Awna, Bermuda.'"

I smile. *Why did I sign the log every time? What was I thinking?* I never thought anyone would be around to notice.

I have to produce something to say. "As I've told Will, my family has been a part of Bermuda for a very long time. Do you mind if I look at the signatures?"

"Oh, sweetheart, please do. I'd love for you to!"

I act amazed at how my signature is so much like my ancestors of six generations ago and how much I look like the woman in the photo. I throw in as much overwhelming amazement as I can.

"Oh, Ms. Banks, do you mind if I take a picture of all of this and the signatures? After all, my mother told me that Awna is a family name." That was the truth.

"Oh, no, dear. By all means."

I pull out my smartphone and begin taking pictures of the signatures and pictures. Will quickly shifts to the idea that I have gotten a phone. I ask the two for their phone numbers and try to change the subject as much as possible. I take pictures of them as well as selfies of us all.

"Well, thank you so much for sharing this astonishing information with me. As Will has told you, I have no remaining family, so this is just huge for me," I say as I allow my voice to quiver and tears to escape my eyes.

"As far as the signatures, I can only imagine that my family wanted to keep a family name from past generations."

I am trying to make my escape when Will says, "Okay, all that makes sense. We know that person in 1846 couldn't be you, but Awna, what about my wound? I know what I felt and saw. I mean, the blood was on my hands and shirt and even on a towel."

I stand there pondering my next words carefully. "I honestly don't know what to say, Will, or what you want me to say."

My words float out so delicately that I know it is the Lord speaking through me. "Will, do you believe that

God can heal you? Do you understand where His healing comes from? I sure don't. All I know is that I'm thankful for His healing, and I claim Isaiah 54:17, which says that no weapon formed against us shall prosper. Then in Isaiah 53:5, Scripture says that 'with his stripes we are healed.' We live in a world of mysteries, Bermuda being one of them. Where is your faith, man?"

Will stands there dumbfounded, as does Ms. Banks, although I catch a bit of a smile that develops on Ms. Banks's face.

I leave the two to think about this. We say our well-wishing goodbyes, so I know all will be fine.

CHAPTER 9

IMPENDING DANGER

That night, I toss and turn; neither dreams nor sleep will come. I get up and watch the news. I download games on my new phone. I go to the shed and work out for hours. I then pray and read until daybreak. I sit outside and watch the sun come up. Selah runs all around the yard until she can't stand it any longer and demands food.

"Selah, you're becoming a hungry little dog."

I stop. This is also strange, as Selah never begs for food. I mean, maybe when I'm dangling a treat in front of her she will beg, but this is different. Things are changing for us, and I do not know why. I need to pray more and pay close attention to the details around me, so I decide to start a fast, shutting myself off from the world. I need to hear from God.

I've been in prayer and fasting now for four days; I feel renewed, although my thoughts still drift to *God, where are the Keepers? What is happening in the spirit realm? Why is everything changing? What does all this mean? Give me what I need to endure this and still make a difference. Please send the Keepers, if they can make it through. If not, show your presence in my life. Only you can lead and guide me now.*

On the fifth night after leaving Will and Ms. Banks, I must have fallen asleep on the sofa. I awake with a start. As soon as my eyes open, I have a vision of a cliff. Darkness is all around. Ethan and Will are standing there, and behind them stands Rosie. The evil smile tells me everything I need to know. She has been overtaken by the enemy, and not just any enemy but a stronghold has possessed her.

My heart pounds as I come out of the vision. I frantically race up the stairs, wash my face, pull on clothes, brush my hair into a bun, and then grab my new phone.

I glance down at the phone. "Oh no!" I turned it off days ago to get alone with God.

As I turn it on, I already know what I will find. Ms. Banks has left many voice messages, but I can barely understand them.

"Selah, stay here. I will be back."

I grab the scooter and take a moment to pray.

Dear God, please protect my new friends. Please do not allow the evil to overtake Ethan. Bind satan's hands so that he will not overtake Rosie and Ethan, and please watch over Will.

I make my way up to the lighthouse. It is dark outside; it must be the wee hours of the morning. I stop and look up at the cloudless sky to estimate the time. The heavens tell their story with the position of the moon and stars. It is around 2:00 a.m. I hesitate but text Ms. Banks anyway to let her know that I am here. She meets me at the side door. We go upstairs to her apartment, where she closes the door.

"That man came back—the man at the lighthouse who was staring at you. He had the same girl with him, and they wanted to know how to find you. We told them we didn't know, trying to protect you. Awna, they took Will."

She bursts into tears as she staggers through her words. "I tried to call you."

"I'm sorry, Ms. Banks. I didn't have the phone on. Did you call the police?"

"Yes, they're looking, but he's been gone for over twenty-four hours now."

"Okay, I'm going to look too," I assure her.

"Oh, honey, you shouldn't do that. These people are very dangerous. That big man had a gun!"

My heart sinks. I know I have to get going; there is no time to lose.

"Ms. Banks, I want to pray with you before I go."

I know I am taking a chance praying with a human; she may be able to feel me pass the peace and may even see what I see. I am not sure.

As I touch her hands to pray, the power of God begins to flow. Time stands still, it seems, as we storm Heaven's gates for Will. As we pray, there are tears and chills, and the power of the Holy Spirit can be felt by us both. I think this might be too much for my newfound friend, but she holds tight to my hands.

She drops to her knees as I pass the peace to her; then we finish the prayer. I close my eyes, not sure of the impact the prayer has had on her. I have taken a significant risk here; I truly do not know why I am so drawn to these two humans.

Still shaking, she looks up at me. Her beautiful face shines as a glowing light surrounds it; it is a light that only I can see. The kindred spirit envelops us both, and she knows that there is something quite different about the prayer. There is also something quite different about me.

As tears creep down her cheeks, she smiles and only mutters these words: "Go, sweet child, and may the power of God overtake you and flow through you. May His hand of protection be upon us all."

I do not know how much she understands, religiously speaking, or how close she is with God, but I have peace about it and know it will be all right. I smile at her and leave, and I hear her thanking God for His hand of protection. I know her joyful and thankful worship will comfort her and bring a prayer cover over us.

When I leave the lighthouse, God allows me to see where Will is. I know the area but not the exact spot. It is just a feeling drawing me to a cliff. It is indeed a place near Cambridge, way too near my cottage. It's a cliff that I can see as I step out back on my veranda. It is a place where many weddings take place because the photography is breathtaking.

I arrive near the place, stop the scooter, and hide it in the bushes. I leave my helmet beside the scooter and then run to the spot. Just before the cliffs are a few bushy trees. I hide in the trees and listen. The waves forcefully crash along the rocks; the air feels different. I immediately realize I am early. I climb the tree and focus. I close my eyes and listen. There is something wrong, but I have no idea what. I know this is the spot I saw in the vision, but in my spirit, I am tense.

I sit silently for around twenty minutes, just praying. I hear voices in the distance coming toward the hill. I hear weeping, not from Will but from Ethan. Rosie is bossy and in charge. Ethan has the gun while Rosie holds a knife, the shiny, long, slick blade shimmering in the darkness. As they make their way up the hill, I feel it before I see them. A storm is brewing, the winds pick up, and the thunder rolls in closer and closer.

Oh no, dear God, no!

I never saw this coming; I knew a stronghold has taken over Rosie, but not this!

The water sprays upward as it hits the rocks. The waves have increased on this side of the island, and the chill in the air is unmistakable. To the naked eye of an observer, it only appears to be an approaching storm. For me, it is far more sinister.

How could I have missed this? Levi always warned me before the fallen ones, the offspring, or even the demons entered a territory.

The spiritual shock and the human fear all try to overtake me. It is then that the spiritual side of me kicks into gear. I am about to meet the accusers of man's soul, not just one fallen one but three.

How did they get through the perimeter?

Lord God, I need your presence!

They must have overtaken the Keepers, but how? Maybe this is why I have not seen Levi.

I am in big trouble and way outnumbered.

God, how were the Keepers hushed? I have not even been warned! These words keep flowing through my mind. This has only happened once in all my existence, and that was when they killed Levi while he was in a fleshly state.

My questions are silenced as they all approach the tree. *Holy God, please protect me from the evils of this world,* I pray aloud. I then leap from the tree.

These beings are not offspring and demons but fallen ones, the ancient ones working with satan. They are the destroyers of men's souls. They are able to take on human form and possess humans, and they hold great power.

The laughter is deafening as they see me.

"Aww! There she is! Good morning, little sister. We hoped you would make an appearance, and here you are," Dagon smirks. He then jumps forward a few steps, as if to try to take my hand. "We have missed you so many times when we come to visit you, little sister. Oh, look at her. Isn't she a pretty little thing?"

All three agree, and then Dagon lets out a laugh that sounds like pure evil.

The welcome is brief, and hatred follows. Their glaring eyes turn red as blood drips from one of Dagon's eyes. The shouts and eerie laughter become deafening, and Ethan covers his ears.

"Tell the voices to stop," he yells at Rosie.

"Ethan, you're such a wimp. I don't hear any voices!" she scolds and smiles demonically.

The three fallen ones are immensely powerful as they stand behind Rosie, prompting her to accuse Ethan. No one sees these accusers but me, for Ethan's, Rosie's, and Will's eyes are blinded to them. They have a veil of protection covering their human vision. These fallen ones are men of old renown and are part of the original fallen ones sent by Moloch. Their appearance comes and goes as they will it. Right now, they have control over Rosie, and without her believing in Jesus, they have complete control over her.

Ethan is new to his salvation and has no clue about the power he could have over the enemy. *Did he even mean it when he said the Sinner's Prayer?* I tell myself that his decision was between him and his Maker and is not for me to judge. Although he has prayed the Sinner's Prayer, he is a baby to the faith and teachings. The Word may have fallen on shifting sand, or he may have been overcome by his past and the pressure from Rosie.

Maybe his salvation prayer was only out of desperation after all, and not real, from his heart. Whatever the possibility, he is now letting the enemy beat him up. Any time a human alters their senses through alcohol or drugs, they open themselves up to the enemy. It is like an open door and invitation, you might say, welcoming in the enemy as well as the torment to the person.

Ethan's eyes are glassy. Obviously, he is high on drugs as he holds the gun against Will's back. Ethan's eyes dance wildly at the noises around him, and he looks frightened, as if ready to pounce.

Will's hands are bound. He has been beaten. His eyes are swollen, his lip is bleeding, and his body looks weak with the twenty-four hours of torture.

"Will, do you trust me?" I ask him.

He shakes his head slightly to signify a yes.

"Stop talking to him," Rosie shouts at me and then hits Will on the side of his head with the butt of the gun she has jerked away from Ethan. Will falls forward but regains his balance.

"Oh dear. He's almost fallen again!" Dagon teases.

"Should I help him up, brother?" Molokai asks Dagon. Molokai and Zagiel smirk at Dagon.

"If you must," Dagon says through his white lips.

Molokai and Zagiel prompt Ethan with evil thoughts. Will winces in pain as Ethan grabs his arm, jerking him to his feet.

"I'm not a wimp, Rosie! I told you we'd find her, and here she is," Ethan scowls.

Rosie smiles. "You are so right, my love. I never should have doubted you."

I lift my hands to God, and the battle begins.

"No weapon formed against me shall prosper. God has given me authority over the enemy, and satan, I rebuke you in the name of Jesus."

Where two or more are gathered, Lord, you are in the midst of us. Dear God in Heaven, Will and I agree that this evil must be terminated.

Will is hurt and bleeding, yet he notices the prayer and starts repeating everything that I say in agreement. As I draw my spiritual sword, the armour of God does not appear to cover me yet, but at least I have my sword. I hear Will continue to pray, and I know I am not alone in this fight.

This battle is different than the one with Roman. Roman was part of a Moloch's clan but like a distant cousin, an offspring, or a fallen one. A fight with offspring is fleshlier. With these three fallen ones, it is definitely spiritual but could also become more physical with them possessing Rosie and possibly Ethan.

It also may be more deadly. That is what took Levi away from me in the brutal fight long ago.

Where are the Keepers? Oh, God, how can I fight this battle alone?

Molokai steps forward. "I got this, gentlemen. This shouldn't take long."

Zagiel and Dagon step near Will to watch Molokai close in action.

Ethan raises his gun toward Will. Just as he is about to pull the trigger, he swiftly directs the barrel at me. I smile at Ethan as God gives me direction.

"Stop smiling at him!" shouts Rosie.

I am trying to break the barrier, trying to pass the peace to Ethan. As I hear Will's prayers turn to praise, I feel my friend the Holy Spirit wash over both of us. Zagiel and Dagon stumble backward and are taken off guard. Then the fighting heightens.

"You must fight, Awna, spiritually and physically. Lives and souls depend on it," I hear the Lord speak to me.

The words filter through my brain, my mind, and all through my body and spirit. I know my Lord's voice. I draw my sword on these two as the power of the Holy Spirit gives me strength. Now before them all stands a warrior of old, fully dressed in armour, ready for battle.

The rain pelts down on us, the wind howls, and the thunder makes such furious sounds that it shakes the ground beneath us.

The fallen ones are shocked to see God's armour covering me and shriek backward a few steps. I advance forward in one quick motion and place a roundhouse kick to Molokai's face. As if in slow motion, he falls backward, rolls in the mossy grass, and disappears.

Ethan stumbles sideways a bit as the power of the fight brushes him.

I come up behind Molokai as he is hiding near a bush. When he sees me, he rolls over, trying to get away, but I stand over him with my sword jutting into his throat.

"Yes, Molokai, you are so right. This shouldn't take long!" I peer deep into his large, bulging eyes and look into his nasty presence, his pointy face, and his giant-like, grayish body. Yes, these fallen ones may be men of old who look humanlike, but they are far from the human design of God.

Terror rips through Molokai's face as my sword hits its target and ends yet another age-old battle. The whirlwind around him is brisk; it blows harder than with the offspring. I can see everything that is going on around us outside of the whirlwind, yet I cannot get out of it. I try with all my might, but I am not strong enough to physically remove myself.

I cry out: *Lord, please allow me to step from his whirlwind as you judge Molokai so that I can protect Will.* The wind is so strong, and as I struggle to free myself from it, I surely know God's judgment has been great against this fallen one.

I can see Rosie trying to grab the gun from Ethan, but she fails and drops her knife in the process. Will quickly limps toward Ethan, unnoticed by the two, and then tackles Ethan to the ground, where they struggle. Will takes control, pulls the gun from Ethan's hand, and pushes the gun away. Will may not be as big as Ethan, but I can see that he is regaining some of his strength, and it matches Ethan's strength.

I try with all my might to escape the whirlwind. Its power is that of hurricane force, and my strength is waning.

Just then I see Rosie with the gun. "Oh no!" I scream.

Instantly a small space opens within the whirlwind, and I try to step back into the fight. My ears pop and my head hurts, but I kept pushing forward against the force of the whirlwind. My hair blows all around, and I can barely lift my foot to take a step. I concentrate, close my eyes, and feel the Spirit of the living God gently push me from the whirlwind. It is then that I am able to step back into the fight.

Will sees the gun in Rosie's hand now and lunges toward her. Rosie's hand is shaking, and the gun almost slips. Zagiel leaves Dagon's side and races toward Rosie. Zagiel grabs hold of Rosie's hand, steadies the gun, and then laughs while looking my way.

"Oh, little sister. You are stronger than we thought. Just imagine: if you had been this strong years ago, your sweet Levi would not have been overtaken. What a shame, dear one. We all grieved so over the loss."

My heart skips a beat as Dagon speaks of Levi. I lose my footing and slip. In an instance of regret, I drop my sword, and as I fall, Dagon steps over me.

Rosie's foot is now on my neck, and she starts applying pressure with Dagon's help. Will's prayers can be heard in the background, getting louder. Rosie then kicks me in the face, and I taste salt and warm liquid spilling down my cheek and lip.

Oh, God, protect us from this evil. Take down the strongholds of the enemy, in the mighty name of Jesus Christ your Son, who bled and died but rose again for the sins of this lost world.

Rosie's foot loosens its grip just briefly, long enough for me to see the gun pointing at my head. In the distance, I turn my head to see Ethan hit Will with his fist. He then jumps up from the ground, leaving Will stunned.

Ethan grabs the gun back from Rosie. "I'll do it," he screams.

"Ethan, I'm so proud of you. You do love me after all. Shoot her. Do it, do it!" she shouts, stepping away from me but still trying to hold onto me.

At that, Zagiel's laughter can be heard above the waves. The thunder rolls around us, and lightning strikes nearer, coming closer to the fight.

I do not want to hurt Ethan or Rosie, but I need to stay alive to protect Will, myself, and others. I will protect good from evil, for I never want to hurt the humans. I close my eyes and pray, and the utterance of my prayer is heard by the Lord.

"Ethan!" I shout. "Put the gun down, please! I don't want to hurt you!"

Zagiel steps in front of Ethan, surrounding his body, and overtakes any attempt I might have negotiated with Ethan.

I take a deep breath. "In the name of Jesus Christ and the blood that was shed on the cross for the sake of humankind, Ethan, the gun that you hold in your hand will burn you with fervent heat, just as the heat from Hell is near you now."

Ethan screams out in agony as the smoke becomes like fog all around him. The burns on his hand become red and blister instantly. He drops the gun, and it sizzles on the ground. The grass around him becomes hot as his feet begin to burn.

Rosie loses her grip on me, running to help Ethan. I jump to my feet and retrieve my sword. Zagiel covers Ethan's body with himself, but Ethan's arm and right leg are now on fire.

I lift my sword and command Zagiel's end. My sword hits its mark. "Into the pit of Hell with you, Zagiel, where you will stay until God's judgment meets you."

As the fire consumes Zagiel, Ethan drops from his talons onto an unscorched patch of grass. I jump from the whirlwind as it starts to cover Zagiel.

In a flash, it is just Dagon standing over Rosie, looking at me.

"Oh, sweet little sister. How you so easily kill and wound your brothers and human counterparts. We should just forgive and forget this mess. Join me. We can rule the darkness and principalities, and all Bermuda will be ours."

"You are no brother of mine, Dagon," I scream out.

"Oh, why deny your heritage, little one? Even if you take me out, which you won't, Moloch your father will find you, and you will return to us. We will fight this war against the humans together."

"Dagon, that is where you are wrong. My Father has found me; He is the Most High God, and when His Son, Jesus, died on the cross, the human part of me was given redemption, and it covers all my DNA. I have made it my lot in life to protect my human brothers and sisters. I have been pardoned from any relation to you."

Will stands on shaky legs beside me and grabs my hand. "I am her spiritual brother, and I accept this protection in the name of Jesus."

I turned to Will. "You can hear them speaking? Can you see him?"

"Yes, glimpses through my swollen eyes. I understand that we are in this spiritual battle together," Will says.

"Then together we will finish this. Stay behind me and pray."

I step forward as Rosie stands holding the gun. As the heat dissipates, she still holds tight.

"Oh, Lord, with thy loving mercy and kindness, take away my enemies. Destroy them, for they hunt me down. I am your servant, and I love you," I shout through the storm. "Please, Rosie. Give up before it's too late," I plead.

Behind me, Will is shouting the same pleas to God but adds, "We bind you, satan, in the name of Jesus. You and all your imps and legions be cast down."

As Rosie pulls the trigger, the smile on Dagon's face fades. As my shield repels the bullet, the bullet is sent backward into Rosie's heart. In that same instance, I see a white light from my peripheral vision as it strikes a metal sign behind me.

Dagon screams out in agony.

"What's wrong, Dagon? Did you lose your host? Now who will do your dirty work?" I shout.

Dagon looks past me at Will; he races toward him and then stops abruptly a few feet away and frowns. The blood of Jesus is on Will's forehead; it glows through the night like a beacon that would guide a thousand ships to safety.

Dagon frowns, looking around. He sees Ethan now standing on shaky legs, limping toward Rosie. Dagon searches desperately for another host. Will breaks out of the stormy darkness and then runs and tackles Ethan to the ground. He can barely see out of his swollen eyes, but he is able to make out a form.

"Leave Ethan alone, Dagon!" I shout. Dagon chuckles as he watches Ethan wince in pain from the choke hold that Will has on him.

"Little sister, look what you've done to your human friend. You've put him in great pain. Let me see if I can make it better."

Before I can get to Ethan, Dagon arches himself over Ethan and Will, but Ethan calls out: "Oh, Jesus, help me. I'm sorry!"

Although Ethan said the Sinner's Prayer weeks ago, this time when he calls on the name of Jesus, I see a glow appear on his forehead, and the light shines around him, protecting him against Dagon. The cry for Jesus this time is real, not just out of desperation.

Dagon screams out again with the agony of nearing defeat. "Sister, please, just let me go. I will not tell our brothers or Moloch where you are, I promise!"

For a moment, I feel sadness and sympathy for Dagon, but it lasts only for a split second. I then swing my sword in a swift, forceful movement. The power of God covers me, and I feel His shield and hand of protection. It is Heaven's hand upon my own hand that sends Dagon to his demise as the whirlwind starts to form around him and judgment starts. As my sword cuts through this demonic creature, lightning strikes the ground where we stand, and he is gone.

It is God's goodness that ends this battle rapidly. Will releases Ethan as he runs to Rosie. Rosie lies on the ground, and the stillness of her lifeless body draws Ethan slowly toward her. He weeps over her body as if he is a child while his drugs wear off.

"Oh, Rosie, my sweet Rosie. Why wouldn't you listen? I never wanted to hurt you or these people. Oh, Rosie," he sobs.

I think how incredibly sad it is that she never found Jesus. The enemy toyed with her mind, spirit, and body, and now, as she lies lifeless, I wonder if she was sorry. I watch the talons of the demons drag her spirit with them into Hell. I see a tear escape Will's swollen eye and wonder if he saw it too.

My armour vanishes along with the storm. Will, overcome with a moment of emotion, walks over to his captor and lays hands on Ethan's back to pray. Prayers fill the air as forgiveness is accepted by both men.

Will calls 911, and the Bermudian police are here within minutes. The sun starts to rise as the storm clears, and the birds chirp as if nothing at all has happened through the night

Ethan confesses to taking Will hostage and explains the foiled plans to kidnap a child. The police come over to talk to Will and me; we confirm what Ethan has said.

The officer listens intently and then scratches his eye as if something is in it. "There is only one problem with this story," Officer Ishaan Ferbert says. "I can understand lightning striking the ground. There was a storm in the area; lots of thunder could be heard all around. I also understand your hands burning from the strike where the ground is scorched."

He points all of this out to Ethan as we stand by listening. "I can understand from looking at you, Will, that you've been brutalized, and you say you were kidnapped."

A shaky Ethan raises his hand as if he were in school about to answer a question. "I'm sorry, Officer. I did that to him, and we did take him hostage."

Officer Ferbert raises his finger to indicate that the men should wait a minute. His eye continues twitching, and he puts his finger in the corner of it to make it stop. "I'm trying to wrap my head around this."

Will sits beside me now, bruised and battered. His left eye is now swollen shut, and his right eye is closing rapidly. His lip is swollen and bloody. As other police officers take pictures of the crime scene, an officer gives Will an ice pack.

"So, you were kidnapped and assaulted?" Officer Ferbert points to Will. He then looks at me and says, "And you found him?"

I nod, trying not to say much, my mind racing to the fact that some of the dots do not connect with this story. All I can do is pray. I've never been part of a human getting hurt or killed, so my heart is sorrowful and filled with anguish. *Oh, Lord, come quickly to rescue us. If I am to speak, give me the words.*

"If someone could just tell the truth, that would be amazing!" Officer Ferbert says.

Instead, we stand silently, waiting for him to cross the t's and dot the i's.

Officer Ferbert steps back and puts his hand on his chin, pondering. "So, who shot the deceased woman, Rosie? She is still holding her gun. Where's the gun that shot her?"

Silence for one second, then two seconds.

Will finally speaks up: "She was the only one with the gun, Officer!"

Officer Ferbert is about to say something when another officer yells for him. "Hey, we found a knife near the deceased woman."

He leaves us momentarily, so we all just stand there. Ethan is still in pain and weeping. Will is savagely beaten and bruised, and as for me, I know I do not have a physical scratch on me. Or do I? Something does not feel quite right, but I cannot put my finger on it.

Officer Ferbert returns. "Okay, it looks like the bullet ricocheted off the metal plate that was holding up the warning sign behind us." We all look as he points. "The sign warns of danger to the tourists who want to explore the cliffs just ahead. The deputy found the bullet embedded in the metal plate, but it is missing its core. If the coroner finds the core in the deceased woman's body, then the case will be closed. We will follow the ambulance to the hospital to get the rest of the statements and take . . ."

He looks at Ethan. "After you take this one to the hospital, take him to jail. And you," he says, pointing to me, "leave your information with the deputy at the squad car in case we have further questions."

The ambulance shows up, taking Ethan and Will to the hospital.

Bracyn, the EMT, looks over at me. "Looks like you need to go too, ma'am."

I frown and shake my head. "Oh, no, no. I'll be fine."

He pauses for a moment and then moves forward to pack and load his patients.

I call Ms. Banks and tell her what has happened so that she can meet us at the hospital. When we all arrive at King Edward VII Memorial Hospital, I park my scooter at the ER. As Will and Ethan are taken back for treatment, I try to accompany Will, but the doctors won't let me in the examining room. I am not family.

While waiting for Ms. Banks to arrive, I go to the restroom to wash my face and compose myself. To my horror, I gasp, "My face!"

I have never bled before, nor have I ever bruised on the outside. My injuries are always on the inside, and now both are staring back at me. I truly look like I have been in a horrible fight.

I touch my face. "Ouch!" It is sore. I have never experienced that either. My insides start shaking. I feel weak and then feel myself falling. I try to catch myself, but to no avail, and then everything goes black.

Muffled sounds surround my body. I can almost make out voices, but what are they saying? The words are jumbled and seem to join as one. I open my eyes, but blurry vision gives way to dizziness, and the brightly lit room makes me shut my eyes tight.

My head feels like it is spinning around the room, and I cannot make it stop. I faintly hear Will's voice.

No! It is Levi's voice.

For a second, I open my mouth and say, "Levi!"

But it is only a whisper. My eyes flutter as I try to open them. Trying to focus, I see Will and Ms. Banks.

Now the lighting is dim, spinning around and around. Their faces become distorted.

No, it is not Will and Ms. Banks. It is the Keepers.

Shock runs through my being as I struggle.

"No, not yet!" I say. "It's not time for a dormant state. I want to stay in Bermuda. I need to rest a while longer."

"Oh please, oh please!" I beg them. I cannot tell if I am speaking this aloud or in my mind.

Memories inch their way through my thoughts. I have just made friends; I have never made friends except for Levi. These people care about me.

"Please do not take me now. I have so much more to do!"

Something wet is on my face. It is hot and stinging my eyes.

I heard a voice say, "She's crying."

A gasp escapes someone close to my body. "Is it pain? Tell me, is she in pain?" a frantic voice bellows.

Do I know this voice? My thoughts are disrupted as I hear a humming sound and force my eyes open. I see a light that starts at my feet and then goes toward my head. I feel an electric pulse, a tingling, deep within my body. It moves from my head to my toes. Every part of my body feels it. I open my mouth to scream but cannot. I cannot move my body; I feel paralyzed.

I hear another one say, "No, she's not in pain. The scan shows her tears are from emotion."

Silence. More silence. Suddenly I remember Selah back at the cottage alone with no one to take care of her. Oh no. She will die in the house without food or water.

With all the strength I can muster, I whisper, "Selah!" It is faint, but Ms. Banks hears my plea.

What is she doing here with the Keepers? I must just be disoriented.

Confusion swirls, intertwining in my thoughts.

Now Will is speaking. "I'll go get her. It has been a week, so don't get your hopes up."

Oh my goodness, why can't I speak? Why can't I move?

I try to speak again. It is a whisper, but I hear myself say, "Please help Selah!"

Do not get your hopes up? A week? What are they talking about? What is wrong with me? It is then that I see the light start at my feet again and travel up me through my body. Then sleep once again overtakes my body.

CHAPTER 10

Fighting Between Heaven and Earth

As Will drove toward Sandys Parish, he was apprehensive about what he would find. How he had forgotten about Selah was beyond him. With his brief hospital stay and now trying to recover, yes, it had certainly been a week. Then there was having to deal with the police. And Awna, poor Awna. No one knew why she could hardly speak or why she could not move or wake. It baffled everyone.

Will drove on; it was not that much farther. He had taken Awna's house keys from her pocket to get into the cottage. When he visited her last, he could barely hear her breathing. At least she looked peaceful, but he wished she would soon wake up. Her internal injuries were so bad that it was like she was in a coma, yet no one had induced it. This new friendship with Awna was so uplifting, but his concern for her had grown over this past week.

It was a beautiful day. A gentle breeze brushed his face as the wind blew his sun-kissed hair all around. He loved driving with the windows down; he did not care if he looked disheveled. When he got out of his car, he did not care if his hair was all over the place. It just made sense for him to breathe in the ocean air while he could.

He took a deep breath as he stood at the cottage door and turned the key. He heard the door click as it unlocked the deadbolt, but silence returned to his ear. There was no greeting, no barking, and no toenails tapping on the hardwood floors. He looked all around.

There Selah lay on her side on the floor by the French doors that led to the patio. Indeed, she had tried to get out. As he rushed to her, she lay so still. Her big brown eyes looked fixed and open. At first, he thought she was dead until he gently laid his hand on her head. She was still warm. He put his ear to her chest; she was breathing, but it was very faint. For a second, he thought she looked just like Awna, lying there with hardly any reaction.

Will looked around and found her doggy bed by the fireplace. He gently put her in it and took his time cleaning up the mess left behind from the week when she was not let out. He scrubbed the floors and sprayed disinfectant. He rechecked the doors, making sure they were all locked, and reset the alarm, sighing as he gently shut and relocked the main door.

Selah was now on the seat next to him. He drove slowly with this beautiful four pounds of precious that Awna loved so much. He drove past the vet clinic. There was no need to stop; he would just go back to the lighthouse.

Ms. Banks checked on Awna, cooling her brow with a damp cloth. There was nothing else to do but pray, wait, and have faith. She thought about the recent events and the disturbing evil that had once again touched the island. She brushed a tear away but could not make the sadness disappear from her broken heart, sadness not only for the evil but also for the lost soul who had perished. It was sheer human emotion on her part; that was all it was.

She heard a car pull up in the distance. She had better make her way back upstairs; she was far beneath the lighthouse. She climbed the dimly lit corridor, holding tightly to the railing. When she reached the top of the stairs, she paused, listening for a second before she scanned the cross that she wore around her neck. An elevator door opened and took her to the ground floor of the lighthouse. She emerged just inside the walls of the old iron lighthouse.

The human eye would never see the secret doorway hidden at the side of the lighthouse. To them, it looked like a solid iron frame with only one front entrance leading into the lighthouse. It was a veil that hid this door, protecting human eyes, for it was another dimension into a different world.

This too was part of Heaven's secrets. Not only in Bermuda but all around the world were many doorways for the Keepers to enter and exit. Ms. Banks felt sorry for humanity, even though so many of their problems were created by themselves. Still, walking among them gave her a sense of purpose.

Will pulled into the lighthouse parking lot next to the apartment out back. He smiled when he saw Ms. Banks at the side of the lighthouse, and she smiled back. They never spoke a word. There was no need to; they already knew what the other was thinking.

Will went straight to Awna. He lay Selah right beside her; the two would do better together. He scanned the pup; her vitals had already started to improve just being close to Awna, but she lay and slept, just as Awna did. After all, she was made for Awna by the Keepers. She too had dormant sleeps which enabled her to also live a long life.

Two weeks passed. Then two months. Meanwhile, Awna lay dormant alongside Selah. They were both very still, their breathing shallow and almost undetectable. The police had closed the case after the findings showed that the ricocheted bullet matched Rosie's gun. It was a good thing, Will thought as he looked down at Awna. God had led him to know how to handle it all without any more statements from Awna.

Will and Ms. Banks fasted and prayed, sang songs of praise, and spoke the Word of God over Awna and Selah. Still, they lay sleeping. The Keepers had not induced this sleep; they did not know why this had happened except to say that they must trust in the Lord's will for her life and wait.

Ms. Banks and Will were faithful and kept a diligent watch over Awna and the pup. They had become human friends with Awna and were allowed to talk with her and build her trust to help fight the battle that had broken through the perimeter. The two never left her side, until . . .

They felt them coming down the stairs, and instantly, they both knew and moved away from Awna. Two more Keepers stood before them, clothed in white robes. A white glow shone around them both. Still, no one spoke.

A sadness enveloped Will and Ms. Banks as they thought that they would be taken from Awna. They pleaded to stay a little longer until she woke. They'd taken on human form to help her through this fight, and now they wanted to see it through.

"This is why we do not take on human form around her very often. The spiritual side of her draws us to her," said one of the Keepers as he stepped forward.

The other Keeper behind him emerged from the shadows, moved toward Awna, and stood beside her. He pushed his hood back and stared down at her.

"Levi, please don't!" Will begged.

A tear formed in Levi's eyes as his hand lifted over Awna, never touching her but moving over her face and then stopping over the apex of her head. A blue glow came from his hand and illuminated her face and hair. The luminous light could be seen shining through her skin. Her whole body was now enveloped in this glowing, soft blue light. The glow shone upon Levi's face too as he turned to the other Keepers.

Levi had not answered Will's plea but returned his hood over his head and stared into the dim light that was still shining over Awna. It glowed even after he took his hand away.

When Levi spoke this time, it was with audible words. "She will not remember you. This battle, as with all the other battles, has become stronger as evil grows in this world. As we fight for the perimeters, the battle gets harder, and we need more warriors and human prayers. Therefore, Dagon and his imps were able to slither through. I did not warn Awna this time, knowing that she had become stronger without me. Nor did I visit her dreams for the same reason; I knew she must be strong on her own."

After Levi spoke, Ms. Banks chimed in. "She must always depend on God, just as we must. She should never depend on me, you, or any of us. We cannot even let ourselves become distracted by the flesh. Maybe it was a mistake to portray ourselves as human."

Will added to the conversation. "Yes, but at what cost? She also became stronger with us. She is just lonely for human companionship; don't you see? I thank you, Levi, for giving her Selah, but, my friend, she has come to a point of concern. Levi, she bled, she bruised, and she cried. And . . . there is more." He paused. "She's started to age again. Look at her!"

Levi dropped his head after Will spoke as the heaviness of his words moved through them all.

Ms. Banks stepped forward to have an audience with the group. "Levi, all of this is true, and it is getting harder to keep her from aging. The dormancy can only do so much now. She has never bled or bruised before, or even noticeably aged. The time will come when her strength is heightened, just like we thought it would be, and she becomes all spirit with no fleshly side. We must prepare for what is to come."

Levi took his turn to speak. "All of what you say is apparent. For her to become more of a spirit like us, though, she must die a human death, just as all humans do, for her spirit to return to Heaven. The sleep that she is in now is all her own. This is not of us; her fleshly body is just growing tired."

There was now silence in the room as they pondered the conversation.

"These things must come to pass," said the Keeper who had not spoken yet, as he stepped from the shadows. All the Keepers moved back in reverence to him. He walked toward Awna; his stern nature gave way to a smile as he looked down at her small, frail body.

Alon remembered how she had looked as a child and the questions she had constantly asked. The memories flooded back to him, playing like a movie in his mind. He had watched as she changed through the ages. His memories saw her mother and the injustice that sin had plagued upon her from the sons of God, the fallen ones. He had been a part of the fall, his biggest regret.

He knew there was good in his own heart; he had just been in the wrong place and time when his Maker had cursed those who betrayed Him and cast them to the earth. He had thought his existence was over until he met Anissa and then Awna. He knew Awna was the apple of not only his eye but also God's eye.

This little one had fought hard down through the ages to keep the peace and to protect man from the evils of this world. She had always felt unworthy, but God said she was indeed worthy. She never honestly believed it even though she felt it in her heart, and doubted even when God preserved her for humanity. There was always a bit of doubt left in her heart about her origin.

Alon laid his hand on her forehead and spoke to the Most High; his prayer was short but powerful and only between him and God. He spoke in the Heavenly language he had taught to Awna.

Peace and light filled the room as he turned to the others. "I must go, but you three will stay near her for now. Our Lord will guide her, but she will have a choice to stay here on earth and fight or go on to Heaven and completely become all spirit with no flesh."

The group hung their heads as Alon continued. "If she chooses to stay on this earth, I will form a troop within the Heavenly army who will protect this territory while she recovers. We have thrown off the offspring and the fallen ones from where the deaths of their brethren have occurred. They will not come this way for now. Awna's future is all up to her and her Maker."

Alon turned to Levi and smiled. The softness edged his almost human-looking eyes as he looked teasingly at Levi. "If it is decided that she wakes, she may or may not remember you. You know how she is. She may also continue to age, but you should not worry. Even if she does not remember you, or if she dies a physical death, do not be discouraged. Love is bigger than death, and we will see her again on the other side."

"Let it be so," they all spoke and agreed. Levi was hesitant but nodded.

When Levi finally spoke, the silence that fell seemed like an eternity. "Alon, may I ask you something? Of course, you do not have to answer. Why did you come back after her first battle when the Israelites overtook the enemy for their promised land? That was the battle you helped Awna fight to the victory. You could have stayed in the Heavenly realm after your pardon from God. You were a part of the Heavenly army once again, and no one would have blamed you for staying. This world is . . ." Levi paused. "The evil is vast here, more so than at any other time in the history of the earth."

The Keepers focused on Alon. Alon was silent for a moment and then glanced back toward Awna. "I came back for her and for humankind!" He looked at Levi. "You could have done the same thing. Why did you become her guardian angel after your death?"

Levi dropped his head, knowing the truth. "Yes, for her and humankind."

There was silence for a moment as they all pondered their mission that surrounded Awna.

Alon broke the silence. "If she lives, you will visit her dreams once again, when it is time, of course. Memory is a powerful tool. She may have an audience with Heaven during her decision time. If she decides to stay in Heaven, then her mission here on earth will be finished."

The silence felt heavy around the group as they pondered what had been spoken and the consequences that it would bring.

Alon continued. "Levi, you have intrigued her human side of emotions. To tell you the truth, you two may have also," he said as he looked over at Will and Ms. Banks. "She has been alone far too long. It has been proven that her fleshly side needs companionship, even if her spiritual does not."

Alon looked at the three of them and continued. "Only time will tell, of course. Remember when we realized that she remembered you, Levi, after every eradication of her memory?"

Levi lowered his head. "Yes, even though we had fully eradicated her memory, she always knew me after each awakening. Sometimes it took a while, but she always remembered me. Then she started remembering her past awakenings, even putting the timeline of years together."

Alon's face showed deep concern. "There is something else. Now that her flesh may have grown stronger, the secret of who she is and what she does may be too much for her to keep to herself. And that cannot be tolerated, even with my Awna."

Will spoke up. "I believe she can hold the secret. She is loyal, very loyal! Ms. Banks and I questioned her about the signature at the lighthouse and how it looked like the one from over a hundred years ago. We also questioned her about the time she was caught in the picture of the lighthouse when construction was completed. We forced the issue of how it looked like her."

Ms. Banks added, "Yes, she kept the secret even when we prayed together when Ethan kidnapped Will. She felt that it was different. As she passed the peace of healing to Will's injury, and when we questioned her, she said nothing, but she gave God the glory. If I may say, I know she becomes stronger when we eradicate her memory, but imagine how much stronger she might be if we did not. She is not like the others."

Alon was taking in what he had heard. Closing his eyes, he prayed silently. The Keepers bowed their heads as well. The silence lasted for a time, and all the Keepers raised their heads in unison. Heaven's language at its best touched Heaven's ear. Without a word, they all nodded.

The Keepers took Awna back to her cottage, where Ms. Banks cleaned her up, washed her hair, and adorned her in fresh linen. Then they laid her in her bed. Selah woke from the deep sleep first, with a yawn and much stretching. Then she felt the urge to go outside, so she decided that jumping up and down and then barking and licking Awna was what she needed to do.

But Awna lay quietly, her breathing shallow. She heard Selah, but she could not make herself lift her eyes. Selah sniffed Awna's hair, which smelled freshly washed and of cherry blossoms. Selah pulled at the shimmery white linen gown, willing Awna awake. Selah still had no luck, so she lay on Awna's stomach while keeping a sharp eye on her.

Awna did not want to wake; she was tired and just wanted to sleep.

Selah jumped off the bed when she heard a noise in the living room. Standing there was Levi, who guided Selah to a new built-in doggy door. Selah wiggled her nub at Levi and bolted out her newfound door. When she returned, food and water sat on the kitchen floor awaiting the little friend. As soon as she had her fill, she returned to the bedroom where Levi stood over Awna.

Selah jumped, trying to get up on the bed until at last, Levi reached down and put her next to Awna, where she resumed her protective position over her. She too was still a little bit weak, so she shut her eyes and fell asleep. With her full belly, she could take a long nap.

Levi raised his hands and spoke in his Heavenly language. He asked the Lord God of Heaven to lead and guide Awna as she slept and while she made her decision either to stay here on earth or to go on to Heaven.

When I awake, I am in the Spirit. As I look around the Heavenly realm, a fog surrounds me. My mind quickly gathers the scene. Awkwardly, I begin walking down a long hiking trail. The fresh smell of pine fills the air as birds chirp and fly around me. I walk farther along to be met by the fragrance of roses, lavender, and jasmine. The smell seems to stroll along with me as I walk, just as the birds join me. Soon the trail changes to a more tropical scene. I lean over to touch gigantic, beautiful tropical blooms. The brilliant colors are mesmerizing; they are so alive. At the end of the trail is a large river that feeds into a massive lake. It shimmers and shines with ripples of moving water skipping over jutted rocks. I walk toward a large rock on the bank and climb to sit.

I sit gazing, enjoying the scenery, as peace and comfort fill my spirit.

I sense him before I turn to look; it is Levi. He strolls toward me, staring for a moment at my frail frame. Then he sits down next to me. The sound of the moving water echoes in the valley. The birds pick up a song and chirp to the heartbeat of the flowing water. Everything seems as one, alive and energetic. I am a part of something bigger. I feel a force pulling me, yet Levi and I sit listening, engrossed in the moment. We never turn to look at one another.

Levi speaks first, but it is as if he has to drag the words out. "I know you are tired, Awna, and I want you to know that you do not have to go back to the earth. You can stay here in this place; I will stay too. Physical wounds heal more quickly than spiritual wounds do. The cost is great for these types of wounds. No one will fault you, Awna. The choice is yours."

I sit pondering, thinking, remembering nothing, only fragments of something. It all seems very foggy.

Confusion stirs within me. Who is this person speaking to me? What is my name? Yes, I'm Awna. But what is his name again? I know I just remembered it.

Levi drops his head, and sadness surrounds him. He has always been able to see into Awna's thoughts with each awakening, but this time is different. He is not even sure of what he sees now. He does know with each recent awakening that she has become a little more human. From what he perceives right now, she does not remember anything about him. For some reason, though, he feels like it all could change.

"Look, Awna, you have a choice. Right now, we are in the corridor of Heaven. It is the very first place that all the righteous humans go. You can stay in this place and keep moving toward God. I know you can feel Him drawing you."

He pauses. "You will never have to suffer again. Your body will give way to your spirit, just like mine. I'll walk you to the gates myself; it is just over the ridge." He points. "Awna, please say something. I can't bear to see you suffer like this."

A soft light dances toward us as peace rests on us both. The light shimmers with sparkles that look like glitter blowing in the breeze, spraying over us simultaneously. The light clothes both of us with white robes made for royalty. It is drawing us, but I stand still until my companion touches my elbow, and we start to stroll toward the ridge.

The light grows stronger and more powerful, lifting us off our feet to quicken us to our destination. Love and acceptance are all around us; it is what I have craved my whole life. Now that I have it, I cling to it. I feel alive, really alive, more than when I was alive on the earth.

Others are here. They smile as we pass. Some clap their hands while some sing the most beautiful songs with no words. As we near the gates, the crowd grows, and more glitter circles them, making their robes light up.

A woman is moving near me. I know her.

"Oh, can it be?" I hear her say. "Awna?"

"Eema!" I say.

We embrace for what seems an eternity, but no one cares. Time is endless.

"Oh, child, you made it through. I am so very thankful. Praise be to God and all His glory," Eema says, smiling.

The three of us walk on together. Levi looks down and says, "It is over, Awna. You have fought the good fight. You saved many throughout the years and generations. Evil is behind you now. There will be no more worries."

I stop. "But who will fight the fallen ones, Moloch's clan, and the offspring? The evil is all around those poor humans."

"Around whom, child?" Eema inquires.

"Around the humans," I speak.

Levi stops as well. "Go on ahead." He motions to Anissa. "You'll see her soon," he assures her.

She smiles and turns without dispute.

"I love you, Eema!" I shout.

"I love you too, child!"

With that, my Eema begins walking without ever glancing back.

A noise from the distance gets my attention. The moans and screams echo in a distant sound; they are faint, but I still hear them. I let go of my companion's hand and run toward the sounds. I see the spirits as the shadow of death stands near them, and the death angel keeps them from stepping over into Heaven. The spirits are walking toward the light just like I had. Then suddenly a force begins pulling them back down deep into the darkness. The death angel stands very still until the time comes. He quickly pronounces each death as he awaits God's voice.

The voice I hear is that of sadness as God speaks: "Depart from me, you worker of iniquity. I never knew you."

At the sound of God's voice, the spirit who had almost made it through to Heaven is dragged down into the darkness. The screams finally drift off into the distance and never touch Heaven's corridors. The sounds are only for my ears.

The death angel stands silently as he lifts a set of weights and passes them to another that I cannot see. The weights are used for judgment.

The death angel moves on past the gates. For some reason, I did not see the death angel when we entered the corridors of Heaven, and he shows no joy in his job. It is just a matter of fact.

Tears stream down my face. Now my companion is back by my side. I look up into his eyes. "I can't go," I stammer. "I can't go to the gates!"

Levi is silent.

"You go! Go on through the gates! Please just go. Hurry. You can stay here in Heaven!"

Levi stands still, not moving.

Then in the blink of an eye, we are back by the rock where we started, a gentle breeze brushing over the water. A figure or shadow stands near the bank. From the shadowy figure, a light touches our faces as we start to back away.

A gentle voice speaks out of the light. "I am always with you. Do not be afraid."

I know in my heart that this is part of the trinity head: God the Father, God the Son—Jesus, and God the Holy Spirit. I honestly feel like this is Jesus, God's only Son, speaking. Yet it also feels like them all, just like everything else that seems connected here.

I only have time to nod and say, "I won't be afraid, Lord. Just please give me strength," as I bow my head.

"Strength will be granted unto you tenfold from what you had before; it will come to you when the time is right." I know that tenfold in the Bible means ten times more. That is encouraging. I know I will one day become stronger.

After the Lord speaks to me, the dancing light touches my head, and I cannot explain it except to say that I feel instantly happy. I know that my friend is standing beside me. I feel joyful, and I cannot wipe the smile from my face. I turn to Levi, my companion, and say, "Go, before the light leaves."

"No, Awna, I can't. I cannot go without you."

"Why? Just go! Hurry . . . go!" I shout as the light retreats, and we are left alone.

"Why didn't you go, Levi?" I cry out.

Levi looks startled that I have recognized him. He bows his head and prays. After a short time, he is given the confidence as to what he can share. "Awna, I'm about to tell you something, but you may not remember this later. It is only for this moment in time. I am assigned to you. Where you go, I go. This last battle has taken its toll on you. The battle called for other Keepers and myself to fight."

He pauses. "I was separated from you for only a brief time, but God was always there with you. He never left you to fight the battle alone. He sent others when He knew the battle would be great."

Levi pauses again before going on. He does not want to place memories of Will and Ms. Banks into her mind. He chooses his words carefully. "I always know where you are. I know what is going on with you, what you think, and how you feel. I try to protect you as much as I can from the evils of this world, just like you protect the humans. We will win the war; the Holy Word of God says so."

It is only for a second, but I see my reflection in Levi's eyes, and I see a new gleam in my own. "Then let it be so," I say, knowing in that instant what I must do.

I turn and run as hard as I can from Heaven toward the evil. I run until I feel myself falling into the spiritual fog that separates humans from Heaven.

The fog overtakes me. It is a thick fog; I can barely see. I stumble through the trail, holding on to the razor-sharp branches that pierce my arms and swat at my face. The wind howls around me, daring me to keep going. My arms are wet and red; my white dress is drenched in blood. My feet are so sore that I can hardly stand. Stumbling, I fall to the ground. My legs will not carry me; my feet betray me, so I crawl. I crawl through the miry clay until I see an opening in the fog.

And now, within a split second, I lie here in my bed with the warmth of my precious Selah beside me as Heaven and what Levi has spoken are already leaving my memory.

Selah snuggles closer as I try to open my eyes.

More than ever, I know I must wake up. *I have work to do. My spirit is willing, but my body does not want to cooperate,* I think, as sleep wins one more time.

The Keepers stayed close to the cottage, taking care of Selah and waiting. More days passed, and then weeks. Still Awna could not wake.

The dreams continued to plague Awna, even though she was back in her bed. She was still stuck between flesh and spirit. The foggy haze prevented her from waking.

She could not move away from the fog. The opening only took her in a circle toward the fog once again.

She whispered aloud in her sleep as she tried to fight her way back through the fog to become awake.

"I will get to you if I must crawl until my fingers bleed. I refuse to let evil win!" I whisper.

The Word of God says in Ephesians 6:10–11, "Finally, my brethren, be strong in the Lord, and in the power of His might. Put on the whole armour of God, that ye may be able to stand against the wiles of the devil."

In my mind, I start quoting Scripture, and a Bible appears in my hand. Then it turns into a golden sword, and the Word of God echoes from it through the fog.

"Oh, Lord, heal me, and I will be healed," I shout.

A bronze and gold breastplate of righteousness forms over my torso, covering me.

"No weapon formed against me shall prosper," I shout.

The Keepers came close as they heard her shouting. They knew she was fighting her way back through, and they began to pray.

A bronze shield of faith appears in my other hand; it will quench fiery darts from the enemy.

"I resist you, devil, and you must flee, for the Word of God says this, and it is true." I toss and turn in the bed as I shout.

I keep on praying as bronze boots appear on my feet for the preparation of the gospel.

"I am a child of God."

I can feel a helmet of salvation on my head as the belt of truth buckles around my waist. "You have no power over me, satan. You do not control me as you do others!"

As she said this, the Keepers knew she was getting close to breaking through the boundaries of Heaven to earth.

As I try again to stand, I can feel the power of God around me.

The fog clears, and I now stand at the threshold of where the earthly and Heavenly realms meet. I investigate a slow-flowing creek beside me and see a warrior's reflection staring back at me. Clothed in the full armour of God, I am a sleek, beautiful warrior of old, ready for battle, dressed in armour with a flaming sword raised high in the air as the Word of God echoes through the blade.

As I touch my face in the reflection, I notice that I look amazingly strong, ready for battle. Peace flows through my whole body. I weep with thankfulness over my decision to return to help the humans and not to go forward into Heaven. I fall to the ground, and at that very moment, the light returns and touches my face.

A voice speaks out of the light. "Stand up, my child, and walk! I will bless your journey to prevail against the evils of this world. The Holy Spirit will lead you."

"Thank you, Lord," I say through tears of joy.

"Remember, when you are weak, I am strong."

At those words, the light becomes a whirlwind as I cross over into the earthly realm.

FLESH AND SPIRIT MEET

The Keepers watched as Awna's spirit stood over her body. She was fully dressed in the armour of God, and the light of Heaven spun around her like a whirlwind. They sensed that Awna was aware that if the whirlwind ceased, she would not be able to get back into her body.

Her human body lay sleeping. Her long black hair lay draped over her arms. Her skin looked pale and sickly as the shell of her body illuminated her frailness.

The Keepers knew that Awna had already made her choice to return to earth and retain her role as a warrior protecting the humans, but they observed that, for some reason, she could not stop herself from staring at her human shell lying before her. They also knew that Awna might be calculating the fact that she felt more alive standing over her body than if she were in the body that lay there.

The time had come. The whirlwind was changing, now slowing down. The Keepers observed Awna as she lay the tip of her sword over the heart of the still body. A jolt occurred in Awna's body as the sword echoed the Word of God, and it flowed through Awna's earthly body. The warrior was gone from the sight of the Keepers, but they knew that the warrior was tucked into Awna's earthly form once again, waiting for God's appointed time to reappear.

I awake with a start and immediately sit up, gasping for air. My lungs take in the heaviness of the air around me. This life force that sustains humanity feels so heavy upon my body. I breathe in deeply as Selah greets me, first by licking me and then by spinning around and jumping up and down on the bed. She jumps down, and I can hear her little toenails running around the house, up and down the stairs and then into the kitchen. Goodness, I feel terrible. I must have had a bad, bad dream. I shake my head, trying to clear the feeling.

"Oh my, Selah. You must be hungry. I must have overslept this morning. I know you have to go out. How long have I been lying here?" I look at the windows, but it is still dark outside.

I raise myself to get out of bed, positioning myself with my elbow, but I cannot find the strength. Pain envelops every part of my body. My breathing is rapid as I wonder what to do. I try again and make it to a sitting position. When I glance at the clock on the wall, I see that it has taken me forty-five minutes just to sit up and hang my heavy, aching legs over the side of the bed. My hands and arms look perfectly fine, but they are very sore, and I don't know why. I look at my gauzy white gown but do not remember putting it on. I think about this, shaking my head.

Then I try to stand but fall to the floor. *What is wrong with me?*

I move my legs around to sit up straight, but the pain will not let me go. My whole right side from my back and down to my feet is on fire with pain. Tears stream down my face. Selah comes running back and begins barking at me.

"Shh . . . Selah, come here."

She leaps into my arms, where she is perfectly content. It does not seem to matter to her that I am on the floor and cannot get up.

We sit here for over thirty minutes together, savoring the moment.

"Okay, Selah, I've got to try."

When I am weak, you are strong are the words that keep coming into my mind.

I pray, *Lord, be strong for me, because I'm so weak right now, and I have no idea why.*

I roll over onto my knees and will my legs to move. Finally, with all the strength I can muster, I grab onto the bedpost for balance and stand on shaky legs, but I have to hold on to everything within reach to continue to move forward.

Each step I take is a task that takes time. The weakness and pain continue as I crawl and then scoot down the stairs. I finally make it to the kitchen an hour later and stand at the kitchen island, slowly getting Selah's food ready.

Out of the corner of my eye, I can see that she is here one minute and gone the next. "Selah!" I call, looking around. There is no Selah.

"Selah, where are you? Here's your food!"

It is then that I see the door: a doggy door. I stand here trying to figure out when I had it put in, but I just cannot remember. Everything this morning seems foggy in my head and shaky in my body.

After a few minutes, Selah comes barreling through her door, happy as can be.

"Well, Selah, I guess you needed your own door!"

Honestly, that door was not there before I went to sleep last night, was it? My head hurts, and I need to eat and get some water.

I open the cabinet doors, which are stocked with food, as is the refrigerator. I am so confused. I do not remember going to the grocery store. I drink a glass of water, make a cup of hot tea, and then make my way to the veranda. I take baby steps, holding on to the wall for support until I reach the outdoor table.

The sun is coming up, and the warm morning breeze greets me as I sit down to rest. The sky is still as I remember—the same brilliant blue with streaks of pink and red running through the clouds. The ocean is adorned with green and blue water.

I close my eyes and try to remember other things but cannot. What has happened to me?

I finish my tea and then go back to the kitchen to find something to eat. Nothing looks good or recognizable. I have no appetite. I grab another bottled water, eat some nuts and an apple, and slowly struggle back upstairs.

I retrieve a pale pink eyelet sundress from my closet and sandals for the day. I lay the dress on my bed; everything looks new to me, but I do not remember buying any of the clothes. My other surroundings are familiar, except for that doggy door. I disrobe in the bathroom, where a tall floor-length mirror stands. I catch sight of my reflection in the mirror and gasp in horror. Holding on to the sink, I turn on the water and splash it on my face. What has happened to my face?

Oh my gosh, my hair! Gray hairs spring from my head. And my youthful skin, where did it go? Have I always looked this way? I touch the small but noticeable wrinkles. I do not remember these or the crow's feet that outline my eyes. A new frown line runs across my forehead. My eyes look tired. Small, weak eyes replace the large dark eyes and lashes that I feel I used to see. Or is this how I think I saw myself?

The reflection looks like a stranger to me, an older-looking stranger. Am I still dreaming? None of this makes any sense. How can a person go to sleep looking youthful and then wake up looking old? I shake my head, looking away from what I see. My stomach feels in knots. Fear and uncertainty fill me as I try to wrap my mind around all of this.

Then I am hit by this question: *Who am I?*

The house is familiar, but something is off. I make my way through every room, still having to hold on to the wall for balance. I open doors and drawers. I see the studio, but nothing on the walls or easels looks familiar. Did I paint these?

I grab my robe from the bathroom, hobble downstairs, find the remote, and turn on the TV. No clues there. I turn on my computer and search the internet.

WHAT!!! Recommended updates start popping up on my screen, so I click the downloads to start the process. Another pop-up wants me to set the time, date, and year. When I notice the year, I shake my head.

This can't be! A year has passed since I last updated my computer. . . . A year?

"Selah, come here!"

Selah pops her head through the doggy door.

"Come here, girl!" I hold her to look at her closely. She too looks older; her hair has a grayish hue to it with wiry sprigs springing up here and there, just like mine. We must both be losing our melanin production, but at least Selah is still jumping around, while I can barely walk.

I slowly travel back upstairs to look in the mirror again and gaze at this unrecognizable person staring back at me. My hair has no shine. The ruddy appearance of my skin looks frightfully concerning. I step onto the scale—85 pounds!!! What is happening? *No wonder I am weak. I've lost 20 pounds. But how do I know that I previously weighed 105 pounds?*

To clear my head, I take a long shower, letting the water run over my shaking body. I pray for understanding. I weep, but it only makes my head hurt worse. I wash and condition my hair, thinking, *At least I know my God, if I know nothing else.*

How could thousands of years pass with my appearance unchanged . . . to this fiasco?

Wait! What was that thought? A thousand years? Maybe I'm still dreaming?

I must be crazy. I am really losing it. This is crazy! "A thousand years," I laugh aloud.

My shower leaves me feeling drained. I need to rest while my body pulsates from pain.

Eventually, I put on my "new" clothes and lie across the bed until I have the energy to dry my hair. Two hours pass before I make my way back downstairs again. This time, the stairs aren't as difficult as when I first attempted them.

I open the computer again and start looking up women's ages—those who look thirty, forty, and up. Yep, the age I look is more like thirty-five to fortyish.

Overnight, how could this happen? It is impossible! I've always looked twenty-five, and not a day over.

Another thought races through my mind. *Maybe I've always looked like this?*

No, something tells me this is not the real me.

Okay, I'll make a plan: first, I'll gain some weight. Then I will work out to build my muscles. I could join a gym?

I raid the refrigerator. I can accept looking older, but I at least want to be healthy. I am far too thin; my ribs are showing.

I pray. I sleep. I eat lots of food for days, but I am still very weak. After three days, my biggest accomplishment is that I can sit outside on the veranda a couple of times each day.

I can't walk far without getting tired and winded. I pray but don't feel or hear anything. I find an old, tattered Bible and ponder the words I read over and over. Yes, these words are familiar too.

Now a month has gone by since I awoke to this nightmare, and I know I have to do something. I determine that tomorrow will be a new day with a fresh start. I have been feeling a little better each day, but now I need to get more food. I have to go out. I research my symptoms, and the internet suggests that I may need vitamins. Yes, that's what I'll do. I will go to Somerset Pharmacy in the morning.

Wait. . . . How do I know the name of the pharmacy?

Making my plans for the days ahead is exhausting. My eyes feel heavy, the room spins, and I feel my body giving in again. I quickly fall asleep on the couch. When I awake, it is dark. The curtains billow with the breeze. I watch them until, somewhere between sleep and consciousness, he comes to me. He stands just inside the French doors, and with the curtains flowing in and out, it seems as though the curtains are one.

Soon he steps from the shadows. I turn from him, ashamed at how weak and old I've become. Vanity at its best covers me like a glove. I tell him to go away, but he stands still.

I have always been happy to see him, haven't I? Who is he, though?

The dream scares me, and I am afraid, not so much of him but of myself. This darkness is wrapping itself around me and trying to pull me down. Sadness fills my spirit. I feel that I need him, but when I turn back around, I am alone.

Yes, thank goodness! It was only a dream.

Then I drift back to sleep.

Levi, Will, and Ms. Banks were just outside on the veranda.

"She is slipping from us, Levi. The flesh is taking her mind, body, and spirit," Ms. Banks said. "We must do something before the flesh takes her life. She does not know who she is anymore. If Moloch's people came for her now, there would be no fight left in her. They would win, and she would die. Then our mission dies with her."

Levi pondered this and prayed. Minutes ticked away, and he finally said, "You may go to her again as before if you choose. We will see if she has enough spirit left in her for friends; it may lift her. We are just so unsure of her current condition. But remember, she will not remember you. You must start all over with the relationship."

Ms. Banks and Will looked at one another and nodded; they would pray for what the Lord would have them to do.

The morning sun shines through the cottage; I haven't moved since last night.

I remember the dream and someone named . . . what was his name?

I cannot remember, and at this moment, I don't even care. Maybe I know him, but I guess it was just a dream.

What is wrong with me? Maybe I am sick? I am so weak and can hardly move. I force myself to sit up, but dizziness overcomes me as my head pounds and spins around. I make it to the refrigerator, where I force myself to make a cup of coffee and eat a small bowl of cereal.

I hobble to the veranda, make it to the seat, and sit here looking out to sea. Now the thoughts start to flow. *I don't know who I am, and I do not recognize myself. I'm weak, and I don't know why.*

I force a spoonful of cereal into my mouth, and then another. Once I finish, I feel a little better. As I get up to go back inside, I see a flyer on the French doors that is held in place by the breeze. I reach for it.

Hmm. . . . "Relax in the Bermuda Breeze Spa," the flyer reads. "Hair, makeup, nails, vitamins, and supplements—all for a healthy you." The flyer announces that a spa has opened within walking distance of Cambridge Beaches. Maybe I'll go there to get my vitamins instead of going to the pharmacy.

Still, as the morning wears on, thoughts come inadvertently. *I've never done anything like a spa visit. I don't think I have, anyway. I wonder what it would be like to go to a spa.*

Maybe I'll try it out. I sure could use a boost.

"What do you think, Selah?" She only wiggles her nub and rushes from her bed by the fireplace to head back out the doggy door.

The day is much like the others, except this day, I pick up my tattered Bible and start to read. By evening, I've read the stories that feel familiar. Instead of just seeing the words, I study and memorize them and then speak them aloud. I rehearse chapters, as this all seems to come so easily.

Did I forget the words that feel so familiar? I start to feel the words, which pick me up and change me. I start feeling different, as though coming out of a dark place.

After a good night's sleep (thirteen hours' worth, which is not like me at all, or is it?), I feel better. I am still moving slowly and looking very thin, but my mood and attitude are better.

I eat, shower, and attempt to do something with my hair and face, but the outcome is not great. I look sallow and sad, but I know I want to feel and look better.

After pondering the flyer, I know what my answer will be concerning the spa. Yes! I will go to the spa today, but I know there is no way I'll be able to walk there.

The flyer states, "Walk-ins Welcome." Okay, I don't need an appointment, but do I have gas in the car? Do I even have a car?

Yes, I do have a car and scooter, but I don't remember filling the tanks.

I go to the garage to check, and yes, there is a car and a scooter, both with full tanks of gas. The car is an older-looking sporty one, but both vehicles look like they have just rolled off the showroom floor.

I go back inside and change into a ruffled, soft ivory-colored cotton sundress. I want to look as good as possible. I've never thought about my looks before; I know that for a fact. What has changed? I used to put on a little lip gloss with a messy bun, and I was ready to go.

Another thought runs through my head: *Now I have unruly hair, gray sprouts pop everywhere out of my head, and my face and neck show fewer wrinkles, maybe because I've put on a few pounds.*

Selah twirls at the door. "No, sweet girl, you can't come today. I'll be back soon." She walks over to her bed and lies down by the fireplace, cutting her sad eyes up at me in hopes of changing my mind.

I grab my purse, make sure I have money and keys, and off I go to the spa.

As I drive my sporty car near Somerset Village, I spot the place instantly. I could have walked but didn't want to chance it. I still feel too weak.

As I park, a couple begins staring at my car. The man asks me, "What year is your car? They didn't make many of these. You're a lucky woman."

I just shrug and retort, "Not really sure."

He looks confused but continues on his way, looking back several times.

I walk into the beautiful spa, which has a welcoming and relaxing feel and lots of beach décor. There is no one in sight. Maybe they unlocked the doors and are busy opening up everything else. After all, this spa is a rather large place, and it is not even 10:00 a.m.

I decide to explore until someone finds me. A young man comes out of one of the rooms and almost bumps right into me. He is tall and lanky but a bit muscular. He has a nice demeanor about him and looks like a surfer. He has sun-bleached blondish-brown hair and friendly blue eyes.

"Oh, Miss. I'm so sorry. I didn't mean to startle you."

"I'm fine, thank you."

"You are going to love this place," he says.

"Thank you. I'm looking forward to it. I could use a boost," I say, very embarrassed at how I must look in front of this cute fella.

"Well, Miss, this is the place to get rejuvenated. My name is Will." He reaches out his hand to me, and I shake it.

"My name is Awna," I say shyly.

"I might see you later. I'm doing some work here. Have fun."

"Thank you. It was nice to meet you, Will."

"You as well, Awna."

Hmm . . . at least I know my name. That's a start.

The spa walls are decorated with nets full of brightly colored fish and seashells, adding an island appeal. Wind chimes hang near the outside French doors connecting a deck that overlooks the blue waters. All the windows are open; the curtains are sheer white and move gracefully, and the music playing is a serene, peaceful instrumental. The walls are white, and the floors are a shiny light-color hardwood.

The large reception desk is made of mahogany wood, hand carved with what looks to be the finest of quality and craft. The desk stands in the middle of the main room, while adjoining rooms can be seen on both sides, each offering a unique appeal. The styling room has multiple long mirrors that touch the floor and a welcoming styling chair that awaits the next customer.

Another room is arranged for doing nails. The nail tables look like the receptionist's desk but are much narrower, with comfortable cushioned chairs for the technician as well as the guest. A glass top rests upon each station, while a matching built-in table cart holds the manicure products. There is a nail polish rack adorned with at least two hundred bottles and all manner of products needed to make someone feel pretty.

Another room off the nail area holds the pedicure paraphernalia. Massage chairs made of the same shiny mahogany wood with adjacent basin baths are set up for the feet. All of the French doors are open so guests can see outside to the Cambridge beaches. The pinkish sand has a relaxing yet inviting aura.

It is a while before I realize that I've been walking around exploring this magnificent spacious spa by myself. I can't help it. No one seems to be around, so I continue exploring, finding massage rooms, each as plush as the rest of the place. White sheets drape each bed. Essential oils and lotions hang on the wall racks for easy access, and the same spa music can be heard in each massage room. Each of the rooms looks similar but with personal touches here and there to make them unique. Candles burn in each room, smelling of coconut, almond, or other essential oils. The dim lighting makes everything feel relaxing, and peace fills my soul.

There is a color bar in one of the rooms with an array of hair colors and developer products ready for action. A computer is aligned to the side of the bar to keep guest records. The adjacent room is where the hair color operation takes place. The chairs and mirrors look like everything else: extremely expensive.

A tearoom opens up to the most picturesque view of Bermuda. Teas from all over the world are displayed next to a tray of wrapped crumpets. Teatime is usually from 2:00 p.m. to 5:00 p.m. The magnificent plush couches and chairs in the room are made of white damask fabrics and shine brightly against the shiny floors. There are Harbor Breeze Baja Palm ceiling fans in every room, giving off a soft, gentle breeze that makes one feel caressed by the ocean breeze. The tearoom has wet, warm cloths lying in heaters for each guest to put over their face while they lounge in the chairs.

Just past the doors, the outside deck has a roof covering so that, regardless of the weather, the guests can enjoy the comfort inside and out. The other side of the deck has tables with brightly colored red umbrellas that stand at attention. This deck was built to please everyone.

I see Will working on the other side of the decking. He waves with one hand while he holds a hammer with his other hand. I wave back and smile. A tool belt is draped around his waist. Embarrassed for staring, I quickly turn back inside.

Still roaming around, I find to the left of the building a hair removal room where waxing, threading, tweezing, and sugaring take place. Attached to that room is a makeup area. Shelves are stocked with skin care products, foundations, blushes, concealers, eyeshadow, and lip colors. The large, low light bulbs shine around each mirror, just light enough for the makeup artist to see to work.

This place is exquisite. Even the restrooms are unbelievably beautiful, with mirrors from the floor to the mid-ceiling. The ceilings have the same mahogany beams. There are tissues, hand creams, mints, burning candles, and freshly laundered white robes lining one side of the wall. Hidden inside the walls are bins for robes and towels once a guest is finished with them.

I hear footsteps and turn back toward the reception area. I didn't notice when I first walked into the spa, but behind the huge reception area is a staircase made of the same mahogany wood which swirls up to the top floor.

I look up to see lofty ceilings I didn't notice before. A beautiful, slender young lady comes down the stairs; her smile is as breathtaking as her poise. Her long blonde hair is brushed back away from her face and falls to her waist. Her skin is mildly tanned but has a flawless porcelain look. I guess she is in her twenties, the way I probably used to feel but not what I've been seeing in the mirror lately.

"Hello, my friend. I'm so sorry to keep you waiting. I didn't hear you come in," she says in a long Southern drawl.

She must be from the States, I think. *Hmm. How would I know this?*

As she steps off the last stair and walks toward me, I can feel the love spill from her. As she takes my hand to welcome me to the spa, I feel a surge of energy that almost makes me lose my balance.

She smiles and holds my hand a moment longer. "Oh my. The floor is a little slick from the morning cleaning. My name is Grace, and whom do I have the pleasure of meeting today?"

"Umm, my name is Awna," I respond. I feel small and inadequate.

"Okay, let's go to the appointment desk, Awna, and see what we can do for you."

She opens her appointment book. "You're in luck, my sweet friend. We have time today for whatever you want. The cruise ships will not port for another few days. I may have a local guest who said they might call for an appointment this afternoon, but that's all. I'm free just for you."

There is something familiar about Grace, but I can't put a finger on it.

"Okay, precious, what would you like today?"

I just stand here as she continues, not knowing what to say.

"You can get a haircut, color, manicure, pedicure, or maybe hair removal, lash extensions, or hair extensions. BUT, how about a massage first?"

As I stand here faced with her questions, I have no answers, but I sure like her accent. "I'm sorry. I'm really not sure."

Grace smiles and tilts her head, laughing and looking at me with her beautiful ocean-green-colored eyes. She is gorgeous with extra full lashes and a flawless face with pouty, full lips.

When she looks into my eyes, it is as if she is looking into my very soul.

I feel incredibly awkward and a bit uncomfortable, not knowing what to say to her. She sweetly announces, "Okay, then. How about the works?"

I feel the heat of my embarrassment but shake my head yes.

"It's been decided, then."

I have no idea what the "works" includes, but I agree wholeheartedly, shaking my head yes a second time!

Grace guides me to the sitting room for massage therapy first. She explains that it is just her and another person working today, as everyone else has the day off to relax before the cruise ships port.

I am given an herbal tea that does wonders for my anxiety. I don't even realize that I am anxious until I feel the weight lift from my soul. Grace then places warm, moist towels on my face, hands, and feet. I already feel as if I've met up with an old friend; peace surrounds me.

After thirty minutes of listening to spa music with warm, moist towels on my face, hands, and feet, we venture into a welcoming, dimly lit room where the massage bed with crisp white sheets beckons me. I undress and climb onto the table. I am already so relaxed from the tea and warm sheets that my body feels heavy and light at the same time. The low classical spa music plays with ocean sounds in the background as Grace begins the process of relaxing my sore, worn-out body.

It seems as if I've spent hours on the table. I sleep, I dream, I wake, and then I fall back to sleep. I drowsily awake again, lifting my head. Grace is there and asks me to sit up slowly and drink the bottled water on the table next to the bed.

"After you drink the water, take a few minutes and then meet me in the facial area. Here's a robe for you." She points to the white robe hanging on a hook next to me. After drinking the water and giving myself a few minutes, I make my way to the facial area.

After a vigorous facial massage with lights and steam, Grace applies a Bermudian mud mask on my face and freshly cut cucumber slices on my closed eyes. Grace says that the mask was blended with the secrets of Bermuda.

I relax in a massaging chair as Grace pushes me to the nail area and starts the manicure massage, massaging from my hand to my elbow. I hear someone rolling a mobile cart toward me. Grace peels a cucumber back from one eye for me to choose a nail color. I pick a pale pink.

"Good choice. This will look perfect with your olive skin tone."

She then places the cucumber back over my eye, pushes and clips my cuticles, and then files each nail. There is someone else in the room because my other arm and hand are also being massaged. As I lay there with the soothing oils on my face, the chair tilts slightly upward, and someone else begins brushing my hair. She informs me that she is applying a thick pack of black henna on my hair that will cover the gray naturally and bring a glossy shine to my hair.

"Hello. By the way, my name is Mercy. I will also be serving you today. Please relax and enjoy."

As the henna processes, it seems that multiple hands and fingers are at work in unison as they target the areas in need. My feet and calves up to my knees are being massaged. My feet are cleaned and exfoliated. My toenails are clipped, filed, and polished in the same pale pink color to match my fingers. I can feel that my two feet are being pedicured in unison.

Yes, I am truly getting *the works!*

I never once hear anyone speak, but they work together silently, as one. After the pedicure, another light is shone over my face, going back and forth from my neck to my forehead. I can feel a warm heat and then something cool pulsating all around my wrinkles.

I then feel the light's soft heat all over me, from head to toe, even to the soles of my feet. I am feeling rejuvenated. Another facial steamer blows its mist not only on my face but all over my body. I am then wrapped in warm towels and told to rest. My hair is gently shampooed, conditioned, trimmed, brushed out, and dried with the quietest blow dryer I have ever heard. All of this is happening while I relax. I cannot keep my eyes open.

I wake slowly to the sound of the healing spa music and the breeze blowing from the shore. When I open my eyes, I see the sheer curtains dancing a jig and think it is funny. I want to laugh but hold it in. I hear the water rushing against the rocks as my eyes continue to open ever so slowly.

I can hazily see someone standing over me, watching me as I attempt to wake. I blink when I realize that both Grace and Mercy are standing there. I think I am seeing double. Then they both smile.

"We get this all of the time; we're identical twins," Grace says with a wink.

Their eyes sparkle, looking like the Bermudian waters. They both help me from the chair as it is righted into its natural position. I honestly cannot tell the women apart; their beauty is incomparable to anything I've ever seen.

They hold my arms until they know that I can stand on my own, and then they walk me to the skincare room. They lay me back again as they attach lash extensions, foundation, blush, and lip gloss. This establishment is amazing, not only because of its architectural beauty held within these walls but also by the peace and love that surround the stylists as they gently and lovingly guide me to the dressing room where my clothes are waiting on a rack.

"Grace, what do you think?"

"Yes, I'm thinking the same thing, Mercy."

Mercy leaves, and when she comes back, she carries an entire outfit with matching jewelry, a purse, and sandals for completion.

"Mercy, you're just so extra. Honey, you're all fun and fluff, but this is absolutely gorgeous, sister. Well done, darlin'."

Mercy beams as the women lead me to the magnificent bathroom with a changing room that I didn't notice before. It is set off to the side of the bathroom. After I change, they lead me to an enormously tall mirror. In fact, everything seems to be enormous and luxurious here. I didn't even notice the boutique in the front corner of the spa. It holds anything a girl could want to feel pretty.

When I look at myself, I gasp at the sight. I've been transformed. It is how I thought I should look. Once again, I feel like it is me when I look in the mirror.

I touch my hair; it shows no signs of the dull gray appearance. It is silky and shiny with soft black strands that Grace has hidden with a touch of henna. I have a glow around me that I've never seen before, or is it this mirror that makes me shine? I run my hand over my arm. My skin is so soft and smooth, and its olive color has a tanned look once again, unlike the ashy tone from this morning.

My nails and toes match with a pale pink color, and the tips have a hint of shining glitter. When my nails catch the light, they look like diamond chips. They are all even, as if they have been artificially sculpted, but Mercy assures me they are my own, all-natural.

I step closer to the mirror, and the wrinkles I saw earlier are gone! I no longer look like a woman in her thirties or forties but look in my twenties. I look at the two stylists, and tears start to flow.

"Oh, my dear, don't cry! You'll mess up your makeup."

"Quick, sister!"

Mercy hands me a tissue, and I dab at the tears. It is as if they can read each other's minds.

Grace takes me in her arms as Mercy stands close with a hand on my shoulder, patting me gently while smiling. "Tell me what you are thinking and feeling, sweet girl."

"Well, I've just been feeling so bad, and I don't know why. I've been in a lot of pain; I just felt so worn out. I am so grateful for your help. You've made me feel pretty. Honestly, I never remember thinking or feeling that I was pretty."

Mercy steps forward and tilts my chin up to look at her. "My dear, you are a beautiful soul, inside and out. Besides, we all need a little help now and again. What in the world would we ever do without each other?"

Mercy wipes away my tears. "Now, no more crying. You'll mess up your lash extensions," she says and dabs once again at my tears.

"No more tears," I say as I take a deep breath.

"I agree with Mercy. What would we ever do without one another!" Grace says and smiles as she leads me to the door. "Remember, we are always here for you if you need us. All you have to do is knock on the door, and we will answer."

I walk toward the door, but as I touch the doorknob, I remember I haven't paid. I turn around, but the girls are gone.

"Grace! Mercy! Where are you? I forgot to pay!"

There is no response. In fact, the two said they might have another guest this afternoon, but no one is around. I find that odd.

As I look at the price list on the wall, I open my purse and count out seven $100 bills. That should cover it. I put the cash on the reception desk with a note of thanks and gratitude. After all, they've spent hours on me.

I get out more money and fold it into another note, saying,

Grace and Mercy,

Here's a tip for each of you. Thank you so much for all you've done for me today. I truly appreciate you both.

~Awna~

As I am leaving the spa, I feel light, like a feather. It is such a beautiful day, and I feel so much better. I have no pain and lots of energy. My mind is clear without any lingering foggy feeling. I don't feel like I even need the vitamins now.

I am still standing in the doorway of the spa and have just closed the door as a lady passes by. I smile as she strolls past me, and then I pipe up and tell her about the spa and what an amazing experience I've just had.

Then I walk to my car. And I mean I literally walk without any fatigue or pain back to my car.

I can see the woman looking around, peeping in the windows. She then shakes her head and goes the other way.

Hmm. The girls probably took a break after all the work they did on me, I think.

As I reach my car, I wish I hadn't driven. Who would have known that I would feel this relaxed, pampered, and rejuvenated, with no more pain! I backed out of the spa's driveway and see the woman I've just spoken with about the spa. I smile, wave, and drive away.

The lady moseyed to the front of the abandoned building. She peeked into the windows to see if maybe there was a spa there, but there was no spa at this location. It was only a defunct building. Debris covered the floor, and old, broken furniture was strewn all around.

Well, maybe it used to be a spa, or maybe the spa is another one of the businesses here in this building. I sure would like to be beautiful like that girl, she thought.

The lady peeked into every storefront window on the street, but once again, she shook her head and walked away. She returned to her husband, who was gazing out at the ocean. His gray hair lifted with the breeze, and his tanned face lit up as he saw his wife approaching.

"Well, Lanie, are you ready to sightsee, or are you still looking for a boutique?"

"Yes, I'm ready. I thought I'd found a spa down the street but must have misunderstood the young lady."

The couple walked along and spotted a café.

"Let's stop here, Jake. It looks so quaint."

"You betcha. I was getting a little hungry myself."

As they turned to enter the café, Lanie spotted something from the corner of her eye. She looked in that direction and saw a very dirty child peeking from behind a bush. She grabbed Jake's arm.

"Oh, honey, look at the child!" The couple stopped in their tracks and tried to coax the little girl from behind the bush.

"Come here, little one. Are you hungry?" Jake inquired.

The little girl pushed closer to the bush, hiding within its bushy limbs.

They assessed that the child was maybe three or four years old and probably a beautiful child without the tangles, dirt, and tattered clothes.

"Let's go on in. She's not coming out. We can ask them inside if she's one of the homeless children who come here to beg for food," Jake suggested.

"Okay, but she's awfully young to be out here by herself," Lanie frowned.

"You remember what the hotel manager said earlier in the week, that sometimes the older children or parents send the younger children to get food because it appeals to tourists' heartstrings," Jack added.

"Yes, but she's just absolutely precious. I don't want anything to happen to her," Lanie proclaimed.

They asked to see the manager and told him about the young child. The manager said that he hadn't seen a child like the one they'd described, but there could be new ones in the area.

Upon leaving the café, the couple left a box with a grilled cheese sandwich, chips, and water near the bush, hoping the child would at least eat. The manager said he would call the authorities to report the child and would check on her during his next break. Who knew if he really would?

As the couple walked away, the little girl snatched the food and water and ran to a nearby bench. Crawling onto the bench, she arranged her food on her little lap and then bowed her head to pray and started to eat. Her large brown eyes looked tired from lack of sleep, yet she smiled, kicking her little, short legs back and forth while enjoying the food she'd been given.

CHAPTER 12

FINDING MYSELF AND MORE

The next morning, I wake up with a new sense of purpose. Looking in the mirror, I feel that I am back to myself, whomever that might be. I feel and look like I am in my twenties. I feel so free from pain that I want to explore. I ride my scooter to the ferry and then into Hamilton alone. Selah doesn't object. I wore her out with frolic and play the day before, after my spa experience.

I park my scooter and walk around Hamilton. I find a coffee shop, the Mocha Café, on Burnaby Street. It is a nice, cozy place with not only coffee but also delicious desserts and food. I lounge around watching people. There are moms with their children, and couples who stroll by the window, only to come in and buy a tasty treat or have a rest from shopping in the nearby shops. The more I watch people, the more I feel alone and wish I had someone to share my life with, or a family to laugh and giggle with, like these people do. Maybe I want someone just to say, "Hey, you want to go get a coffee with me?"

I look down at my coffee, staring into it, deep in thought.

"Is this seat taken, dear?"

I look up to find a sweet older woman standing nearby. I smile. "Sure, you can sit here."

"Oh, thank you, dear. It's just that all the other seats are taken, I've been walking all morning, and I really need to sit down. I'm sorry. Let me introduce myself. My name is Faith, Faith Banks."

"Hi, my name is Awna. It's so nice to meet you!" I smile from the inside out. "I was just sitting here thinking how nice it would be to have some company, and here you are!"

"Isn't it funny how things work out?" Faith shakes her head, smiling.

I smile, thinking how I'd like to be friends with this lady but have no earthly idea how.

We make small talk about the weather, the growing number of tourists, and how she and her grandson are here on visas. She mostly does all the talking because honestly, I don't remember much about myself that I could add to the conversation. She orders a decaf coffee and sips it as we talk. I like her and feel that, even with an age difference, we could possibly be friends.

Faith is looking at me, and there is a slight pause in our talk. "Awna, might I say that you are an exceptional young lady. You know, my grandson is around your age. I would just love for him to meet you."

Panic stirs within me, and she can see it on my face.

"Oh dear. I didn't mean to be so forward. It's just that he hasn't met many people his age while we've been on the island. He just works all the time. He teaches, and he's doing a side job this week working on a spa deck in Somerset Point. He does carpentry work."

"Is his name Will?"

Faith looks stunned. "Why yes; how did you know?"

"I met him. I was in the spa yesterday having a pamper day."

"Oh my goodness. This is amazing; we will have to get together. Here's my number. Feel free to text or call me to talk anytime." She hands me the napkin with her number on it. "Will and I are managing Gibbs Lighthouse, so he actually has three jobs. He's just the jack of all trades, so to speak. Please come and see us; we'd love the company!"

Faith finishes her coffee and puts her used coffee mug in the dirty tray bin. With that, she stands, hugs me, and leaves to catch the ferry.

I finish my mocha, thinking that things are looking up for me. I decide to look around the city, feeling like I am a bit lighter indeed. I look through the windows of the boutiques. I am so intrigued at what I see that I enter one and purchase a cute, gauzy white eyelet skirt with a sewn-in slip. I match it with a plain olive-colored tank with lace on the straps.

I make my way back toward the coffee shop, being sure to peer into the storefront windows as I stroll. I don't want to miss anything.

Passing the Mocha Café, I find a pet boutique called Paws and Claws. I purchase a cute pink doggie shirt for Selah with "Little Diva" written on it. As I stroll through the shop, I locate a small squeaky toy and doggy shampoo. I have to curb my spending because the scooter's basket and storage will only hold so much.

I stop by the grocery for a few supplies and then drive to Queen Elizabeth Park on Par-la-Ville Road. I pass a moon gate made of limestone and am captivated by the majestic scenery. Jasmine fills the air, beckoning me to stop. I have nothing perishable in my basket, so it wouldn't hurt. I lock my basket and storage and set out on a small adventure.

There are approximately forty moon gates in Bermuda. The beautiful architectural designs are wonderful photo opportunities. There's also a legend on the island that lovers who walk through one of these gates holding hands will be blessed with eternal love and happiness. I stop, thinking, *How did I know that?*

What a beautiful day in paradise. No sweater is required, and the temperature is around seventy degrees with sun and only a hint of humidity. I feel like I could spin circles and dance. Strolling past the blooms and trees, taking in my surroundings, now I wish I'd brought Selah. She would have loved this.

I sit for a moment on a bench adjacent to the perfectly manicured grass and shut my eyes, soaking in the sun.

Then I feel the stare of someone. I open my eyes to find a child just gazing at me. She looks maybe three or four years old. I have no idea how to judge a child's age, but that guess was my first thought.

Her skin is a beautiful olive color. Her hair is straight and mostly black with massive tangles, but I can barely see the golden sun-kissed highlights that frame her little face due to how matted her hair has become. She is very dirty. Her eyes are big and brown with a sad, hollow look about them. Her pink shirt is tattered and dirty with rips and holes throughout. Her shorts are so filthy that I can't even distinguish the color, and her dirty little feet have no shoes on them.

"Hello," I say.

There is no response. She only stares.

"Where's your mommy or daddy?"

No response.

My guess is that she is a homeless child. I read about this issue just the other day while trying to orient myself with Bermuda's history. I've never seen a homeless person before, especially a Bermudian. At least, I don't think that I have. The country is full of wealth everywhere I look, but some of the common Bermudian folks either can't find work or have lost their jobs. The cost of living in Bermuda is far more than these people can earn. Thus, Bermuda deals with a lot of homelessness in parks, abandoned buildings, and in the caves.

How do I know this? I ask myself silently.

The little girl continues to stare. I stand and look around, but there is no one except tourists and a few people strolling during a high tea break.

"What's your name?"

Still, no response.

"My name is Awna. Okay, let's walk around together and maybe we can find your mommy."

I reach out my hand; she hesitates but takes it. We stroll together, and I look everywhere for her family, calling out, but no one answers.

We stay at the park for hours, walking and playing a game of "toss the rock into a cup," just hoping her mom, dad, or someone who knows her will come by, but to no avail.

I have only one helmet for the scooter. How could I even dare put a child on my scooter? The police would rake me over the coals.

Well, the child has to eat, and I have to do something. Doing nothing would be pure negligence. I hold her in front of me on the scooter seat as best as I can, and she grips the basket as I slowly drive the short trip to a deli.

I buy us a peanut butter and jelly sandwich, a pint of milk, water, and chips. We picnic under a willow tree, and the child eats like she is starving.

I've never been around a child, let alone fed one. *How do I know that?* This makes me pause.

I hesitate but decide it is best to go to the authorities about the girl. Maybe they have information. After all, I've just seen the police station on my drive here; it is only a few blocks away.

At the police station, the young officer who helps us looks barely out of the police academy. Officer Cantrell asks for my driver's license. I search my purse and, luckily, find it. I tell him the situation.

"What do you mean, there's nothing you can do right now? She's a small child, for goodness' sake!"

Officer Cantrell stands his ground. "Look, lady. We see this every day. A lot of the women and families hope that tourists like yourself will at least give their child a meal. If you take her back to where you found her, her mother will probably be waiting. Or the child may just run off and go back to her family."

"What? Are you out of your mind? How can you say that?" I glare at him, trying to keep my cool.

"Okay, look. Just leave her. There's some paperwork for this kind of thing, but I'll fill it out, and DSS will come get her."

"And how long will that take?" I retort.

"It could be the end of the day, or maybe two days. They are extremely busy trying to keep families together or keep them from leaving their homeland. This has become an epidemic," Officer Cantrell says. "We see this daily. Four Bermudian families left yesterday; they'd finally earned enough money for the plane trip and had a little extra left to start a new life in Florida. These families are in hopes of keeping their family together before they are torn apart by authorities."

Officer Cantrell drops his head as he draws closer to me and whispers, "Look, I grew up as one of these children. I was finally assigned to some missionaries at the church. That's where my life turned around. The missionaries are long gone now, but they were incredibly good people. There's a new pastor and his wife at the church. They are very friendly people." He looks around before speaking. "You're a resident here. You've seen the church, haven't you?

I just stare back at him, not knowing what to say. "What church?" I ask. "How can I help this child?"

He leans over the counter and whispers, "The Evangelical Church."

An older officer walks into the room, and immediately things change. Officer Cantrell suddenly starts spouting rules about DSS and picks up the phone. I hear a door slam and look around. The little girl is gone.

Officer Cantrell places the phone down and says, "We'll take it from here."

A small handwritten note lies on the floor just under the front desk of the police station. Eyes will never see the written report of a three-to-four-year-old child being seen just outside of a small café near Sandy Parish.

I press my lips together and shake my head, leaving the building and trying not to let frustration get the best of me. I look all around but don't see her. My heart sinks. She'll be hungry again soon, and she's all alone. I search up and down the street, but she is nowhere in sight. I ride around this part of the island, from the police station and beyond, but still, I don't see her. I drive back to Queen

Elizabeth's Park and sit there until almost dark. There is no sign of the child, so I go back home. Maybe Officer Cantrell is right and the parents sent her out for a meal.

My heart sinks.

When I arrive home, Selah is extremely glad to see me. We play for a while, but no matter how hard I try, I cannot get the child off my mind. *Who is she? Where is her mother?*

Officer Cantrell said something about a church? I go over to my computer and resume my research on homelessness in Bermuda. The results are staggering and make my heart heavy. *When did this paradise become a place of such hopelessness for so many?* I ponder these things in my heart.

Selah and I go down to the beach. Darkness covers us, but neither of us seems to care. We frolic in the water until I look like a prune. I go to the shed and try to open it. *Wait a minute! A shed?* I close my eyes to think. *Yes, a shed, and a hidden key.*

I find the key under a large white stone and open the door, but it is so dark outside that I can't see inside. There are no lights in the shed. Turning, I stumble over a couple of towels and feel around as my eyes adjust to the dark.

I find some wood for a fire.

I return to the beach and build a fire. I stretch out in a lawn chair, throw a dry towel on us, and watch the fire until way into the night. I fall asleep praying for the child as Selah sleeps in my arms.

The sun is coming up when Selah and I awake. She runs around, kicking up sand dust as she digs in her heels.

"Oh, girl, you are working your way up for a bath."

We hike up the stairs leading to the cottage. I bathe Selah to get the sand and seawater off and then dry and feed her. I shower and don shorts, a tank top, and sneakers. I throw my hair into a messy bun and blast it with a little hairspray. I grab my cross-body bag that holds my keys, lip gloss, and ID.

Hmm. . . . What is that at the bottom of my purse?

I find a cell phone in my purse, but I have no idea why I have a phone. I don't have anyone to call, or do I? Maybe there are clues on the phone! I find no contacts programmed into the phone, but it is good to have, I guess. I look at my search history, but there is nothing there either.

I make some peanut butter crackers and grab a banana and a water bottle. Then I think, *Yes, I'll add Faith Banks to my contacts. Now I have at least one person to call.*

I am about to leave, but Selah is not okay with me leaving her again. When she looks at me with those big brown eyes, I can't say no. I grab an extra water bottle, treats, a harness, and a leash, and off we go in the car.

I look at the sky. The cloudy weather might bring storms and hinder my search. *Oh, Lord, please hold the rain back so I can find her.*

"Selah, keep a lookout." She wiggles her nub as I lift her little body to where she can see out the window of the Benz.

Oh, Lord, lead us to the little girl so that we can help her. She's probably hungry and scared. Thank you, I pray. One good thing is that I still remember my God. I hope that memory will never leave me.

I start noticing every church we pass, looking for the Evangelical Church. *Lord, show me the church Officer Cantrell was talking about, the church that helps homeless people and their children.* We stop at several churches; it seems that they are doing what they can with the funds they have.

One church stands out; it is like a beacon standing out amongst the others: the Evangelical Church. I'd found it. "Thank you, Lord!" I say aloud as Selah spins in circles in the seat.

I walk to the front door and find a brochure. The church is pastored by a young "newly married" couple of almost five years. Derik and Catherine Drake are in their early thirties. They got married in college and then continued their journey in foreign countries, ministering wherever they were needed.

Upon meeting them, I find them to be kind, loving people who seem far older than they appear. They have a heart and vision for the community. We talk for over an hour, and they give me a tour of their church. The building is a beautiful reflection of Bermuda's architecture with its limestone roof and cisterns to capture the rainwater. The smell of the ocean seas along with a tantalizing breeze make it even more beautiful.

In talking to the couple, I learn that the church is helping many people, whether homeless or from the food bank, and that they host fundraising events for the cause.

"You know, Awna," Catherine says, with her brown curls bouncing as speaks, "We would really like to help this little girl if you find her. Some of the children are left in hopes that a rich family will take them in. DSS, the authorities, and our churches are working together on these issues. We are doing as much as we can, but unfortunately, it's just not enough at times. It's a rich country for non-Bermudians. Poverty has no place here, yet it's all around us."

As she speaks, I notice her dark blue eyes show such gentleness, and her demeanor speaks of her commitment to her cause.

"There are not enough jobs, and with some of the children growing up homeless, they have no skills to find jobs, let alone good-paying jobs. We've heard it's become a problem for many of the islands," Catherine finishes.

"The homeless situation isn't the only struggle. There are abductions too," Derik pipes in. "Just last year, there was an attempted child abduction in the area. That couple also kidnapped a man. The situation escalated, a woman was killed, and someone else was hurt in the altercation. For the life of me, I can't remember the rest of the story."

As Derik speaks, chills run down my body. *What was that all about?* I think. I can hardly say a word, so I sit silently for a moment before nodding my head. "Yes, if I find her, I'll be sure to let you know," I respond quietly.

Catherine then suggests, "Take a picture of her if you find her. We are well versed in most of these children. We may be able to help connect the dots."

"Awna, we hope you'll join us in our service this Sunday," Derik interjects. His green eyes and tanned face seem to light up as he speaks of their church.

Catherine joins in: "Oh, please do, Awna. I feel . . . well, a kindred spirit with you."

As she speaks, she grabs both of my hands in hers. As our eyes meet, it is as if she looks right into my very soul. I feel a tingle or small shock as she holds my hand. Then a smile crosses her face, as if she knows something that I don't.

"Umm, yes, I'll have to come visit. Well, come on, Selah. We have to continue our search."

"Oh wait, Awna. Let's exchange numbers," Catherine suggests.

"Oh, that's a great idea." I type her number into my phone as she does the same.

Derik bends down to give Selah a pet before we leave. As he does, his bangs fall into his face, but he pushes them back as his smile widens toward Selah. I observe his unruly blonde hair. Honestly, I don't remember noticing people's features as much as I have the last few days. Truly, he and Catherine make a fine couple.

We say our goodbyes, and I lead Selah to the car. I sit for just a moment, trying to figure out what just happened.

Lord, lead and guide me, I pray.

I stop to think for a second: *Lord, why can't I remember anything else, but I know you? I'm truly glad I do; you and*

Selah are all I have. I can't remember my own life. Do I have a family? Friends? Please help me, Lord.

"Who am I?" I say aloud and sigh as I close my eyes, taking a deep breath.

After a few moments, we are on our way back to Queen Anne's Park.

I walk Selah around on the plush green grass, where she whirls and twirls, happy as a lark.

We search for the little girl all around the park, but to no avail. When we finally give up, it is nearing evening time. I decide to go to the lighthouse in the hopes that we will see my new friends.

We drive the twenty minutes to Gibbs Hill Lighthouse. It is such a beautiful evening: eighty degrees and not a lot of humidity. The sun is hanging lower, and the orange and blue intertwine to bring about brilliant clouds in the evening sky. It is a busy evening at the Lighthouse Diner; a crowd starts to trickle in. I decide to get a to-go order, so I tie Selah to a small tree and go inside to order food.

I look around but don't see Faith Banks or Will working. It must be their day off. I retrieve Selah and venture to a bench at the side of the restaurant, where I eat a club sandwich with fries. I finish and put my trash in the dumpster. Selah sits watching me from the bench and seems very content, unlike me. I am very unsettled. I sit a while longer, enjoying the view of the water and city below, thinking that the little girl is somewhere not far away, but where?

I am lost in my thoughts, thinking maybe I will just leave, when I hear a voice behind me. It is my friend Faith.

"Well, Awna, I'm so glad you decided to visit. I saw you throwing your trash away. I'm sorry I didn't see you in the dining room; I was taking my break. Do you mind if I sit? I still have a few minutes."

"Oh, no. Please do. I know we just met, but we were out driving around and thought we'd just stop by."

"And who do we have here?"

"This is Selah."

"Oh, what a beautiful Yorkshire Terrier you are, Selah." Faith turns and asks, "Her name is from the Psalms, isn't it?"

"Yes. It means to pause, ponder, or wait. I feel like I had to wait a long time for her."

Hmm. Another thought: *I waited a long time for Selah.*

"It's a perfect name for her; it just fits," Faith says, smiling at Selah.

Selah jumps beside me onto Faith's lap and starts licking her face. I am a bit embarrassed and try to get her away from Faith, but Faith absolutely adores her and only encourages her behavior.

"She is perfectly fine, aren't you, little girl." Faith cuddles Selah and holds her up. "Well, you're a tiny thing, just like your mommy." Faith then smiles at me. "So, what's on your mind, child? You smile, but I sense a bit of a heavy heart."

"Is it that obvious?" I ask. I tell her about the little girl and all that has happened while trying to find her. We both sit there pondering what I've just shared.

Faith finally speaks. "You know, the Bible says in Isaiah 55:8–9 that God's ways are not our ways. The verses say: 'For my thoughts are not your thoughts, neither are your ways my ways, saith the Lord. For as the heavens are higher than the earth, so are my ways higher than your ways, and my thoughts than your thoughts.'"

I listen intently because I know the verse. It speaks to my heart. I am so excited to hear Faith speaking God's Word because that is one thing I do remember. My heart feels glad.

She continues, "Certainly, Awna, we don't even begin to understand everything. It seems that there are problems all around this world, and we don't have the answers to those problems. I believe that to find the answers in our own lives, we must figure out how we can help others with their situations. This is where prayer comes in. I believe the Lord will show you what you need to know when you need to know it."

She sighs before continuing. "Maybe the officer was right. Maybe it is a way for the homeless to feed their children. It's sad, that's for certain, but it is a way of survival. Will and I haven't encountered anything like this at the lighthouse yet, but if we do, I'd probably go broke feeding anyone who shows up."

We both shake our heads in agreement. I feel my mood lifting just by talking to her.

"I sure hope you find her and can help her. Let me know if there's anything I can do. You have my number. Don't be afraid to use it," Faith says.

"It is just good to be able to talk to you about it. Thank you."

With that, we hug, and I go on my way. I know Faith is busy, and I don't want to intrude on her kindness.

Selah and I return home around 6:30 p.m. I feed her and then walk around the house to see if anything will trigger my memory.

I end up in the art room. I thumb through the paintbrushes, paints, and supplies, hoping to remember something. I look at the finished paintings of beach scenes, the sky, and clouds. I don't even know if I painted these items or if they were done by someone else. Regardless, I am drawn to it all, so I sit down and begin to paint. When I am finished, I realize I've painted a portrait of the little girl from the park. I am so amazed that I am able to paint and draw like this. The painting is an amazing likeness of the little girl and looks so real.

It is well after 10:00 p.m. when I finish, and I pull the easel closer to the French doors. I leave one door cracked so the painting will dry but not too close to the door that the breeze could blow it off the easel.

The next morning, I wake feeling refreshed and ready to take on the world. I determine in my heart that I will find the girl or her family and see how I can help. I hang her portrait in the guest bedroom and stand staring at it until Selah barks and reminds me that it is time to go. It is almost 7:00 a.m.

We take the Benz, and I decide to take the longer route. I keep my eyes alert, hoping I will see her. We drive past Hog Bay and then Gibbs Hill Lighthouse. I take the adjacent road that swings back around near Horseshoe Bay Cove. As I drive, I keep looking for those big brown eyes. I take some back roads and cut through East Avenue, which gets us to Middle Road. I then turn onto Harbour Road, which takes us to Queen Elizabeth Park.

The crowds grow all around the island. There are tourists everywhere these days, and traffic moves slowly, even at this hour. It normally takes thirty-two minutes to drive to the park, but today it takes an hour. My guess is that tourists are out looking for breakfast eateries.

As I drive, my mind starts to wander, thinking of matter-of-fact things. Then Queen Elizabeth Par-La-Ville Sculpture Park enters my mind. It was renamed in 2012 during the queen's Diamond Jubilee in celebration of Queen Elizabeth II. I shake my head, thinking, *How do I know all of this?*

I rub my eyes after we park; it feels like a headache is coming on. I don't think I've ever had one of those, but this is probably how they feel. The more thoughts and memories that enter my mind, the more I am confused. There is no rhyme or reason. If I could only put everything together like a timeline or puzzle, it would help. That's what I need to do, I decide.

I put Selah's leash on her, and we start our walk along the stone sidewalk. I am awed by the mixture of flowers and their smells. Their brilliant colors remind me of the colors I used last night to paint the portrait of the little girl. We stop by a goldfish pond and sit on the rocks around it to watch as the fish swim. This calms me and my body down. Selah goes wild chasing the fish around the small brick pond. Luckily the leash is long enough to support her amusement as she dances around the rocks. She finally completes her adventure, breathless, so I retrieve water from my backpack and fill her little bowl. She drinks and, satisfied, sits watching the people.

After resting, we resume our mission. I look behind trees and under bushes, but the girl is nowhere I look. I am deep in thought when Selah begins pulling on me. I mindlessly follow the way she tugs me, nose to the ground. She leads me to a large rock, her nose leading the entire way.

"Selah, what in the world has come over you!"

I reach down to pick her up and am met face-to-face with the child. I gasp quietly but hold my composure, not wanting to frighten her.

"Well, hello. I've been looking all around for you. My name is Awna. Do you remember? What's yours?"

No response.

"Would you like to share my lunch again, even though it's still breakfast time?"

Her dark eyes light up with hope. We sit on the rock, where she eats the crackers and banana and then looks at me for more. I've given her everything I brought.

"What's your name, sunshine?"

She looks as if she is thinking but still says nothing.

"Where's your mommy?"

She stares and shrugs.

"What about your daddy?"

She looks up and points as one tear falls from her eye. I frown, wondering if she means he died. I fear my assumption is true. She brushes her tears away and lowers her head. The poor little thing is filthy— no shoes, tattered clothes, and in dire need of a bath.

I close my eyes. *What should I do?*

I'll take her to the church. I've only been at the park searching for a couple of hours this morning. I look at my watch: 10:30 a.m. I need to get this taken care of as soon as possible.

I reach out my hand, and to my amazement, she takes it. We walk to the car, where I strap her in. I don't have a car seat and have no clue if I even need one. Well, this is the best I can do.

I drive to the church and knock on the church door.

No answer.

We walk around the back of the church to the parsonage, and I knock on that door.

No answer.

Goodness. What to do now?

"Well, sunshine, I guess you're stuck with me."

I strap her back into the car, and we take the ferry home. It will be quicker than moving slowly in the noon traffic.

I feed her a peanut butter and jelly sandwich for lunch, which seems to be her favorite, along with Goldfish and applesauce I picked up from the store. I fill the bathtub and give her a bath, which she does not like, not at all.

Selah is so excited that someone else is getting a bath. She barks, spins, and runs all around the house, up and down the stairs from the kitchen to my office. I look at the sad-looking child and say, "I think she's showing off for you."

She cries and pushes me away, but I scrub her from head to toe, washing her straggly hair and then conditioning it for fifteen minutes while combing it through. She sobs but plays with the cup that I am using to rinse her. She is still whiny as I towel her dry and comb through the tangled mess.

"You know, my mommy used to wash my hair and comb out my tangles with her fingers."

The child frowns but searches my eyes for information. I catch myself, but the memory just keeps coming.

"My mommy used her fingers to get my tangles out because we didn't have a comb. We lived in a faraway land and didn't have very much. Alon provided well for us and was finally able to make me a comb from a tortoise shell. I kept it for many, many years until I lost track of it."

The child looks very interested now, so I continue searching my thoughts.

"It was such a special gift from him, because Alon felt like family to us, yet he was of no relation."

The child smiles as if she understands my story. The memory flows as if it were yesterday. I can see the comb in my mind, and even though I said the name Alon, I still do not know who he is. Is that a thought or a memory? How can I see the comb so vividly in my mind?

I must have lived in poverty if we could not afford a comb. Somehow, these thoughts make me sad, and my mind races for more, but there is nothing else. I let out a sigh and continue grooming the child's hair. Despair fills my heart for a moment, but then I adjust my thoughts to the present.

I have no clothes or shoes for my guest. I thought I could just wash her clothes, but the holes and dirt are too much.

"Okay, sweet girl, I've got to be creative."

I find a tank top from the top drawer, tie a pink ribbon around her tiny waist, and cinch the straps of the tank into tied knots, as tight as they'll go. Big dark eyes just stare at me.

"Tomorrow, I'll take you to get some necessities like shoes, clothes, hair-bows, and some toys. Would you like that?"

She drops her little head, looking at her tattered clothes on the floor. She picks up her pink top and hugs it in her arms.

"Me like this."

"Oh my goodness. You can talk! What's your name?"

She frowns, stares at the ceiling, and then says, "Sunshine!"

I laugh, knowing that is highly unlikely. "Okay, then. Sunshine it is."

We go down to the beach and sit at the table, where I hope her hair will dry quickly.

I put the umbrella up to keep the sun off us. Even though it is early evening, the sun is still high enough in the sky to cause my skin to feel sticky from the humidity.

Dusk will soon take over and give the moon its place, not caring what is going on in the world but holding true to its commitment.

We drink lemonade, and I talk while she listens. Selah sits on her lap, absolutely enthralled by Sunshine.

As the girl sits looking out into the green-blue water, I take in her beauty. Her black hair glistens with those sun-kissed highlights that adorn her little face. Now that it is clean, her hair shines in the light. Her dark eyes look like big pools of sparkles that light up as she sees something new; they look as if they are dancing.

She finally looks at me and smiles. "Ow-na."

"Yes, that's me."

She then points to Selah and says, "Silly."

"Very close. Selah." I say slowly.

"Silllya."

I smile as she snuggles Selah tight. Selah is such a ham, sitting there sporting the new shirt I'd gotten her. When I put the shirt on her, she pranced around like she was in a parade. She cuts an eye over at me to see if I approve, and I pat her head in confirmation.

The sun starts to make its way down as we make our way back up to the cottage. Sunshine stops and says, "Up" as she reaches her little arms toward me. My heart melts as I hold her all the way up to the cottage. By the time I get to the French doors, she's laid her head on my shoulder. I suddenly feel a sense of protectiveness over her, my mind wandering again to a feeling of something I've missed or never had. I know exactly what this feeling is—a child. I've never had a child to love.

I shake my head again. Maybe my memory is coming back. I am not sure what is happening, but I do know that the thoughts and feelings are strong. *I will never let anything or anyone hurt you*, I think as she hugs me around the neck.

After dinner, I turn the bed down in the guest room closest to me. I decide to read to her from the Bible since it is the only book I've been reading lately. She seems to love it as much as I do. I read to her the story about Jonah and the whale.

"Me!" she interrupts and points to the wall where I'd hung the portrait of her.

"Yes, that's you. Do you like it?"

She shakes her head yes, smiling ear to ear. She giggles and snuggles closer as she points to the words I am reading.

As she feels the pages, her eyes grow heavy. We say prayers, and she puts her little hands together like mine. Then together, we say a sleepy "Amen," and I tuck her in as she yawns deeply. I kiss her forehead goodnight, and she falls asleep immediately.

I sit in the living room again, watching the curtains dance around from the breeze. It seems this is one of my favorite things to do lately. I try to remember if I've ever been around children before, but I have no recollection. It does, however, seem to come naturally.

I wish I could remember something about my life. I google my symptoms on the computer and, after a while, determine that I have amnesia. My memory may or may not come back, and it was probably caused by trauma. I walk around the house looking for things that might trigger my memory, as the internet instructed. Although I've already been doing that, I am now on a mission. My heart wants the truth.

I go upstairs to check on Sunshine, who sleeps peacefully. I move into every room: the studio room and the two extra bedrooms. I stand in each room looking around, going through the chest of drawers and the nightstand.

I stand here thinking, *I don't even remember decorating any of this. Nothing in the drawers seems like I know any of it. Nothing in this beautiful home looks familiar, yet it does.*

The beach theme decorates every room. It doesn't look tacky but instead looks graceful and purposely put together with a peaceful feel about it. The furniture in my room is distressed antique-white, accessorized with white pillows with a touch of turquoise around the edges, reminding me of the ocean waters of Bermuda. There are white down comforters and matching pillowcases with small hints of turquoise décor on a vase. A throw blanket is spread across the side of the chair. Everything looks perfectly new and unused but speaks of an older era.

I finally start getting myself ready for bed. I shower, dry my hair, and look around for my pj's. I think I put them in the vanity drawer but realize I've left them on the closet door hook.

As I put on my night clothes, I notice a small seam in the wall. That is strange. Upon getting closer, I realize there is a small crack in the wall. When I run my hand along the edge, something clicks, and a door opens. I step through and find the light switch. When the light shines on the room, I feel the wind sucked out of me.

What is this place?

It looks like a boutique full of clothes. The decorations match the feel of the cottage yet have a twist of past and future. There are ball gowns, parasols, modern dresses, formal and casual apparel, sundresses, glasses, sunglasses, handbags, and gloves. There are wigs galore: blonde hair, red hair, multicolored hair, black, and brown. There's long, short, shoulder-length, curly, and straight hair, and all manner of hair extensions. I find theatrical makeup and jewelry that look expensive. There is even costume jewelry. A desk made of distressed white antique mahogany wood sits in front of a large octagonal window.

I touch and feel everything, but still nothing triggers my memory. I grab the iPad lying on the desk. It is dead, so I plug it in to charge. I turn it on and search for why a person would have such things in a hidden room. After reading all the scenarios, I decide that I must be in a witness protection program or that I am a spy. Then I read that criminals would also have such things. I don't seem to have a job, so I know enough to think that something is amiss, especially with the kind of house I live in.

I look out of the large octagonal window positioned to look at the Bermuda shore. I stare out at the tiki torches lit in the distance off to the side of the cottage, far enough away to look like flickering flames.

Who am I?

I sit, trying to remember. I pace. I pray. My stomach aches. I fall asleep.

Later, I awake to the cries of the Cahow bird and peer out the window to see it sail along the shore. My heart races, and my arm is numb as I pull myself up from the desk.

Thoughts race through my mind. *The Cahow is our national bird. Its picture is also on Bermudian currency. It breeds in Bermuda, and it is on the endangered list. It resembles a seagull.*

How do I know all of that? I must have read it somewhere.

I watch the bird as it glides through the air with such grace and smoothness. It is free. I want to be free from wondering. I deeply yearn for the truth.

I look around and realize I've slept here all night. I take another look around in the daylight. Indeed, this room looks like I've awakened in an uptown boutique. I exit back through the hidden door and make sure I don't close it all the way. I want to come back later tonight to look around.

I have just enough time to shower, brush my hair, throw on a sundress and lip gloss, and then check on Sunshine.

She rubs her eyes sleepily, crawls out of bed, runs to the window to peer out, and then tugs at my hand.

"What do you want, Sunshine?" I laugh and wander with her as she leads me downstairs to the French doors. "You want to go outside?"

She shakes her head yes. It is somewhere around 6:00 a.m., and Sunshine starts pointing to the sky.

"Oh, thank you, Sunshine. This is one of the most beautiful sunrises I have seen, well, ever since this last awakening." I stand here in awe of the beauty, not realizing I've just spoken aloud.

Sunshine quickly turns her head from the sunrise to look up at me. I stand frozen in place. Where did that come from, and what does it mean? Awakening?

Sunshine rubs her sleepy eyes and lifts her arms. "Up," she says, and our day begins.

We take the Benz out of the garage and start by taking the ferry to Hamilton to find clothes for Sunshine. Daisy & Mac's is a unique little boutique on Queen Street and sells everything imaginable. The owners know children and what they need.

As soon as we walk in, a dark-haired young woman greets us. "Aww, looks like you have a three-year-old. My goodness, how cute she is."

She stoops down to Sunshine, looks back and forth at us, and then determines, "You look just like your mommy. Now, you two come this way, and we will get started. What are you looking for today?" she asks casually.

Still taken aback by what she said, I stammer over my words. "Umm, we need everything."

I look closer at Sunshine; thoughts run through my mind. *Oh my goodness. What if she is my child? What if I have been in a car wreck? Oh no. My husband, did I have one? Has he died?*

No, there are no photos of anyone around the house, not even of me. I remember how Sunshine looked up toward the sky and a tear streamed down her face when I mentioned her father.

My thoughts are running rampant. *What if I abandoned her, not even knowing?*

I need to calm down and just be in the moment, I tell myself.

The young woman is sizing up Sunshine, not paying attention to my reaction. "Kids grow like weeds, so do you need everything for a new summer wardrobe?"

"Yes, please," I say.

"Looks like someone was playing dress-up. My little girl does the same thing: grabs my tops, and they look like dresses on her. She also hates to wear her shoes. Kids are so free; we should be more like them."

"Yes, absolutely," I agree.

"Don't you worry, Mom. I'll get her all fixed up."

Shock again runs through me as I stand staring at her pulling items off the racks, asking Sunshine if she likes this or that.

"This is what happens when you wake up one morning and nothing fits. It's like they outgrow their clothes overnight!" she states.

Well, at least that is one explanation for Sunshine's outfit and no shoes.

The young woman is doing all the talking, so I don't have to say much. "My children hate to shop for clothes. It's a good thing I own part of the store; that's about the only way I can outfit them, after store hours." She smiles, remembering her children. "Oh, where are my manners? My name is Britt, and what is yours?" she asks chipperly.

"My name is Awna," I say, still trying to process everything.

"Do you like this, sweetheart?" Britt asks, holding up a dress.

Sunshine actually answers her with a shy, faint voice.

Britt does everything with ease until Sunshine is completely outfitted.

"Look, Mommy!"

I am stunned that Sunshine has spoken those words. She twirls around in an all-white dress decorated with a green-stemmed, yellow-topped tulip that flows from the bottom of the dress to the top of the shoulder. She has matching sandals on her tiny little feet. Britt has added a white and yellow ribbon to her hair. Sunshine is the most beautiful child I've ever seen. Her little white teeth shine brightly against her olive-colored skin, and her eyes light up like light bulbs. She hugs the dress happily, skipping around and twirling.

We leave the store with sundresses, shorts and top sets, lacy socks and everyday socks, shoes, sandals, undergarments, hair bows, a doll baby, learning toys, books, tearless shampoo, and conditioner. Anything a child or parent wants to buy is sold at Daisy & Mac's place.

Sunshine no longer looks like a homeless child but like a child who has just stepped out of a magazine in New York City.

In the car, we ready ourselves for the rest of the day and then take the dreaded drive to the police station. I have to find out if Sunshine is a missing child. Even if her mama is a homeless person, maybe I can help them both.

But what if I am her mother? Whatever the outcome, I must know the truth.

Sunshine and I sit waiting our turn. I hold her on my lap so she won't run away again. As before, Officer Cantrell talks to us. "No, this child has not been reported missing, and this honestly does not look like the same child you brought in the other day."

He pauses, looking at us. "There's no picture of her in our database, and no one has contacted us."

"I've spoken with the Evangelical Church, and they are going to help us, but I wanted to see if anyone has reported her missing?" I respond.

Officer Cantrell looks around before he leans forward and quietly speaks. "She's better off with you, ma'am. Trust me. Like I said, she doesn't even look like the same child.

I know what she'll go through if we try to place her. There are so many who are homeless."

He juts his head around to see if we are alone. "Our islanders are in a panic over all of this; you don't want that for her. We have homeless people living in abandoned buildings, and our foster care is always beyond capacity."

He feels comfortable and continues. "Just the other day we had to break up a group living in the caves at Horseshoe Bay. One tourist said they were begging for money. Look, you're a citizen here. Are you financially and mentally stable? It looks like you're willing to help this little girl?"

I pause, shocked at what I think he is about to say, so I interrupt him. "Yes, I am capable. Listen, I know Derik and Catherine from the Evangelical Church. I know they are in tune with the homeless. Their church helps feed and clothe them. They know more than we do concerning the homeless. Can you give them a call and tell them I'm here with the child? Here's their number."

I write down the number Catherine gave me. Sunshine and I wait for another ten minutes before Officer Cantrell comes back.

"Okay, we called DSS, and of course they are full. They too suggested that we call Derik and Catherine since you're a citizen. I contacted them, and they vouched for you to care for the little girl at this present time. Catherine acted like you are an old friend or that you feel like an old friend. Honestly, I'm not sure. The phone was crackling during our conversation. Anyway, she asked that you come by her house to complete some temporary paperwork to cover the foster care side of things. In the meantime, I've got your information. I'll contact you if we find out anything more."

"Thank you so much, Officer. I just want what's best for the child. Truly, I do."

Officer Cantrell stands there staring at us, looking from me to Sunshine. Finally, he shakes his head and announces that the person behind us should come forward to the front desk.

"Okay, thank you very much." I smile, and we leave.

With that, I look at Sunshine. "It would appear that we are to become family, at least for now."

She smiles a big smile and giggles. My heart soars as we walk together out the front door.

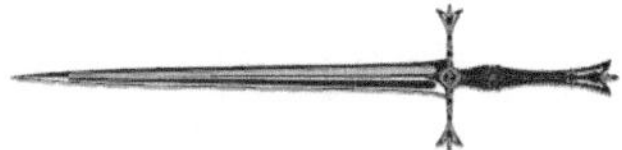

Catherine and I sit on her veranda while Sunshine colors in a larger-than-life coloring book from the children's ministry. We talk over a hot cup of mint tea, and then I sit by myself and fill out the paperwork while she entertains Sunshine. I remember enough about myself to fill out my address and phone number. I have my driver's license in my wallet and found a social security card in the desk in the hidden room. I think it may or may not be real.

When Catherine returns, she looks the forms over. "I used to work with Kemper, the lead DSS supervisor. She's going to get the paperwork rushed through to get you legal. They'll need to fingerprint you and do a background check, but in the meantime, just take care of Sunshine, like I see you are doing already. Sunshine showed me all her pretty clothes, toys, and everything else you bought for her. Your car is overflowing. There's barely enough room for the two of you." She wrinkles her nose as she laughs.

"Umm, was it a little too much?" I question. "I had no idea what a child would need, but Daisy & Mac's took care of us."

When Catherine laughs, she does it with such warmth as she looks from me to Sunshine. "Jesus has brought you two together. I feel it in my bones. I mean, you even resemble each other. This is a good thing, I'm sure."

The chills make their way all over my body. It is as if she knows a secret that I have no idea about. In this moment, I feel as if I've known Catherine forever.

On Sunday morning, while Sunshine is still asleep, I read from the Bible. I feel complete peace as the words comfort me. They feed me somehow.

As I turn the page to Psalm 91, I start reading: *"He that dwelleth in the secret place of the most High shall abide under the shadow of the Almighty."*

I know I am in the secret place of the Most High, and Catherine's words about coming to church flow through my thoughts. *Yes! I need to wake Sunshine; we are going to church.*

CHAPTER 13

SEARCHING WITH PURPOSE

Sunday service is filled with joyous singing, happy faces, and all manner of diversity. The place is packed with a lot of friendly and talkative people. Sunshine joyfully goes with Catherine as she leads her to the children's church. I do not know what to think of all the friendliness and smiles.

It has been a while since I have been to church, and around humans.

Hmm. There is another thought. I close my eyes to process this. *Around humans? Who or what am I? If people could only be as nice as they are in church all the time, we would have a rather good world, and I would not have to fight the enemy with every twist and turn.*

There it is again. *What enemy? What fight? I fight people? What are these thoughts?*

As I sit here listening to Derik bring the Word of God, he speaks of that very thing, that we fight an unseen enemy. He points us to Isaiah 54:17: "No weapon that is formed against thee shall prosper."

He goes on to speak about the book of Ephesians. "Ephesians 6:12 says, 'For we wrestle not against flesh and blood, but against principalities, against powers, against the rulers of the darkness of this world, against spiritual wickedness in high places.'"

I am captivated and want to hear more. He continues reading in verse 13. "'Wherefore take unto you the whole armour of God, that ye may be able to withstand in the evil day, and having done all, to stand.'"

Goosebumps form on my arms. I feel like I know about this somehow.

"Verse 14: 'Stand therefore, having your loins girt about with truth, and having on the breastplate of righteousness.'"

When he speaks about the breastplate, a vision of a warrior appears to me. The warrior is a woman, but I cannot see her face. I see an emerald jewel that is absolutely beautiful on the breastplate, and for some reason, all of what Derik says feels familiar.

Derik continues, and I listen intently. "Verse 15 says, 'And your feet shod with the preparation of the gospel of peace.' Church, we must be ready to go where God wants to send us. We need to be ready to move on His behalf when He prompts us. It could be missions, teaching Sunday School, or even sending a card to someone, but we must obey his call."

He pauses, letting his message sink in. "Church, we need to follow verse 16: 'Above all, taking the shield of faith, wherewith ye shall be able to quench all the fiery darts of the wicked.'"

In my mind, I see the warrior fighting a battle, and as fiery arrows shoot toward her, she lifts her shield, and the arrows are extinguished.

My heart rate increases, and perspiration beads on my forehead. The audience shouts, "Amen" and begins clapping. This encourages Derik to move on to verse 17. "'And take the helmet of salvation,' which means having Jesus in your heart, letting Him cover your mind and heart against the enemy, 'and the sword of the Spirit, which is the Word of God.'"

As he speaks of the sword of the Spirit, I see before me a golden sword, and the Word of God echoes from it, the words flowing from the sword like a waterfall. I look around to see if anyone else sees this, but no one appears to be shocked or alarmed if they do.

Derik continues preaching. "You are a warrior!" and he points to me.

I sit up straighter in my seat and feel lightheaded.

Then Derik points to a man on the other side of the church. "And you are a warrior!"

The man smiles and shouts, "Yes, I am! Hallelujah!"

Derik is bringing home the point that we are all warriors if we love and serve God and that we all are able to fight against the evils of this world.

Still, my mind races. What does all this mean—the vision, the sword, and fighting enemies? I mean, I love to read the Bible, but I have never fought anyone. What are these thoughts going through my head?

As we all join hands to pray, I touch the hands of the two ladies next to me, and it is as if an electric shock moves all through the church. I find myself deaf, and I cannot see.

I am speaking, or is someone else speaking? *What am I saying?*

It is as if God silences me and then begins speaking through me.

After a few seconds, I am able to hear and see again. The ladies holding my hands are shouting joyfully. I hear singing. Others are thanking the Holy Spirit for sending us a message on how to be warriors of God. The praises erupt into greater heights just as the doors open in the back and a mighty wind comes through the place. It is not an ocean breeze; it is different.

Then there is silence. I hear faint prayers and sniffles; some people are sobbing from the joyous worship. Pastor Derik returns to the altar and asks people to come forward for prayer, saying that my testimony has touched hearts.

Everything is a blur; I am weak and shaking. I notice that Catherine is pointing to someone to come forward. I turn to look behind me to see who she wants, but no one is there. I look at her again, and she motions me forward. I obey.

She whispers in my ear, "Can you help us pray for these people?"

I have not noticed it before, but the altar is packed full of people needing prayer, reaching out to God, hoping and believing for answers to their prayers, for healing of their bodies or loved ones, and for other miracles.

I look back at Catherine. "You want me?"

"Yes! God has anointed you. I felt it from the first time I met you, and now today it is stronger. Your testimony about people not knowing who they are in Christ . . . all I can say is that the Spirit of the Lord is powerful today."

"Okay," I stammer, walking shakily to the first person Pastor Derik has anointed with olive oil.

The lady tells me her name is Maggie. "My husband is abusive; it is hard for me to do what God has called me to do."

"What do you feel like God is calling you to do?" I ask.

"He's called me to preach, but my husband's abuse gets worse when I go to other churches and share the Word of God. He even tied me up one time for a whole day, right before I was supposed to preach that night. I used that time to fast and pray. After he untied me, he thought I'd learned my lesson, but I snuck out and preached anyway at a camp meeting. Twenty-five people accepted the Lord into their hearts that night, so I know what I need to do for the Lord. I've left my husband before, but he always finds me. I'm at my wit's end."

I am shocked by her story. I've never had anyone truly confide in me, to my knowledge, and am so unsure of what to say.

How do I know that?

There is one thing for certain, though. I do know how to pray.

"I just need him to stop hurting me!" she speaks.

Tears fill my eyes as I feel her pain. It is so heavy; she carries such a heavy burden. I can't even imagine how God will use her once the heaviness is gone.

"You must be strong and courageous, just as the Word says," I remind her.

She shakes her head knowingly.

Pastor Derik lays hands on her head, and I do the same.

I cannot explain what happens next except to say that electricity seems to be everywhere, and a powerful, peaceful presence fills the place. Reverence is all anyone can do.

While Pastor Derik prays for the husband's salvation and Maggie's safety, I pray against the enemy. I hear myself saying, "Hear me, satan: I bind you in the name of Jesus. Loose this man and bring him to repentance. God, wherever he is, whatever he is doing, visit him right now and let him know that you are calling him."

God has given authority within me that I have been unaware of.

I move to another person, and then another. I pray against cancer, alcoholism, unfaithfulness, and promiscuity. I feel myself getting stronger with each prayer. It continues as more people come to the front. By the end of the service, the children are gathered around us.

I did not realize it, but Sunshine's hand has been on me each time I've prayed. She has been there the whole time, and I had no idea.

Catherine takes center stage and starts singing and playing the piano. A guitar player joins in. It becomes a celebration. The sick and downhearted begin feeling better.

A man yells out, "I'm healed." He then throws down his cane and starts walking normally as his family meets him halfway down the aisle.

Just when things are at their happiest, the door in the back slams, and a silence falls across the church. In enters Tacket, Maggie's husband.

"He's come to get her," one man whispers.

Derik braces himself as Maggie stands up as straight as she can.

Tacket is a big man.

He is a descendant of the evil within the world.

Is that another thought or memory? If I had no memories before, I sure am having them now. The trouble is, I have no idea how any of this ties to me or my life. What does "evil within the world" mean? I know what evil is, but this seems to mean a different kind of evil.

Tacket's face is ablaze with anger; his deep brown eyes seethe as he lays eyes on her. "Maggie!" he shouts. "Get out of my way," he yells as he pushes a deacon out of the way.

I stand watching the scene unfold. He approaches her, one big arm lifted. I can see the bulge of muscles against his tee shirt. I step forward just as his fist comes down to hit Maggie in the face. I touch his fist, and I pass the peace. I know exactly what I've done but nothing else.

Maggie, Tacket, Sunshine, and I all fall to our knees. The Spirit of the living God surrounds us, and an unseen whirlwind envelops me and then Sunshine and Maggie. Finally, the Spirit of the Lord moves to Tacket.

I see the lives of these people before me, like a movie. I see the abuse, the hurt, the pain, the seething anger, the bruises, the hospital visits, the stitches, and the blood.

I feel water on my face; it is tears that flow like a river as the peace passes to the couple.

The biggest hurt for Maggie to let go of and forgive her husband is what happened many, many years ago. Tacket had beaten her so badly one day that she miscarried their unborn son. It was the only child that would ever live in her womb.

As all of this is happening, the peace keeps flowing from Maggie. She cries out, "Father God, forgive me. Heal this pain that I've felt from my husband; help me forgive him for killing our unborn baby."

Her cries lift to Heaven, and God gives her a vision. We see the vision too, for we are still in the whirlwind. There is a Hall of Babies. The doors to the room are large with windows that start at the ceiling but stop midway down. The light that shines in the Hall of Babies is soft, but as it touches the hardwood floors, they appear as glass. Hand-carved wood is everywhere, including the doors and trim. Even the cribs seem to be built from the same material.

There are babies on the left side and babies on the right side. All are in cribs with the finest of furnishings surrounding each baby. Some of the babies are tiny, while others are older, too young to walk. We all know which baby is the Tacket baby, for there is a glow all around the crib. As the Lord speaks to us, He prompts us to see the baby, and we walk toward that crib. The funny thing is that we never see the Lord, but we hear His voice in our minds.

"Your baby is safe with me; you will see him again, one day, at an appointed time."

We watch the baby as he coos and smiles, and we all know he is in the arms of Heaven.

Tacket groans and weeps bitter tears; he shakes with rage against himself.

I've never seen this before in a human. I saw it more with Moloch's clan or offspring when their demise was near.

I shake my head with these new thoughts, but I cannot connect the dots. They are so scattered about in my mind.

When the grips of the enemy start to fall, I see the chains that have bound both Maggie and Tacket fall immediately. In this vision, I take out my sword. It is golden like the one I saw earlier. I am now the warrior dressed for battle. I slay the demonic force that held Tacket, and I cast it down into the pit of Hell.

Tacket starts to cry and begs for forgiveness for killing his unborn son and for hurting Maggie all those years, asking Jesus to forgive him too. I have no idea how long we have been in the whirlwind, but the people in church whisper prayers, knowing they are in the presence of God's Spirit. No one wants to move or leave because the presence is like a thick fog.

I feel the total release rush into Maggie and her husband, and it is finished.

I sit for a moment, clearing my head, and then look up into the whitest little teeth smiling at me. "Come up, Mommy."

I take Sunshine's hand, and we all get up, weak and drained. We help each other to stand and go back to our seats, and the church erupts all over again, for a sinner has come home. Tacket smiles yet still sheds tears, not really knowing how to be forgiven. Forgiveness and whatever small amount of love left between two people have conquered satan's power.

I hear Pastor Derik inviting the couple to counseling sessions, and they agree.

Derik then returns to the podium.

"Well, church, you've just witnessed an old-time revival. We hardly ever see this anymore, but we sure are thankful for the Spirit of God visiting us today. Let's give the Lord a round of praise."

The church claps and praises God. Minutes later, the service ends, we say our goodbyes, and people flock toward Sunshine and me to shake our hands.

"Please come back!" "We wish you well." "Peace be with you!" These are the kind words spoken to us as we leave for our car.

As Sunshine and I drive away, I feel tired and exhausted but also ecstatic and somehow stronger.

I don't speak, and neither does Sunshine. Instead, she lays her little head on the seat and falls fast asleep.

I carry Sunshine, still asleep, into the house and lay her on the couch. I make some tea and lunch for when she does wake up. I sit down on the veranda in a lounging chair but leave the French doors open so that she will see me and not be afraid if she wakes up. I lean back to think about all that transpired and what it means. Then the tiredness overtakes me too, and I fall into a deep, paralyzing sleep.

I dreamt that it was a calm and peaceful day. The birds were singing, and the ocean breeze was a welcoming warm touch as it fanned my face. I was in a long pale pink Victorian gown with white lace covering an outer layer that hung to the ground. It was adorned with a hint of pink around the sleeves and hem, and I held a matching parasol umbrella. The era in time was not the same as now. There were horses and buggies filled with happy faces.

I stood by a hitching post talking to a man. I felt close to him, but I don't know now who he was. We were laughing, and I felt complete happiness.

We then rode in a carriage. The horse was black. Its mane and tail were silky with a glistening mix of black and caramel which shone brightly in the sunlight. We traveled near the Royal Naval Dockyard, where the carriage stopped. We got out and strolled toward the beach. We stopped for a moment to gaze at the green-blue waters with swirls of turquoise gutting through them.

In my foggy dream, my companion and I were speaking in low voices. I can't seem to make sense of what we were saying, but all seemed right with the world. I wanted to stay in this dream and not wake up.

Black clouds began to gather as thunder rolled in, getting closer and closer, until things turned dark very quickly. I heard sounds that raged on the Bermuda dockyard coastline. It was like people arguing and accusing, but I didn't know what was happening until I turned and faced them.

There on the shore were the demons, Moloch's offspring, and a few original clansmen. I knew who they were in my dream.

The man with me was saying something, but I couldn't hear him. The storm was upon us, and I moved closer to the man to hear what he was saying. The mixture of fear and dread on his face told its own story.

Then I heard his words. "Awna, be watchful as storm clouds gather!"

Somehow, I knew what he meant. As the fog started to descend upon us, my clothes were no longer adorned with the long white lace dress but were changed to the armour of an ancient warrior bearing a golden sword.

He, my friend, no longer wore a royal uniform but wore what resembled armour like mine. His breastplate was adorned with twelve jewels, but one jewel stood out from the rest. It matched mine and was a shining emerald. He lifted his shield as the armour surrounded him from head to toe, and he too was now a warrior.

Although I could not see him due to his armour, I knew it was him. It was the man from the dream I'd recently had where I was ashamed for him to see me. He was ready for battle. His sword blazed like fire. I also had a flaming golden sword, and the Word of God echoed out of it. As I moved it from right to left, the flame increased its size.

This battle was a spiritual one. A light shone around me, and as I fought, I swung the sword high. I heard the words flowing from me: "No weapon formed against me shall prosper. But the Lord is faithful. He will establish me and guard me against the evil one."

I was in the air as my sword met its first mark. The creature fell to the ground and disappeared as a whirlwind overtook him. One by one, the demons approached both of us. We fought until the end—until we conquered them. I turned to watch them pivot into Hell as they disappeared from our sight into their audience with God.

From the corner of my eye, I caught movement. It was him; he was kneeling. I smiled, as it was just like him to praise God after a battle. Then the shock enveloped my body as I saw him holding his own sword close to his body. I didn't understand what was happening until I knelt beside him and saw the blood flowing through his fingers and then dripping onto his sword.

Our eyes met. "I'm sorry. You've got to finish this," he spoke.

A shaky finger pointed to something. I looked in that direction just as I was thrown backward. The speed at which I crashed into the rocks told me everything that

I needed to know. It was four fallen ones from Moloch's clan. They were devils, men of old, and they had come to kill me.

The fight was like no other in my life. The light around me created a fog to confuse my enemies. My blazing sword shone through the fog. I saw the blade of my sword hit its mark as I flipped through the air. A whirlwind and flash of light sent the first fallen one into judgment. The second evil enmity hit me hard from the side, and I fell into the water, where he tried to drown me. I fought hard and knew my air was running out. I kicked, hit, and struggled to breathe as I heard their laughter. I knew my time was short.

I looked up and saw a faint light sparkling through the water, and I prayed: *Lord, please. I don't want to die like this, knowing they are here and what they will do to innocent humans. Help me win this battle; then you can take me home if you want.*

An unseen hand pushed me to the top of the water. Something had stunned the tall one holding me under. My sword ran through his heart, and into the water he fell. A mighty whirlwind lifted the water around him, and a lightning bolt hit him. Then he was gone.

The two remaining enmities started fighting over who would get to kill me. I came up out of the water behind them with the force of a hurricane. I smashed into them with vengeance for hurting my friend. They fell into each other; my sword was ready and hit both in one instance.

It was over quickly, but I was weak. As I lay there in the sand, I saw the Lord cast them into the pit of Hell where they belonged. I never stopped speaking the Word of God during the fight, nor did my sword. It echoed through space and time.

When the Keepers came, I still lay there claiming the promises of God. They never spoke. They just lifted me up without touching me.

My pain was intense. One anointed my head with oil. I heard him say without speaking, "In the name of the Father, in the name of the Son, and in the name of the Holy Spirit." I was instantly put into a deep sleep. I watched in my dream as they carried me away toward the cliffs.

I wake with my heart racing, my mouth dry, and my breathing labored. I am sweating, and my body cannot stop shaking. The warm breeze touches my face. I can taste the salt in the air, and I try to force awake the rest of my body. There is no use trying; the dream is stronger than I am. It continues but shifts backward in time. It is now before the Keepers came for me.

I was kneeling over him; his face was still and peaceful. No more blood poured from his wound. My own heart ached, and my body was weak. I touched his face and whispered, "Oh, Levi."

I wake in the present time, and the wind is howling around me. I shout, "Levi, where are you?"

I am fully conscious now. I look around but see no one. The rain starts to pelt down on my face as I run to my private beach, looking for him, calling out his name: "Levi! Levi!"

Still, there is no one in sight. I run back into the cottage; I cannot stop shaking.

Who is Levi? I must have known him.

I feel a closeness like I have never known before. Grief grips me deep inside my spirit, as if my dream has just happened. Tears stream down my face; I know the man in my dream was someone special, someone who has been slain, but I can't figure out who he was.

Sunshine is still sleeping on the couch, so I run to the hidden room. I look around for clues in desk drawers. I briskly look through all three closets, but there is nothing in this room connected to my dream.

As I turn to leave, there hangs the long pale pink Victorian gown with white lace, with the parasol attached. I touch it, and instantly I fall to the ground.

I wake with Sunshine touching my face. A tear invades her happy little face and then drops to my arm. I watch as it puddles, and then another one falls. I gather myself as best I can and hug her.

"I'm sorry if I've scared you," I say as I look into her big brown eyes. I see no expression, only a blank stare. The stare tells me that this child has most certainly seen tragedy in her few short years.

The rest of the night is silent between us, and a restless night's sleep follows me.

The next day, I feel an urgency to find Sunshine's family and return her. I have no idea who I am, but I know that battles seem to surround me, and the mystery and secrets of Bermuda somehow have a hold of me. I have to find out the meaning of all that has transpired. I am a demon killer, for Heaven's sake, or a warrior with some kind of military training. I cannot be a mother to this child. I am a killer. I've watched those tall creatures who look somewhat human die by my hand.

No, I cannot be a mother. But as the morning sun creeps higher in the sky, my worries seem to disappear. It is as if nothing had ever happened. I don't feel the urgency to find her family; I just feel peace.

We dress for a trip to Horseshoe Bay. I pack a picnic lunch, and off to the beach we go. In the back of my mind, I know what I must do. I will eventually have to search for her family. I should pay a visit to the homeless at Horseshoe Bay. Maybe they know her or her family.

The temperature is eighty-five degrees, and the humidity is high from last night's storm. The wind has settled down to a nice, constant breeze. I stretch out a blanket a few feet from the water, put stakes around the edges to hold it down, and set out a sand bucket and shovel so that Sunshine can play in the sand.

I brought a book but have no intention of reading it. I am on the lookout. The beach holds mostly tourists today, and beach music plays as the sun takes control over the day. I put sunscreen on Sunshine and then on myself.

She hesitates when I suggest that she build a sandcastle while I read my book. She takes the bucket and just sits at the water's edge, peering out into the water. I felt bad for her; I scared her last night. I move closer to sit by her, but she still never smiles or talks. We build a sandcastle together, and as we finish, I see them from the corner of my eye. It is the homeless ones; they sit on the rocks near a cave looking into the crowd.

This could be her family, I think.

One by one they crowd onto the rocks. There are eight of them, and the group looks very young. There are four boys, three girls, and a toddler. The oldest female looks maybe eighteen years old, if that. It is like downward stairsteps after that. They look hungry, hollow-eyed, envious, and broken.

Soon enough, they start walking toward the sunbathers and swimmers, asking for money or food. The restaurant owner comes out and glares at them, and they run away. I wait a little while and then get up, put on my cover-up, and put Sunshine's on her.

"Come on, baby girl."

Her face lights up, as if she knows what I am about to do. Maybe she knows her family is there. I go to the restaurant window and order eight hotdogs, eight hamburgers, eight baskets of fries, and two dozen chocolate cookies. The owner looks at me as if he knows my intention.

I motion to where we have set up on the beach. "There's a lot of us here today," which is true. There are a lot of people out today, especially near our blanket. That seems to be enough to satisfy the owner.

We walk back to where our belongings are. By then, other customers begin ordering food, and the owner forgets all about us.

I grab the food and a bag of water bottles we brought from home. I count the bottles, and there are exactly eight of them. I secure all the food and bottles with Sunshine's help, and we head toward the cave. As we move inside the cave, the children cower together.

"Hi, my name is Awna, and this is Sunshine."

No one says a word, and if they recognize Sunshine, or she them, no one reacts at all. I step in and lay down the bags of food and the bottles of water. The oldest boy, with curly black hair, a lanky frame, and a thin face, runs toward the food and grabs as much as he can. He takes everything to the oldest-looking girl. She starts handing out the food, splitting her own food with the toddler. The oldest boy then retrieves the remaining food and, with her nod, gives the extra to the boys.

"Sunshine, do you know these people?"

She shakes her head no and then grabs my hand.

I look at the oldest girl. "Where are your parents?"

No one speaks; they just keep eating. I walk closer to the girl and can see that she is also very dirty like Sunshine was, but all of them have salt residue on their skin, unlike Sunshine when I found her.

"I wanted to know if you all know about the food bank at the Evangelical Church?"

"No," is all the oldest girl says.

"They can help you," I respond, trying to break through this barrier.

"We don't need no help, miss," she snaps.

I step closer, and they all start to scoot away like scared animals.

"Okay, I get it," I say, putting up my hands and backing away. I reach into my cross-body purse and hand the oldest girl some money. She hesitates but walks over and takes the money. When she counts it out, she gasps as she realizes she holds ten $100 bills.

"Ma'am, we can't take your bills."

"Yes, you can. I want you to have the money for food and to get things you need."

She smiles. "Miss, nobody be lettin' us in their stores lookin' like we do."

"I hadn't thought of that," I say.

"And the Evangelical Church is too far. If the police see us out on the road, they put us in juvie or take my baby away."

She has a point; they are in a fix.

"If you will trust me, I'll help you. Bermuda is my homeland, and I want you to have shelter and food."

She shakes her head as if put out by me. She then picks up her baby, and she and the group move farther back into the cave, taking their food with them.

"You be thinking just like the others, Miss," is all the oldest girl says.

"Well, at least the owner will take your money for food; I'm sure of it."

"Oh, he be takin' it, all right. Then run us away when it's all gone. Thank you, Miss, appreciate yo' kindnis." She hangs her head as if ashamed.

"Wait, do you know this little girl, or have you seen her around the area?" I point at Sunshine.

The oldest girl looks suspicious. "Why would your little girl be around us, Miss? No, we ain't seen her nowhere," she says hatefully.

We back away and leave them alone. I need help with this one. *Catherine and Derik will know what to do*, I think.

Sunshine is beaming and runs back to the blanket to pack up our things.

"Sunshine, what are you doing?"

She stands there looking at me, smiling. "We go see Miz Cat."

I frown. "Yes, but how did you know?"

She giggles and starts running for the car, carrying her bucket while dragging the blanket behind her.

I put everything else into the beach bag, and off to the Evangelical Church we go. Sunshine is now happier than I've seen her since last night's episode. She can't wipe the smile off her little sweet face.

When we arrive, Catherine and Derik are in their yard replacing mulch around the parsonage. Sunshine runs for a hug from Catherine. Derik wipes his hand on his sleeve to wave a friendly hello.

"Come to the veranda for some lemonade," invites Catherine. "Come on, Derik. It's time for a break. Girl, maybe we can have church again like yesterday!"

I smile, not knowing what to say.

"Derik and I were talking about yesterday's service and concluded that if we had fifty more in our church just like you two, we could change the world."

Sunshine and I smile, not knowing how to take a compliment.

"I knew you two were special the first time I laid eyes on you."

"I don't know about all that, but I do have something to run by you," I say, trying to get to the point.

"All righty, so tell me what brings you out on this beautiful spring, summer-like day. I can hardly wait to see what the Lord is going to do next."

I open up and tell her about the children at Horseshoe Bay and how the oldest girl seems to take care of them all, along with her own child. "Is there anything that we can do?" I ask.

Derik speaks first as he sips his lemonade. "Maybe we can take the van over there and drop off some clothes and food. But that's just a Band-Aid. They need a shelter or orphanage. Basically what they need is a home!"

Catherine poses questions as they brainstorm a solution. "What about some of the properties the church has been looking at to purchase for just this purpose? Have you heard anything back from the realtor and bank, Derik?"

Before he can answer, she adds, "This reminds me of when the church received the donation last year. Someone donated condos and properties to place the homeless. They also placed a mother and her child and set her up nicely. They even arranged workforce development sessions to get them started. That's kind of what needs to happen now."

Why does what she just said sound familiar to me? I shrug it off and continue listening.

Derik smiles at Catherine's ramblings and then picks up on her quest. "I haven't heard anything yet from the bank or realtor."

Pondering a moment, he continues, "Now, you know, hon, we'd have to get people to work at the shelter. This could take some time because we'd have to get signed contracts from the house parents for the loan to go through. Finding workers is a bigger deal than finding property. Awna, do you know the 80/20 rule in ministry?"

I frown, and he elaborates. "It always seems that there's 20 percent of the congregation who do all the work in the church, and 80 percent are bench warmers. Or there's 80 percent of the work that needs to be done, and only 20 percent of the finances available. It's a vicious circle." Derik scratches his head as he finishes speaking, looking over at me.

"Oh, I didn't realize this. I would've supposed the percentages were higher, for workers especially," I banter back.

"At times there's more workers, and at times there's more money. Basically, that's the norm for most churches."

I shake my head as if understanding, but I don't know why more people won't help.

"What about that nice couple—Sandy and Burk Jennings? They are interested in the homeless, and they are looking for a bigger place to live. They even thought of converting their own home into some type of shelter, except it wasn't big enough. If we could get them to commit with a contract, then we could get the loan for the building, and we'd be in business." But Catherine's joyous assumption stops when she sees the look on Derik's face.

"Hon, you always are the optimist!" Derik pats her on the leg.

"That's why you love me. I always see the brighter side of things." Catherine winks at him.

"Yeah, I see all the work, and the lack of $2.6 million to buy what we'd need," he says. They laugh together and then stop to look at me and Sunshine. "Let's all pray. Where two or more are gathered, the Lord is in the midst of them," Derik says and leads us in prayer.

We leave them shortly after and head home. Our evening is happy and cheerful. I feel like I've stumbled onto something that I am meant to do. I can't stop thinking about those children. After dinner and bath time, I read from the Bible once again as Sunshine falls asleep, fast as usual.

I immediately go to the hidden room. I snoop around, opening boxes and drawers. I find a small safe, unlatched, which holds passports with many different names, and then I start thumbing through the racks of clothing. I step forward to feel a purple velvet blazer, and my foot hits something. I spread the clothing racks apart to find a larger safe. I step forward and immediately work the combination: 42 right, 47 left, 27 right, and then 3 to the left. The numbers just pop into my head. I turn the lock, and when I reach the number 3, I lift the handle and hear a click. *I remembered the combination. I am remembering more and more.*

When I open the door, I am shocked at what I see. There are more passports and money in Bermudian, American, French, and Swiss currency, and stacks of it. There are also credit cards that have expiration dates years from now.

I sat here stunned. "Who in the world am I?" I say out loud.

I start counting the Bermudian currency. I know Derik said $2.6 million, but they will also have to renovate any place they purchase by putting up walls to make smaller bedrooms out of the large bedrooms, and then purchase whatever else might be needed to house the orphans and other people.

I count the bills until I reach $3.6 million in the right currency. Stacks of money are all over the floor, desk, tables, and even the windowsill of the octagonal window. Even after I've taken the cash out of the pile, there are still stacks of money, and then more stacks left, as if the money hasn't been touched.

I put the money into a small carry-on suitcase, write a note with Catherine's and Derik's names on the front, and attach it to the handle. On the bottom of the note, I write, "For Homeless Shelter."

I've been thinking lately, *What if I wake up and can't even remember today or yesterday?* To avoid this, I've started a journal that mimics the many sticky notes I've put around the house to remind myself of things I've remembered over the past few weeks as I try putting the memories all together. I want to make sure things are taken care of the moment I think about them.

I put the suitcase in front of my nightstand and then put a sticky note in my journal saying where I left it.

I turn out the light and go to bed. During the night, I roll over to find Selah snuggled close to me. This is a little strange since she's slept with Sunshine from day one. Still, I love every minute of having my best little friend back in my camp.

I sleep better that night than I have in months.

HOPE FOR THE FUTURE

Sunshine wakes me up by jumping up and down on the bed. "Wake up, Mommy."

"Aww, you're saying 'Mommy' better!" I respond.

Her smile is infectious. I smile, and simultaneously, our feet hit the floor running, making a list for our day while we eat breakfast. I tell Sunshine, "Before we do anything else, we have to get some groceries first. Then I need to call Catherine to set up a time to stop by, okay?"

"Okay, Mommy." She shakes her head yes.

We dress for the day, Sunshine in pink shorts and a white top with sparkling stars on it. I don a pair of jeans with a gauzy pale yellow shirt and a tank top underneath.

I grab my purse and run upstairs to get the suitcase, but it is nowhere in sight.

I frantically search upstairs. I know that I put it in front of the nightstand. I grab my journal. Yes, there's the sticky note saying that I put the suitcase in front of my nightstand. It is not there. Sweat breaks out on my forehead as I frantically look around my bedroom, under the bed, in the bathroom, in Sunshine's room, and in the hidden room. I open the safe, and it is just as I left it. I run downstairs and start looking around, but the suitcase is just gone.

My stomach feels sick. How could I lose $3.6 million overnight? Did I dream this? No, I made a note and put it in my journal. Maybe I imagined that too? Maybe I am mentally ill?

I know that I remembered correctly where I left the money. After all, there is the sticky note.

I take deep breaths, get some water, and try to calm down.

On the way to the grocery, we are silent as I drive, my mind busy trying to figure everything out. Sunshine plays with her doll, singing to her, while I am deep in thought.

Did I dream that I put the money in the suitcase? Maybe I got up after dreaming and put the note in my journal? Or am I dreaming now? What is wrong with me?

I feel foggy, or maybe it's pure frustration. The thoughts roll through my mind until we reach the grocery store. We gather our items and head for the checkout clerk. I notice a mother with a child who is throwing an all-out fit. He wants a pack of cookies that the mother put back on the shelf twice.

The mother tries to calm him down. The child looks a little younger than Sunshine, but Sunshine has never acted like this. It is a war between the mother and child until the child starts rolling on the floor. I have no clue what in the world I'd do if Sunshine acted that way.

Before I can stop her, Sunshine heads over to the fit-throwing child and the embarrassed mother. She kneels and touches the child's face, and as the shocked child looks at her, they both smile. She then takes the pack of cookies from him and puts them back on the shelf.

And just like nothing at all happened, she runs back to me, smiling.

WHAT?

The mother apologizes for the outburst and then picks up the child, who is still staring at Sunshine, smiling. The fit is now long gone; only a curious stare follows us to the checkout counter.

The chills travel down my body as I realize that Sunshine passed peace to the little boy, just as I did in church. We both smile at the women and pay for our items; then we go our separate ways. Riding home in the car, I am more confused than ever.

As we are putting away the groceries, I get a call from Catherine. She is out of breath and can hardly speak. "We have the money for the homeless shelter. We have it and can help the kids at Horseshoe Bay!"

"What?" I respond, in shock.

"God provided what we need and more. An anonymous person left a small suitcase with our names on it on our table on the veranda. The suitcase was full of money, and there was a note attached which read, 'For Homeless Shelter.'"

Catherine takes a breath before continuing. "We found it this morning after a night of praying over those children from Horseshoe Bay. I still cannot believe it! Who has that kind of money, let alone in cash? It was $3.6 million, Awna. Can you believe it? We are checking with the authorities to make sure it isn't stolen or counterfeit, but it looks real to me."

I am speechless. "Wow, that's amazing!" is all I can sputter out.

"It's legit, Awna. We are meeting the realtor today and going forth with the deal if the money checks out. It's the property we have been dreaming of for this kind of venture. It is in Historic Olde Towne, St. George's. The property used to be called Aunt Nea's Inn. We contacted the elders, and they voted unanimously. We can have those teenagers from Horseshoe Bay into the shelter within weeks if they do not mind the renovation and construction we would have to do. Sandy and Burk have agreed to be the house parents, and church families have agreed to take in the kids until they all can move in. Sandy and Burk will also rent their own house out! It is all working out, Awna. It's a win-win for everyone. I must go; I'll call you later."

Catherine has been talking a mile a minute, not even noticing I've made very few comments. "Okay, talk to you later. I am so glad for this. Let me know how I can help!" is all I can say.

Sunshine is happily playing with her doll babies, so I look online for information about the property Catherine spoke of. It is not hard to find. The building is grand and was used as a bed and breakfast, but it recently went out of business. It is not on the touristy part of the island. It is off the water a bit, although it gives views of St. George's Harbour. It has a grand old entrance and appearance that make it hard to believe that no one has purchased it yet.

The building is painted a light-colored yellow with black shutters with columned porches upstairs and down. The windows are large to let the light in. It has ten large bedrooms, twelve bathrooms, two kitchens, two offices, a library, a theater room, a large garden, a swimming pool, a playground area, a gazebo, and beautifully-kept landscaping. It is breathtaking.

As I am about to close my computer, my Bible app pops up with the verse of the day, Proverbs 25:2: "It is the glory of God to conceal a thing: but the honour of kings is to search out a matter."

As the sense of God's presence runs down my body, I also feel peace. I know that who I am and whatever all this means must be kept a secret. It is not up to me to disclose the information about the money found, either.

I drop to my knees and begin to pray. I thank God for the blessing, for finding the money, and all that has transpired.

As I rise to stand, I see Sunshine praying right beside me. She looks at me and smiles. "Awe-men, Mommy."

Tears stream down my face. When I hug her, I notice tears streaming down her face too. I tilt her chin to look at me and am about to ask if she knows anything about the money but stop at the pure ridiculousness of the notion. Questioning her would make me feel untrusting of a small child. Plus, how could someone as little as Sunshine get over to their house and back, all by herself?

But . . . how did the suitcase get to Catherine and Derik?

We go to our beach and spend the rest of the day splashing, laughing, eating lunch, and then floating on floats I got at the grocery store. I tie Sunshine's float to mine, but to my surprise, she slips off the float and starts swimming underwater.

When she comes up for air, she motions her little hand. "Come on, Mommy!"

I am so shell-shocked at what I've just witnessed that I just stare at her. How can this little girl who is just starting to say her words correctly swim like an Olympian? I turn my float over into the blue-green waters, and together we swim until we are both so shriveled up that we look like prunes.

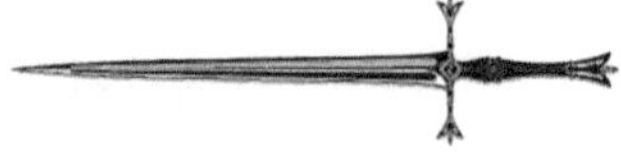

Weeks pass, and as each day ceases and brings forth a new one, my love for Sunshine only grows. There is still no word from DSS on my paperwork, nor do I want to call and ask, afraid they might take Sunshine away when they find an open spot or even find her family.

Sunshine's knowledge is taking off. Her words are becoming clearer, and she acts like a small adult instead of a child. I have no idea how old she is except to compare her to the other children at church, on the internet, or when we go out. Sometimes I have the courage to ask a mother or father how old their child is (only if they look in the same age range as Sunshine).

Still, I believe she is very smart, but maybe all parents think that of their children. I wonder if my mother thought that of me, but I cannot remember if I even had a mother.

The words of Ms. Banks filter through my mind to the effect of "Sometimes God's plans are not our plans, nor are our ways the same as His ways, but His ways are higher than ours."

What we thought was going to be the proposed shelter turned out to be a home for children and homeless teenagers. Not only was it a home, but it had been designed in those short weeks as a Christian-based learning facility. It also provided educational reform, workforce readiness, coaching, and an emotional counseling center for the youth. This home would house more than twenty homeless children from birth through age eighteen. Construction was underway to do even more add-ons, and more people had volunteered to help. People from the church and the community came together to help with Project Love-Last, as it was named.

I would say that the percentages had changed in our church. Now workers were at 80 percent, and so were the monetary tithes and donations.

Sunshine and I helped pick out the furniture, curtains, and floor rugs. We helped paint and decorate every day. We also had the good fortune of being on-site as they moved the young people in.

Their starstruck faces shone brighter than I had ever seen upon anyone's face. The mission of Project Love-Last was simple: to save the next generation, and to love them with a lasting love that would then be passed on to them and their children for generations. These youngsters were to be shown love, and in return, their mission was to return that love to others on the island who were down and out.

The ribbon-cutting day was a long one. The church had prepared food, music, activities with games, and a sermon that dedicated the home to the Lord. Without Him and our faith, this project and these lost young ones may have always been just that: lost and hopeless.

Shona, the oldest of the teenagers from Horseshoe Bay and the one with the child, was given her own room. On the day of the celebration, she motioned for Sunshine and me to see the beauty of her new home. Her bright smile told the story of thankfulness. She looked so different from that first meeting in the cave.

Her long, clean dreadlocks swing side to side as we ascend the magnificent staircase. Her room is to the left at the top of the stairs. She is talkative about having her own bathroom "with a tub!" she says. "So I can bathe my youngin'."

The windows in her room are a focal point as they reach from the ceiling to the floor. They are adorned with long curtains that match the comforter of shimmery ivory. The hardwood floors in her room are dark, shiny cherry wood, just like the rest of the house. The crown molding in the room looks from the distant past, as if it was hand-carved with meticulous detail, similar to the ceilings.

As we look out the window, the room lights up with a spectacular view of the Bermuda waters. The palms gently sway with the breeze, and we watch as a few boats sail by. The birds sing pleasant songs, as if they are also rejoicing.

Shona's bed is queen-sized, which she jokes about, saying, "It's because now I feel like a queen!" She blushes as she says this.

An antique vanity is off to the side of the room with a changing panel for privacy from the open windows.

The carpenters have taken one of the three huge walk-in closets and converted it into a small room. The toddler crib/bed is filled with the most beautiful furnishings in colors of bright pinks for her little girl. A rocker in the corner sits next to a hand-woven basket full of blankets, and a chest of toys sits near the crib. I painted a mural on the wall of the ocean, birds, and flowers that speak of Bermuda's culture and surroundings.

"We are so happy for you, Shona, and for all of the others."

Shona's big brown eyes fill with tears as she turns to me. "Miss Awna?"

"Yes, ma'am," I say.

"Thank you. I never would have dreamed that my life could be like this! Do you really think I can make a difference?" Shona asks shyly.

I smile at her. "Yes, I do. As a matter of fact, I think you will be a leader in the community. You, my friend, will bring change."

She beams as I continue. "Truly, Shona, you already have. Even with a child of your own, you became the caregiver to the others at Horseshoe Bay. You made sure they were taken care of as best as you could. You even denied yourself food in order to give it to them. I do not doubt that you will do remarkable things here. Now you are being blessed for your efforts and struggle."

With tears streaming down her face, she runs to hug me. "Thank you, thank you, Miss." Shona continues, "You made a difference too. You found us and gave us money for food, and you worked with the others to set us up in this home. The church has given me a job helping Mr. and Mrs. Jennings. I be helping with the children. Now I be havin' money to help my own child. I's forever grateful to you, Miss!"

"I'm just glad we found you and the others," I respond as I smile.

With that, we continue looking around at all the other rooms. Shona gladly gives us a tour of the whole house as she reminds us that we have not seen the updates since the others moved in. We soon rejoin the others outside.

Later during the celebration, I look around at the happy faces and smile, knowing that Sunshine and I are big players in God's plan.

Sunshine, who has been talking to the adults, children, and whoever would listen to her newfound vocabulary, comes over to me, beaming.

"Look, Mommy, we did it!!!"

As she twirls around, she gives me a wink, and the twinkle in her eye catches me off guard. The fact of the matter is that she portrays complete, undefiled, pure joy.

She then runs back out to the other children to play for a while.

Later when I look at my watch, I guess that an hour has passed. I think, *We'd better get going. Selah will be hungry.*

I am about to call for Sunshine when she comes running over. "We'd better get going to feed Selah. She'll be hungry," Sunshine announces.

I frown. "I was just thinking the same thing," I say, but she only smiles.

With that twinkle in her eye, she bounces off, saying, "I know."

We get in the car to drive home. I do not want to ruin the happy mood, so I don't ask her how she knew what I was thinking. Plus, it is silly of me to say anything at all; her concern for Selah is just coincidental.

We've had a big day. Sunshine and Selah are still awake in bed, giggling and playing, but I am unsettled, so I roam around the house. I read the Bible, I pray, and I sit on the veranda pondering the events and wondering if I will ever remember my past.

As thoughts flow through my mind, I feel something near my feet. I jump, finding Selah smelling all around the veranda. I pat my leg, and she jumps up onto my lap. As I pet her, she relishes the solace of just us. I smile and look out of the dark waters still glistening in the moonlight.

Hours have passed since I put Sunshine to bed. And then it hits me like a brick: Selah is always with Sunshine these days.

"Selah, where is Sunshine?"

Selah wiggles her nub, jumps down, and trots up the stairs. I am close behind her. We reach the door, and I open it quietly. As I walk over to the bed, I already know Sunshine is not there. I grab my shoes and quickly venture out into the night.

Selah is not at all happy to be left behind, but it is just after midnight, and she is tired, so she goes to her bed beside the fireplace.

Where could Sunshine be? Instinctively, I close my eyes. The breeze touches my face, and as I feel its coolness, I sense that I know exactly where she is.

It is more than a two-hour walk from here for a little girl, so I take the car, which will get me to Gibbs Hill Lighthouse in sixteen minutes.

Part of me feels like I am going on a whim; the other half knows where I need to go. If there is one thing I have learned, it is to follow the half of me that feels certain. I drive with the windows down, keeping an eye out for her.

As I arrive at the lighthouse, I turn off the lights and park at the farthest point of the parking lot. I wait and then wait some more. Maybe I am wrong? Maybe I am overreacting? I should just go home and wait. And why Gibbs Hill Lighthouse?

Then, out of the corner of my eye, I see her heading toward the lighthouse. *What are you up to, Sunshine?* I think as I watch her.

She walks up to the side of the lighthouse and puts her hand on it. A light appears, and she is gone. I get out of the car and run toward the building. My heart races at what has just happened.

The door to the lighthouse is locked. There is not a door where she stood and disappeared just seconds ago. I put my hand where she had put hers, and in an instant, I wake up in my bed. I am bewildered and groggy at first, trying to orient myself.

I get to my feet and run to Sunshine's room, but she is not there, and it is still dark outside. My heart aches. Tears flow down my cheeks. Saddened, I close her door behind me, taking many years of loneliness with me.

Maybe this whole thing has been a dream?

Yes, that is what happened; I fell asleep and dreamed I followed Sunshine.

I have no idea anymore; I cannot trust myself.

Pondering all of this, I decide to go downstairs for some hot tea. As I prepare the kettle and set it on the stove, another thought hits me. I should check the hood of my car to see if it is warm; that will prove I went out in the car. I head out to the garage and feel the car's hood. Sure enough, it is still warm. This is real.

I calm down a bit and drink the tea, asking the Lord to help me remember. I feel like I need to remember to feel whole.

No answer comes, but a sudden sleepiness does.

I wake on the sofa around 5:30 a.m. When my eyes open, everything looks better and brighter. Selah is waiting, so happy to see me, and I her. I run upstairs to see if Sunshine is back home, but she is not. Tears slide down my face, and my heart aches.

I need to take my mind off this, so I focus my attention on Selah, and we play. I mean, we run all around the house playing with her squeaky toys.

I have to do something to keep my mind occupied. I need to call Catherine, but not now. How will I explain that Sunshine is gone? That I lost her?

Maybe she just went back to her family. Every instance where I start to panic, a calmness covers me, and I know I need to wait before I make any decisions.

"Come on, Selah. Come on, girl. Let's go down to the beach."

I skip down the steps to our secluded beach. Seaweed and ocean debris cover the sand, so I find the rake from the shed after stumbling around in the dark. Selah runs all around the beach, and I laugh more than I have in a long time. In fact, I cannot remember the last time I truly laughed, or have I ever laughed? Well, only with Sunshine.

Selah and I go into the water up to my knees, and Selah dog paddles. I turn her toward me, and we swim together. The water is warm and then cool, as if it cannot make up its mind. Coming out of the water, Selah looks like a little soaked rat. I tell her to stay, and she stands still on the sandy beach, where the sand envelopes her little legs like a pair of Bermuda shorts. Her little nub wiggles as if displaying a happy smile.

I jog to the shed to retrieve a towel. Opening the door a little wider, I spot a kayak in the dark. I search for the light switch and find not only one switch but several others. I turn them all on, and I am totally bewildered. I walk around and look at the boat and the pool, and then I find the apartment.

I am drawn to the kayak more than anything else, and as I touch it, I nearly fall to the ground. Memories flood my whole being. I hold on to the side of the workbench where the kayak sits, and my body shakes as a vision plays out in my mind like a movie.

In my vision, there is a young man in the kayak, with the blue-green waters in view. He is flailing about and laughing. Then he is gone. I swim to him; then I am bandaging him. I remember I was laughing with him, and there was a woman too. Who is she? I cannot see their faces or remember.

Who are these people?

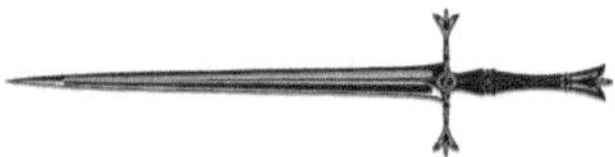

My mood suddenly changes. I step forward and put both hands on the kayak. The name is spoken in my mind, just as if I had said it aloud: "Will!"

I remember I got a cell phone for some reason. I remember the lighthouse. Oh no! I remember the blood and a fight.

"Will!" I speak aloud, but the memory is fading. I touch the kayak again but feel nothing. The cell phone discussion and the guy at the spa, that was Will.

"Come on, Selah. I'll dry you off at the house."

We both run to the house.

The French doors are open. The sound of Bach drifts faintly into my ears as I speed past the living room into the bathroom. I grab a towel for Selah's bath, and then I shampoo, condition, and briefly blast her with the dryer. I brush through her beautiful long blonde-brown hair and then proceed upstairs to my bedroom, where I left my purse the day before.

"Yes, I remember," I whisper as I touch "Contacts" in my phone's settings. I know his name is in here, but there is still nothing else I remember. I look through the messages, but there is nothing. Only Ms. Faith's, Catherine's, and Derik's numbers are programmed in.

I sit on the floor and try to remember more. I close my eyes and wish it to be so, but nothing more comes to me. Selah looks like a movie star staring up at me with her big pink bow. I stroke her head. "Oh, my sweet friend. I couldn't have imagined all this, could I? Sometimes I'm not sure what is real or a dream."

The day has gone by quickly. It is now dinner time, and I still have a lot of energy. Selah finishes drying with me on the veranda as I use my phone to catch up on the happenings of the world and the Bermuda news. The thought comes to me to look at last year's news to see if something happened to make me remember the blood I envisioned early in the day. I remember what Derik said and how I felt when . . .

The chills run down my body, which seem to indicate a memory of something that happened.

CHAPTER 15

FINDING TRUTH

I scroll date after date on my computer, and I am at the point of giving up when I see it. I click on Bernews. com, an online news source for Bermuda. I find a picture of me, and it looks like I have been in a fight or accident. In the picture, a man is standing behind me. I know it is Will; I recognize him, and he looks worse than me. There is another tall man sitting on the ground. The police are all around.

"What happened?" I say aloud.

I know it is me in that photo; that part was clear. The news clip says a woman was shot and killed, there was an altercation, and the case was closed.

I sigh again. As hard as I try, I cannot remember. "Let's go in, Selah. Are you hungry?"

Twirls of happy bliss emanate from my little dog.

"Oh, Selah. I'm so glad I have you. I sure hope we find Sunshine. I'll have to call Catherine tomorrow and let her know that Sunshine ran away."

Darkness descends upon the Bermuda paradise. As Bach plays in the background, I putter around the big house looking for something to do. I keep peering outside for Sunshine. I paint another picture of her, rearrange my office, and then venture into the hidden closet that holds passports, money, and disguises. I thumb through the paperwork and again start to wonder who I really am. I decide to sit down and make a list of all that I know and all that I can remember.

- I think I am a good person.
- I would never hurt a person, yet from what I remember, this is not entirely true.
- I might be a spy or in witness protection.
- I fight. (What does any of this mean?) Maybe I'm not such a good person.
- I have Selah . . . and no one else besides Sunshine and my new church friends?
- I live in Bermuda. I feel like I have been here for a very long time. I am a resident with no credentials, yet I have many credentials.
- I think I may have traveled all over the world from the looks of the passports and articles around the house.

- I live in an amazing, expensive house, but I do not work. I've never seen a bill come to the mailbox, but I still have electricity.
- I remember my secret closet and the dress from long ago.
- I love classical music and old things, and I am hesitant about new things.
- I am drawn to my Bible. (I run and grab my Bible. As I touch it, peace floods my spirit.)
- I can quote Scriptures as if I am a preacher, like Derik. (I start shouting the Word of God loudly all through the house.)
- I can recite the whole Bible, and I have an understanding of what it means.
- I speak many languages.
- I am gifted with a special power, evidently to fight demons or something.
- I can pass the peace; Sunshine passed the peace too.
- I sometimes must change my look with disguises.
- I feel like I am a messenger of God, but I don't know why.
- I think I am some sort of protector.
- I kind of remember Will, and there was a woman. What was her name?
- I never lack for anything. My finances are innumerable, yet I'm frugal. (Well, I was until I went to the spa and pampered myself, got a cell phone, and gave away $3.6 million.)

- I lay asleep in a dormant state until the Keepers wake me. . . . (That's it! I remember them! They were in my dream. Are they family?)
- (I gasp. How could I forget?) I have Levi!

My list stops there.

"Levi!" I speak aloud. "I have missed you! I remember that you came to me, and I turned away. I am so sorry for that."

I spend the rest of the night planning to see this guy Will. He must be the one beaten and bloody. From the picture, his shape and hair color look like the guy from the kayak. Then it dawns on me. This must be Faith's grandson; she said his name is Will.

Things are coming together. As the wee morning hours creep in, I read the Word of God and ready myself.

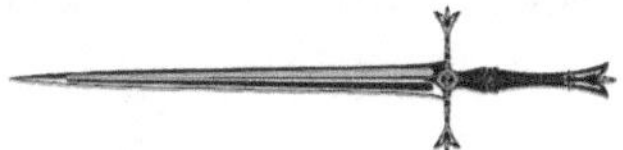

The ocean waters can be heard hitting against the rocks and cliffs surrounding my home. The sheer white curtains dance yet again around the French doors, as I have forgotten to close them. Selah and I eat and dress, and I pull my hair over my head in a messy bun. I grab a poncho in case of rain and jump on my scooter, and off we go. I am going to Gibbs Hill Lighthouse, where I hope to find Sunshine and possibly see Will.

Selah loves to ride. Today, I put her in her basket and close the top since the breeze is a little brisk. I have not noticed the weather, but the clouds tell the story of impending rain.

The scenery is incredible. High atop Gibbs Hill, the wind picks up, and the sea's colors of green and blue look majestic as they play along the shoreline. I stand and take in the signs that spring is ending and summer is beginning in Bermuda. If a tourist watches long enough, they might see migrating whales frolic along the reefs. There could be up to ten thousand a year that pass by Bermuda as they travel north to their feeding grounds.

Yes! I am remembering things!

I can see Hamilton and the Royal Naval Dockyard in the distance. I park the scooter, hook Selah to a leash, and pop my helmet into the basket, and we take off to hike around. Selah and I look around to see if anything looks familiar. The problem is that everything looks familiar, but what stands out?

I stare up at the lighthouse. It looks the same, and when I walk over to it, no one seems to be around. I walk to the side of the lighthouse where I saw Sunshine go in, and I feel something. It is a tug in my spirit. I reach out to touch the old iron statue, and just as my fingers would have made contact, I hear someone coming toward me.

"Hello, we do not open until 9:00 this morning." When I turn, I see Faith. "Oh, Awna, it's you. Well, hello, dear."

"Hi, Faith. I'm just looking around. I can never seem to get enough of the history and beauty of this place."

"Nor can any of us, dear," she speaks.

Faith looks around, breathes in the fresh sea air, and closes her eyes. I do the same. As I do, peace and calmness fill me. I am not in a hurry to grab another clue but simply want to breathe. Selah is spinning circles and skipping forward to see Faith.

"Selah, calm down. I'm sorry, but she sure is happy to see you." As soon as the words are out of my mouth, thoughts spin in my head and transform my memory.

It was nighttime. A soft glow showed in a room, and a lady had her head bowed. We were praying; we had a fear of something. I left in the dark to go find . . . Will.

I open my eyes and try to play it cool with Faith. I drop the leash and let Selah run to her. Faith kneels and welcomes the bouncing furball.

I step closer and watch as a flood of memories fills my consciousness. I know everything now. I am fully myself. I smile and am truly grateful to remember. Nothing feels confusing or foggy; I am clear-minded.

Faith picks Selah up, loving on her. As she looks up and our eyes meet, a frown touches her face.

"Good morning, Ms. Banks. It's very good to see you again. It has been a while—I mean, before our coffee at the café."

A stone face reflects a bit of a shock, but she keeps her composure. It is as if she isn't sure whether she should admit that she recognizes me.

"You had better come in, dear." She turns and starts to walk to the other side of the gift shop, where a small apartment awaits, but I stand still.

She stops. "Are you coming?"

"No."

I turn to the lighthouse, and as I get closer, it calls to my spirit. I touch the building and go through the invisible door. Ms. Banks and Selah are right behind me. The three of us start down the stairs and then down the elevator and more stairs. I lead the way without a word; I know where I am going. As we reach our destination, we stand there and wait. Not a word transpires.

Levi appears first, but he is still dreamlike even though I am wide awake. "Awna, what are you doing here?"

"Hello, Levi. I've come for truth."

Will appears next. I can hardly contain myself, but at this moment, I still have a few questions, so I stay quiet and nod my head toward him.

"Hello, Will," I say, acting casual.

Levi bows to the others, and they do the same to him, but I stand waiting.

Levi breaks the silence. "There is no go-ahead for this; it is completely unorthodox."

"Levi, we had no idea that she would become more like us. She was supposed to become more human and then . . . die," Will says.

"Die!" I speak. "I did die, and I had a choice to stay in Heaven or come back here, and I came back! I am more spiritual than flesh and will always be so. My spiritual side will always be stronger, no matter how many times you take my memory away!" I shout angrily.

If there was any shock about my knowledge or my anger, you wouldn't have known, for no one spoke a word.

"The Lord has not spoken to us to give her this truth," Levi says softly.

"Then we shall pray," Ms. Banks responds.

We all fall in reverence to the Lord God above. The answer comes quickly, and we all hear it. The three lay hands on my head, and truth floods my soul.

From birth, I was fleeing from Moloch to the protection of the Israelites, the Keepers. Levi was an earthly Israelite priest but now serves as my guardian angel.

My mother had spoken to Levi concerning me. Soon after she'd died, he'd taken me under his wing. I remembered the Holy of Holies and Moses coming down from the mountain as he blessed me, asking God's hand upon me.

The truth of the battles against the principalities and the dark forces of this world flooded into me, and truth transformed the flesh and spirit into one force instead of two separate forces. I remembered everything!

At that instant, I already knew this truth, but Levi spoke more truth to explain what had happened. I just listened.

"Awna, the enemy was getting closer to you. Roman's kin moved closer to our area, but we held Bermuda at the three spots of the triangle to keep them out while you were . . . well, being transformed. The Lord confused the enemy, and they left the territory, just as we had prayed for so that you could recover. Your memory had to be wiped clean; you were in no shape to fight, nor could you have withstood the truth. None of us knew exactly what would happen as you became more human. In all honesty, we did think you would die, and that would be it. Through all the generations, we've kept you alive, as well as the others, to fight the evils of this world, those seen and the unseen."

"Others?" I interrupt.

There is silence.

"Yes, there are others like you, but they are very, very few indeed. You and your kind protect many borders of the earth. And when the saved, those redeemed humans, pray, it changes situations. Prayer is powerful. But as they pray, we must fight to get their prayers through to Heaven for the protection of God to cover them.

Will speaks up and adds, "Sometimes we must fight Moloch's offspring too. Sometimes we fight satan's imps and demons, and, yes, sometimes we fight the descendants' crossbred humans who carry evil inside of them. And of course, we fight the fallen ones too. It is constant spiritual warfare to stop evil so that good prevails. We are gatekeepers of good, not evil, yet some of the evil gets through the territory. Sometimes God may allow it for a purpose or a time, only for the good that will come from the bad."

Will stops, as if to let it all sink in.

"Those are the times when the humans have many questions and ask why," Ms. Banks continues. "We brought you home to Bermuda to heal and rest. The battles on the earth have been great for many, many generations. As you became more human, you became weaker, and as you were making the transition, you worried about your appearance. The Holy God had to call in more Keepers to bring peace into this place while you healed. Otherwise, you would not have been able to handle this domain or any other on your own. Either you would become stronger to fight, or you would die a human death."

Levi takes his turn to speak. "We thought that you would die like other similar ones, but instead, you died to the flesh and gained your memory to fulfill your spiritual purpose. Now you are not even like the few others who exist. You are one with spirit and flesh. You may not even need your many disguises anymore. Only time will tell."

Levi stops talking and considers his words. "Some of your kind have died a human death, regardless of our efforts to save them. Awna, to explain it, you have retained a certain DNA that continually regenerates itself. It doesn't grow old like a human's DNA. You age very slowly because of this minuscule fragment in your DNA. Although there are others like yourself, you are the oldest. You have retained this DNA to live and fight the fight, while others have not."

After Levi finishes speaking, they all remain silent.

I am also silent because everyone is taking in all that Levi has said. "Where is Sunshine, and who is she? She has something to do with all of this, doesn't she?"

Will speaks this time. "Yes, she was sent to you as a cover of protection as well as company for you as you became more human. We thought she could keep an eye on you to bring life into you as only a child can do. We communicated through Sunshine as to how you were doing. She watched over you before you ever met her. We then tested the waters as we met you in the spa and the café and as you came to see Faith to speak to her while you were trying to find Sunshine."

"Yes, I was very grateful for that interaction."

Will continues, "If Moloch's offspring came looking for you, they would not think that you could have a child, and if for some reason they figured it out, you two would have been able to handle them together."

"She fights too?" I question.

"Oh yes." Ms. Banks says. "She's a champion at taking down fallen ones, demons, imps, and offspring. She's a natural evil terminator, just like you."

Sunshine walks down the steps, that same little girl with a big smile. A radiant light shines all around her. I know in an instant that she was the ten-fold, ten times more power to fight, promised to me by the Lord while I was in the Heavenly realm. When the Lord speaks to us, sometimes it's different than what we think.

"Hi, Mommy," she says.

I smile, but sadness covers me. "I guess you do not have to call me that anymore if you don't want to."

Smiling, she thinks for a minute. "I would still like to call you Mama. I've never had a mama."

"I'd like that too, Sunshine. I've never had a child before." I say this, meaning it with all my heart.

"Sunshine, what is your real name?"

There is silence.

Sunshine then smiles. "My name is very complicated, but I really like that you called me Sunshine. Why don't you just call me Sunny?"

"Okay, Sunny it is," I say, not wanting to push her. She'll tell me about her real name in her own time.

Ms. Banks comes over and hugs Sunny, who is now holding Selah. Ms. Banks then looks toward me. "Sunny has been raised for this purpose, trained from her birth, you might say. This will be good for both of you. You've already worked well together."

"Is she like me? Is she one of the few?" I ask.

Silence fills the room.

"I will give you as much truth as I can, but yes, she is exactly like you," Levi says.

"So, what happens now?" I mean, "What do we do now?"

Levi speaks up. "You will know when the time comes. Both of you stay in prayer, read the Word, train, and I mean train hard, and God will show you at the appointed time.

"Awna, 'Trust in the Lord with all thine heart; and lean not unto thine own understanding. In all thy ways acknowledge him, and he shall direct thy paths,'" Ms. Banks whispers from Proverbs 3:5–6.

"Now you must go. There's much to ready ourselves for," Levi states.

Sunny and I head up the stairway, but I stop, looking back at the three of them, and finally speak. "Will we see you again?"

"Yes! Most definitely!" they all say simultaneously.

Levi speaks up. "I will still visit your dreams. These two you will see from time to time in human form.

With that, we happily make our way up and through the invisible door.

Sunny and I stand in the parking lot near the lighthouse and look at each other.

"Well, let's go home," I say.

We put Selah in the basket, and Sunny sits in front of me. She now has her own helmet that I keep strapped to the back of the scooter. We slowly make our way back home. The sky, palms, birds . . . everything is brighter and more beautiful. I see everything with a clearer vision. Now that I have my memory back, everything seems to speak to me.

When we get home, I feel drawn to the secret room, and Sunny follows. In the desk drawer, I almost know what will be there before I open it. I pull out the drawer, and there it is—a birth certificate for Sunny naming me as her mother. This is another intervention from the Keepers to connect all the dots. There are also two passports with our names on them and plane tickets to the United States.

"Sunny, look. We will fly into Florida in a few months. Then we will be given our instructions for where to travel next. I must say, I feel it in my bones that where we are going is going to be cold."

Sunny giggles. "Well, Mama, we better order some warmer clothes to take on our trip; we will never find that kind of clothing here in Bermuda or Florida."

Selah wiggles her nub and barks.

"Yes, Selah. I'll order you some warm clothes too. After all, it could be the end of summer or the start of fall when we get there, but we'll be ready."

Sunny giggles, smiling with such love for me in her eyes that I truly believe I could be a mother figure to her. She sits in the old Victorian chair next to the long gown hanging with the matching parasol. She takes the parasol down, opens it, and starts to twirl it around.

"One thing about it, Mama. We adjust quickly to our surroundings, so maybe a nice change of scenery will be good for us."

"Yes indeed, Sunny. We sure do adjust quickly. I guess the main thing is that we must strive to look like others so as not to raise suspicions."

Sunny shakes her head as if processing it all, still playing with the parasol.

"You know, I've been thinking, Sunny. As long as we are together wherever we are sent, it will all be all right."

I look around the cottage, part of me not wanting to leave yet. Seeing the past and present items here in the secret room makes me wonder when I'll return to this place that feels like home.

Sunny picks up on my thoughts. "Mama, we still have a few months to get things in order. We can prepare and still enjoy our remaining time here."

"I agree," I say cheerily.

As if we are thinking the same thing, we turn and head to our bedrooms to change into our swimsuits, leaving the secret room to echo the past all on its own.

We traipse down the stairs to the beach, grab our floats from the shed, and begin splashing and giggling as we play in the water, not a care in the world for now.

"Hey, Mama. We must go see Catherine and Derik and of course our church family before we leave. We will tell them about your amnesia and show them the birth certificate so it makes us legitimate in the system."

"I like how you think, Sunny. To God be all the glory!" I say with vigor.

It is so good to be me again. I no longer have to scrap for truth or fear losing my memory again. The truth has indeed set me free.

Ms. Banks, Will, and Levi stood on the cliffs overlooking the two swimming below. Alon appeared before them. Alon looked over at Faith and Will as they bowed in respect.

"Mercy and Grace, you two did a superb job transforming her at the spa. I have found your knowledge in such matters, umm, should I say . . . excellent. I think it gave her just what she needed to press ahead." The beautiful twins appeared before Alon. They were also Keepers. They too bowed in a show of respect of Alon.

The Keepers have a common goal, to keep Awna and other warriors like her alive as they fight to protect the humans from evil. The Keepers do what is needed to maintain goodness on the earth while keeping the secrets of God.

"It has been our absolute pleasure," the twins said simultaneously.

Alon looked at them both and smiled with as much emotion as he could muster. He then said, "In the future, you are welcome to be whomever Awna and Sunny need you to be to further the cause. Or you can be yourselves. The choice is yours."

"Why, thank you, Alon," Grace said with her slow Southern drawl. "I do like this look, and my accent as well. I am rather enthralled."

Grace and Mercy laughed, sounding like one person as their voices blended.

"And just maybe we should keep Will away from kayaks next time," Mercy announced.

Grace and Mercy looked at each other and laughed, as did the rest of the Keepers.

"I just couldn't help myself; I've always wanted to use that kayak for as long as I can remember. I had my chance and took it." Will smirked, his sun-bleached hair hanging in his eyes.

Alon continued to face Will. "Will, maybe you should go visit Ethan in prison before we leave the area. Indeed, he may need to feel the true forgiveness that only you can give him."

With that, Will nodded and then disappeared.

Alon turned toward Awna and Sunny, swimming in the beautiful waters of Bermuda. He could no longer mind-communicate with Awna or even let her know he was alive. That was his punishment and yet part of his pardon from Heaven. She must always think he had died many years ago in the fight to obtain the Promised Land for the Israelites while protecting her.

Alon was allowed to continue to watch over Awna, as were the Keepers, but she must never see him. Careful attention always had to be administered, since she had become one with her spirit and flesh.

One day, though, when it was decided that her earthly mission was complete, he would be one of the first to greet her. Of course, Levi would also be by her side. On that day, there would be no more battles for her to fight, and no more would she be hunted like an animal by the enemy.

Also, for now and in the future, her memory would never be erased again like it was before each awakening. She would always know her identity, where she came from, and what her mission was here on earth.

Alon spoke: "We have learned that, as Awna changed to become more human, it was her memory that connected her flesh and spirit into one, giving her more strength than she had before."

"Yes, to God be the glory!"

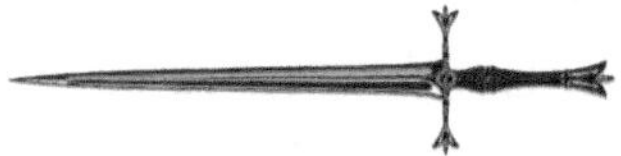

Alon looked over the Bermuda horizon as the others followed his gaze. They all savored the few short minutes they had together at this moment in time.

The breeze changed ever so slightly, and a frown crossed Alon's face.

Nothing ever stays the same for very long, he thought. And they all agreed.

Alon announced, "Something has changed. A storm is coming to the earth, unlike anything this world has ever known before. We must prepare, for this evil will be unfathomable."

By this time, Will was back standing with the others. They all bowed their heads to pray. They knew what was already spoken in Alon's prayer, but out of respect, they remained silent to let Alon speak.

"God says that all the Keepers must be dispersed evenly throughout the earth. They are to use as many underground tunnels and gateways as possible to get to the appointed cities. All of the Keepers must go except for you three." He looked toward Levi, Will, and Ms. Banks.

"Mercy and Grace, you can return to Awna and Sunny when it is possible. I am to accompany you to your next post, and then I will return to help Levi. A heavenly army has been placed around the triangle of Bermuda, and you will be protected from evil."

"And so it is," Mercy and Grace said together.

With a nod from Alon, Mercy and Grace stepped forward, and the three of them disappeared into a spiritual fog that quickly dispersed into the air.

Will and Ms. Banks bid a friendly nod toward Levi and disappeared, going back to the lighthouse until further notice.

Levi stood his ground, overlooking the cliffs. He was alone now with Awna and Sunny; nothing would ever hurt them, not on his watch.

A feeling arose inside Awna to look up toward the top of the cliffs. She did not see anything at first until a gentle breeze blew, and she caught a glimpse of Levi, her guardian angel, standing tall upon the bank. She focused her sight to see him up close.

His breastplate of righteousness glimmered with the shiny jewel. His arms were crossed as he watched the horizon. His facial features were aligned with a strong jawline. His piercing eyes were greenish with a touch of blue, like the Bermudian waters. His hair was covered with the helmet of salvation. A shield of faith hung to one side, and his sword, the Word of God, was sheathed on the other. A shimmery belt of truth surrounded him. His feet were shod with the preparation of the gospel of peace. His head was bowed in prayer as he stood upon the bank. He was indeed a mighty warrior dressed in his armour, ready for battle.

As Sunny and I dry off on the shore, the sun is high in the sky.

Once more, I glance at Levi, toward the cliffs, and think about how peaceful and safe I feel knowing God's hand of protection is so near. I am thankful that I can now catch glimpses of Levi during the day and not just in my dreams.

My thoughts merge not only to Bermuda but also around the world and the many nations of the earth, wishing the inhabitants here, for only a season in time, could see and feel the love of God and witness His furious protection over His creation, just as I feel.

One thing is for certain as I gaze around me . . . Bermuda has never been safer than it is right now.

A Note from the Author

I would like to speak briefly about the Scripture that gave me the idea to write this book. It concerns the sons of God, the fallen angels (fallen ones, as I refer to them in the story), and Nephilim (giants, as they are often called). This subject has always fascinated me but also left me with many questions.

My goal for the storyline in this book was simple: to tell a story related to these Scriptures concerning these entities. This book is my interpretation of these mysterious beings, believing they, along with satan, have brought such evilness into God's creation.

Some Jewish interpretations identify the Nephilim as fallen angels, but this subject has been disputed for some time. Scriptures concerning these beings can be seen in the storyline. It was not my intention to dispute the matter but instead to write a fictional possibility or reason for the evil that continues to plague humanity through DNA and generational curses.

I chose Bermuda for the setting because of the mystery that surrounds the place. It is also special to me because my husband and I were married there. I attempted to declare its beauty throughout the pages of this book.

The Keepers are pure fiction, conjured up in my imagination for how an array of guardian angels may protect our comings and goings.

There are many accounts in the Bible where Heaven and earth seem to have a gateway to each other, so I wanted to bring that possibility into my storyline with Gibbs Hill Lighthouse.

While my characters are fictional, let me show you in the Bible where the thought came to me for angels coming and going from Heaven, just as some of the characters in the book do.

Here are a few Scriptures.

In Genesis 28:10–18, we read of the mystery of Jacob, who, while traveling, dreamed of a ladder that reached to Heaven, and angels were ascending and descending on it. He called it the Gate of Heaven.

Jesus Himself said in John 1:51, while speaking to Nathanael, *"Verily, verily, I say unto you, Hereafter ye shall see heaven open, and the angels of God ascending and descending upon the Son of man."*

Also, please read 2 Kings 6:18. In this Scripture, Elisha prayed that the army that surrounded him and sought to kill him be blinded. The Lord answered his prayer by altering the enemies' eyes so that they did not even recognize Elisha. Their vision was altered in such a way that they were actually led straight into their enemy's camp. In my book, I related this Scripture to where Awna needed protection against Ethan and Rosie in the park, and their eyes were also altered, not seeing Awna but someone else.

I will highlight one more point concerning the gates and doorways of Heaven, from Matthew 3:16–17. Here, Jesus was baptized in the Jordan River. *"And Jesus, when he was baptized, went up straightway out of the water: and, lo, the heavens were opened unto him, and he saw the Spirit of God descending like a dove, and lighting upon him: And lo a voice from heaven, saying, This is my beloved Son, in whom I am well pleased."*

The Jordan River held a special mystery of God, a place for some to go to meet God, see His power, and be baptized in its waters.

There are many mysteries of God that we may never understand. That is why we must search out the Word of God and continue along the path of being a Christian.

May this story cause you to search the Word of God for yourself, and may His full amour be upon you as you do. May you find that you too are like Awna, a warrior for God, capable of fighting spiritual warfare against the enemy. I pray that you will study God's Word and find His truth. May it set you free.

For we wrestle not against flesh and blood, but against principalities, against powers, against the rulers of the darkness of this world, against spiritual wickedness in high places. (Ephesians 6:12)

Be not forgetful to entertain strangers: for thereby some have entertained angels unawares. (Hebrews 13:2)

www.ingramcontent.com/pod-product-compliance
Lightning Source LLC
Chambersburg PA
CBHW022102310726
48972CB00007B/1849